THE HURTWOOD VILLAGE MURDERS

BENEDICT BROWN

Storm
PUBLISHING

Ebook ISBN: 978-1-80508-189-0
Paperback ISBN: 978-1-80508-191-3

Cover design: Rose Cooper
Cover images: Shutterstock

Published by Storm Publishing.
For further information, visit:
www.stormpublishing.co

ALSO BY BENEDICT BROWN

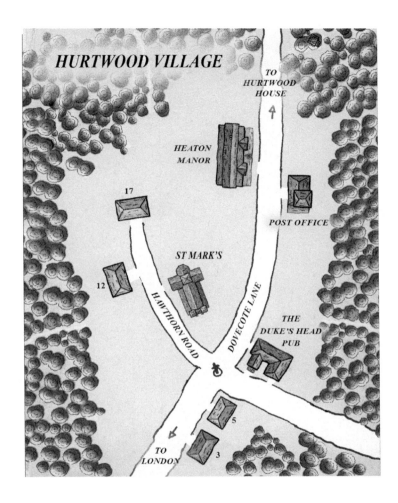

PROLOGUE

Everyone loved Lucinda Heaton. She was one of those people you simply had to adore. It was not just that she was bright, pretty and charismatic. As her neighbours in the picturesque village of Hurtwood often remarked, there was something almost luminous about her.

Lucinda sparkled – that's the very word for it. She could walk into a room, and everyone would turn to stare before she'd even opened her mouth. And when she did, she would sparkle all over again. It had been said on more than one occasion that if they'd put Lucinda Heaton on recruitment posters during the war, the British Army would have been full to bursting in a matter of days.

Along with her voluntary work in the village school, she was a noted ballroom dancer, could sing as sweetly as a West End actress and, in the springtime, her garden bloomed more brightly than any other in the village. I needn't mention all the prizes she won in the local summer fete. Suffice it to say, her marrows were marvels, her damson jam delicious, and her sunflowers were something to behold.

As it happens, she was weeding her front lawn when the

letter arrived. Rushing past as they went about their business, her fellow villagers couldn't help but pause to appreciate her handiwork, even on that cold spring day. The sky always seemed a fraction brighter when she was out there, and even a missed bus or a reprimand for lateness from one's employer was worth enduring if Lucinda happened to direct her pretty smile your way.

The postman himself was something of an admirer and was only too happy to have a letter to deliver that morning. He walked right over, put it in her dainty (though earthy) hand, and received a brief "Thank you, Ned," for his troubles.

"You're very welcome. It's always a pleasure," he mumbled in response and continued his round with a spring in his step as she carefully opened the letter.

Lucinda was just as charming as everyone claimed, which made the two lines of text on that otherwise blank piece of paper all the more disturbing.

BY THIS TIME NEXT WEEK,
YOU'LL BE DEAD.

Everyone loved Lucinda... Well, almost everyone.

ONE

ENGLAND, MARCH 1928

I'd rarely seen my publisher look so ecstatic. Bertrand Price-Lewis appeared to be smiling from the toes of his black leather brogues to the top of his balding pate. It really was a sight to behold.

"I'm so proud of you, my boy." He placed one hand on my shoulder as he led me to the street outside his Bloomsbury office. "I don't say such things lightly, but your new book is the finest mystery novel I've read in some time."

I was probably blushing by now and would have graciously accepted the compliment had one of my least favourite people not barged between us on his way into the building.

"I bet you say that to all your authors, Bertie," the large, gloomy figure exclaimed. My fellow detective novelist, Carmine Fortescue, was a noted bore. His wildly popular books were uniquely dreadful, and he always smelt of boiled pork for some reason.

"Now, now, Carmine," the smooth-tongued publisher responded without apology. "As you well know, I'm fond of every novel I publish."

My rival turned to me instead. "It's a pleasure to see you,

Marius. It's been so long since your last book that I thought you might never finish another. What have you been doing? Travelling the world? Composing a piano concerto? Struggling for ideas?"

I was ready with a pithy response, but when I opened my mouth to deliver it, nothing emerged. This wasn't the first time I'd flopped in an argument with that wretch. Carmine Fortescue had a singular ability to leave me speechless.

With the battle won, he laughed his cynical laugh and strolled gleefully into the offices of Price-Lewis and Aster Publishing.

"Never mind him, my boy." Bertie's voice dropped lower so that only I could hear. "I wouldn't say it to his face, but the man is a charmless know-all. I only represent him because his books make the company a fortune." This didn't make me feel a great deal better about the encounter. "Today is your day. You should be very pleased with yourself."

"Oh, yes? And why's that?" a soft voice from behind me enquired, and I turned to see a ray of sunlight in the middle of the gloomy day.

My childhood friend, Lady Isabella Montague, was taking me to lunch. It was a big improvement on the last time we'd met in that spot. For one thing, I wasn't lying on my back on the pavement.

"Bella, I believe you know of my publisher, Bertrand Price-Lewis?" I said to be polite before answering her question. "We were just counting our blessings that I've managed to complete another book."

Bertie stepped forward and took my friend's hand in his. Although he was a short, round man in his sixties, with oddly sprouting clumps of hair and bright red cheeks, he was somehow more suave than I was at twenty-eight.

"Lady Isabella, it's a pleasure to meet you at last. And may I say that I never doubted your friend here for one moment?

With your help, we steered him through his crisis of confidence, and I'm certain that his new book will be a huge success."

"It's nice to put a face to the name," Bella replied, as the pair had never spoken directly when executing their plan to interfere in my life.

Bertie looked warmly at my elegant companion as he made his excuses. "I will leave you young people to enjoy yourselves." He was already backing off along the street to rush to his next appointment. "Marius, we'll meet again soon to discuss book number three."

I'd like to be able to describe his expression at this moment, but I was rather distracted by the presence of the first girl I'd ever loved. The fact she had a boyfriend was neither here nor there. I was simply happy to have her back in my life after years apart.

"I hope you brought an appetite," she said, putting her arm through mine as she led me around the square to a grand red-brick building on the other side of the road. "The food at the Hotel Russell is ambrosial, and just wait until you see the dining room."

I was eager to discover why she'd summoned me to lunch.

"I will do my best to eat up every scrap we order," I replied as we hurried along the pavement and up to the entrance.

Above the ornate stone arch of the vast hotel, a carved lion peered down at me with a look of apprehension on his face. The unicorn beside him, meanwhile, appeared quite startled and was clearly jealous to see who was on my arm. A doorman ushered us towards a grand foyer that was all marble columns, Moorish ceilings and a zodiac-themed mosaic floor. I had spent the money from my first book – and the advance payment from the second – on a neatly appointed flat in a fashionable part of London. The Hotel Russell, however, was a world of luxury I'd only visited in my dreams. I just had to hope that no one would wake me up for some time.

We entered the restaurant, and the maître d'hôtel didn't ask what we required but took our coats and sat the chic young lady and her tatty friend at a table below an immense crystal chandelier. Underneath her belted mauve cloak, Bella wore a coral silk dress that suited her more than I can say. I, meanwhile, wished I'd worn something smarter than an old blue suit that had once belonged to my father.

"Do you recognise this room?" she asked with a playful look in her eyes as we took in the splendour.

"I can't say that I read a lot of magazines about hotels, my dear." It's a shame I can't erase the words I speak as I do in my novels. "My dear" sounded all wrong, and I instantly regretted it.

"I seem to remember that you like history, though." She relaxed into her chair and stretched her arms out as though the place belonged to her. "This restaurant was designed by the same architect as the dining room on the *Titanic*."

What a good omen, I thought, but I said, "How remarkable."

"Daddy used to bring me here whenever we came into London to go to the theatre."

I replied with a blithe smile and a quick retort. "That's a coincidence. My father took me to the George pub for sandwiches whenever we went to see Dorking Football Club lose to every other team in Surrey."

"You are a tease, Marius." She studied me for a moment, perhaps trying to make sense of the fellow who had crashed back into her life after a decade without any contact. "But then, you always were."

She twisted the stem of an empty glass between her fingers. This very gesture brought a waiter shooting over to us with a wine list and two menus. After a brief deliberation, liquid refreshment was ordered, and she took up the conversation once more.

"I brought you here..." she began, then paused mid-thought.

"Yes?" I poked at her rather rudely with this word, but at least I didn't finish the sentence for her. In my head, I wished she would say, *because I have left my ill-suited, uncouth boyfriend and thought we should celebrate.*

"I brought you here, Marius, because— Oh, look, there he is."

She broke off whatever she was about to tell me as her odious paramour had just bumbled into the restaurant in his usual irritating fashion. I'd been looking forward to an exquisite lunch with my exquisite friend in that exquisite restaurant, and now Gilbert Baines was there, too.

TWO

Bella was pleased to see him, but I couldn't think why. Dressed in a dull brown blazer and matching tie, Gilbert possessed the social skills of an electric eel.

"Quin," was the only acknowledgement I received as he sat down opposite me and extracted a number of files from his briefcase.

"It's lovely to see you too, Gilly, old pal." I truly didn't mean this from the bottom of my heart.

"If you're going to embark on this ridiculous enterprise," he began with his eyes on the papers in front of him, "then I insist you do it properly. Have you chosen a name yet?"

I couldn't imagine what any of this twaddle meant and attempted to convey this with a blank expression. Gilbert was evidently no great interpreter of body language so, when that failed, I put it into words.

"I haven't the faintest idea to what you're referring. Is it possible that you've lost your mind?" I thought I expressed myself rather diplomatically.

"It's my fault for not explaining sooner," Bella helpfully intervened. "Gilbert is here to discuss our sleuthing. He thinks we should set up a company and have everything laid out clearly before we go any further."

"I had assumed that any detecting we got up to would be on an amateur basis."

Gilbert huffed out a reply. "No one is expecting you to be Sherlock Holmes and Watson. I merely think you should know where you both stand and set everything down in writing. After all, you are about to embark on your first official case."

I was speechless. Truly speechless! Well, except for the fact that the waiter returned to the table at this moment, and I ordered the Chateaubriand with béarnaise sauce. But when that was done, I sat there staring at the troublesome pair in front of me.

"Ahh, yes," Bella finally reacted. "I didn't have time to explain that either. You see, we may have another mystery to solve." She smiled angelically, and it was hard to feel grumpy that they had ambushed me. I had barely heard from her since Christmas, when we'd investigated the murder of her film-star friend. While we'd both been keen on the idea of running around after criminals and having adventures, I'd been too busy writing since then to give it another moment's thought.

"So?" Gilbert asked as vaguely as possible and, when I shrugged, he deigned to say more. "What should this new endeavour be called?"

A second neatly waistcoated waiter served us each a glass of Savennières, and I seized mine to take a sip of the pleasantly sharp white wine before ignoring his question. "What will it be this time, Bella? Has some old lord been killed? Are the Metropolitan Police scratching their heads over a case?"

A flash in her eyes told me that she was excited by such prospects. "It's nothing like that, but it is quite intriguing. Lucinda – you do remember Lucinda Heaton, don't you?"

"Of course I do." I hadn't heard that name for a decade, but

Lucinda was not the sort of person one forgets. "Is she in some kind of trouble?"

"You got it in one! I heard rumours in the village and rang her to check whether it was true. You see, she received a poison-pen letter yesterday morning at her home in Hurtwood."

This frightened me a little. It was not that I'm such a coward when it comes to danger and dead bodies. Having spent the best part of a year on the front line in France, I'd seen far worse than most policemen ever would. What gave me pause was the idea that such nastiness had infiltrated the village where we'd grown up.

"What did it say?"

"What most threatening letters say," she replied matter-of-factly. "It promises a nasty death any day now. Cinders says she'll show it to us when we get there."

"I see." The reality was beginning to sink in, and I wasn't certain that I liked it. "I'll have to go to Hurtwood."

Gilbert had been listening with that usual indifferent expression on his face. "It's not so bad, you know. It's actually rather pretty down that way."

"Yes, thank you, Gilbert. It's not the landscape that I mind, but I haven't been back there since I left for the war. There are so many people I haven't spoken to in all that time – all our friends from school, and a few enemies too. I don't know how they'll receive me."

"I'm sure that Lucinda will be only too happy to see you," Bella teased, and the two ends of her mouth became a little sharper. "Don't forget how much she adored you when we were children."

Gilbert was clearly excited by this, even if I wasn't. "A bit of an admirer, was she? Perhaps you can rekindle the flame of young love. It's not right for a man of your age to be alone."

"I'm not alone. Thank you, Gilbert. I live with my mother, aunt and uncle." In my head, this was a proud claim to make.

Once the words were out in the world, I felt like digging a hole and spending the rest of my life underground. At least I hadn't boasted that I also had a dog.

Bella just laughed at me. "You don't know the most interesting part of the mystery yet."

"Oh, yes?" My voice rose a fraction higher, along with my left eyebrow.

"Lucinda wasn't the only one to receive a letter. Her cousin Tilly got one, too."

My gaze wandered around the restaurant as I attempted to make sense of what I was hearing. I barely took in the décor or the other diners, but the gentle hubbub kept me from floating off with my thoughts.

"I could understand her cousins upsetting someone. James and Tilly have always been a troublesome pair, but not dear Lucinda."

"Everyone loves Lucinda," Bella replied in a rather detached voice. We had heard such assertions since we were children. Even though she was part of the otherwise loathed Heaton clan, our friend was simply the most revered person in the village.

I suddenly remembered a rumour my mother had told me. "What does her fiancé think of all this? The last I heard, she was supposed to marry Richard Fairbanks this summer."

Growing more excited with every revelation, Bella leaned closer to whisper. "She called off the engagement just a short time ago. I've yet to discover why."

"Well, I'm not interested in any of these people," Gilbert rudely announced. "All I require is a name to put on the documentation for your new business."

"It's not a business, my dear," his girlfriend corrected him. "It's meant to be a lark, a jaunt. Our sleuthing should be a thrilling adventure to enjoy before we settle down and become boring. It will be something to tell our children about in place of bedtime stories."

It didn't take much to get Bella excited about a new project. When we were children ourselves, we had devised any number of grand schemes. If her current plan came to fruition, it might well be the first we'd completed.

Gilbert, on the other hand, was not the type to revel in fun and games. "You don't have to call it a business if you don't want to. I'm still going to fill out the necessary paperwork in order to protect your interests." I doubted that he was particularly concerned about my interests, but he did have some suggestions for names. "I rather like The Great Adventurers, Ltd? Or what about Marius and Company?"

"*Marius* and Company?" Bella repeated with fire in her voice. I enjoyed seeing her bland boyfriend get her monkey up. "Why wouldn't we use my name when I had the idea in the first place?"

Gilbert put his hand on hers and spoke in a tender voice. "I'm only thinking of you, my sweet." As much as I was loath to admit it, the man did have a kinder side that he reserved for her. "If anything were to go horribly wrong with a case, I'd want the blame to fall on Marius."

To save her from having to respond to this, I jumped in myself. "That's lovely, old chum. You are far more considerate than people realise."

He clearly didn't detect the undertone to this statement, as he nodded gratefully and returned to the main discussion. "Marius and Co. it is then." He scribbled the name down in a few places, then handed me the papers to sign as our meals arrived at the table.

"Do you know what, Gilly?" I asked him with more than a little mischief in my voice as I put the papers safely in my briefcase to be looked at my leisure. "I think this will turn out to be a grand idea. Having everything in writing gives me a sense of what lies ahead. Think of all the thrills that Bella and I will have together now that we've got our very own detective agency. It's just a shame you'll be too busy at the bank to join in the fun."

He suddenly didn't seem so keen on the idea. "Perhaps I was being a little hasty with all this talk of formal entanglements. If you could give me back—"

"No, no, it's a wonderful idea." I turned to our companion before he could object again. "Do you really think someone wants to kill Lucinda and Tilly?"

She sipped her wine before answering. "It's certainly possible. But whatever the reason the sender wrote those notes, this is just the kind of case we should be investigating."

"Has anyone called the police?"

"Sergeant Rossiter has been informed, but you know what he's like. He essentially told Tilly that, if no one has been murdered, she was wasting his time."

"How did you hear about the letters?"

Bella had chosen salmon and took a moment to savour a bite before replying. "Lucinda's neighbour, Jeb Paignton, was passing when she received the letter, and I bumped into him in the street. He said he immediately thought of us."

"Why?"

My questions were evidently becoming wearisome, as she set her fork down and sighed. "Because he'd heard about our frankly sensational investigative work at Everham Hall. We out-policed the police, if you remember, and people in Hurtwood have talked of little else since."

I doubted that the folk back home were really so amazed by our exploits, but I wasn't about to tell her that.

"And besides," she added, "you know what it's like. There is no such thing as a secret in Hurtwood."

I bit my tongue then. This was not an attempt to stop myself talking. I'd missed the lump of meat on my fork and given myself a nasty nip. "I'll call Inspector Lovebrook at Scotland Yard to find out what he thinks."

"Perfect. And I'll meet you at Lucinda's house first thing tomorrow morning. You can stay at Hurtwood House if it makes things any easier."

I couldn't blame Bella for taking such an interest in the goings-on in our village. She spent most of her time caring for her stricken father in the grand manor house nearby. Any excuse to get off the estate would do her good – even if it ended up with several dead bodies and a killer on the loose.

We ate, drank, and I told them as much about my new book as I could without giving away the plot. Bella kindly oohed and aahed at the appropriate moments, and then I laughed at her stories about the unusual inhabitants of the village where we'd grown up together. It felt the same as when we were adolescents and spent our long summer days putting the world to rights. Not even Gilbert's occasional tuts or glum comments could spoil the atmosphere.

"I think we should have a toast," she eventually announced. "To Marius and Co."

"To the good ship Marius and Co. and all who sail in her." I raised my glass and, when Bella's beau failed to do the same, I believe she stamped on his foot.

We finished the last of our wine and, when the meal came to an end, I was rather sad it was over.

"This is my treat," I told them. I thought I should at least pretend I'd made something of myself, even if I was barely keeping a roof over my head. "It's not often I have the chance to wine and dine one of the mighty Montagues."

"You silly thing. It's been so nice to see you again." Bella's face lit up as she rose to leave. She placed a friendly hand on my sleeve before Gilbert led her off through the restaurant and back outside. Feeling somehow over the moon and down in the dumps at the very same time, I sat there and watched them go.

For whatever reason, Bella loved Mr Baines the Banker, and there was no hope for a Johnny-come-lately like me. I'd had my chance to propose to her before the pair of them ever met, but seeing her in any context was still better than the years I'd spent without her. It was a Tantalean punishment that I would have to bear in silence.

"Would you care to order anything else, sir?" The plummy waiter peered down at me through his pince-nez. I had the definite feeling that I was no longer welcome now that my passport to this realm had departed.

"Just the bill, please," I replied, and he nodded in an impressively snooty manner. He was about to scuttle away when I spoke again. "My publisher will pay. I was told that Bertrand Price-Lewis has an account here?"

"Yes, of course, sir." He looked as though he was about to take issue with this, and so I pre-empted the complaint.

"I'm one of his best-selling authors. You can tell him to charge the meal to Carmine Fortescue."

I winged my way out of the restaurant before the waiter could discuss my identity with his colleagues and realise that I was not the twenty-stone blowhard with whom I sadly shared a publisher. Like a soldier escaping from an enemy camp, I shot through the elaborate lobby and out of that luxurious entrance to breathe in the (relatively) fresh London air.

And that was when I remembered that there was another reason I'd stayed away from my home town for so long. I really wasn't certain that I wished to go back.

THREE

Bella wasn't the only one who was excited about my first visit to Hurtwood in over a decade. My mother, aunt and uncle were most animated when I returned to my flat in St James's Square.

"I've always thought you were silly not to have gone back there," my mother kindly informed me when I told them of my plan. "It's not as though the place is haunted."

"Are you so sure, Mother?" I was cutting parsnips for my uncle in the kitchen. The man was a real chef – in that he was very good at getting other people to do the most tiresome tasks for him.

"Now listen here, boy." The bushy-bearded former baker waggled his knife around as he spoke but did not appear to have much interest in using it on the pile of carrots in front of him. "It was *my* brother who went missing from Hurtwood all those years ago. You may be his son, but I knew him a lot longer than you did."

Ah, yes. I always enjoy being reminded of the fact that my father disappeared off the face of the earth while I was defending Britain on the continent. The beloved and ever-friendly Hurtwood Village solicitor walked out of the house to buy a paper one morning and had not been seen in the ten years since. This was surely the most significant reason why I was less than eager to return to my childhood home.

"It's not a competition, Stan." Auntie Elle was sitting in her wheelchair at the table, scrubbing the earth off a few large potatoes. She prodded my uncle with the end of her grabbing stick each time he stopped working. "We all loved Terence. He was a good man and, whatever happened to him, it affected us all."

Our dog Percy howled in agreement, although he hadn't actually been born when my father disappeared. He pointed his large, sorrowful eyes in my direction, but I would not give him the sympathy he desired.

"What I was trying to say," my mother continued, "is that nothing in Hurtwood is more frightening than what you'd find in any other town. We had a happy time there together, and the house where we lived is just a building."

I knew this made sense, but there's often a gulf between what's true and what's comfortable to hear.

"I don't have any choice now either way." I sighed, which rather undermined my stoic declaration. "I've agreed to go, and I won't disappoint Bella by changing my mind."

I was expecting a stronger reaction to this. My family were not entirely supportive of the idea of my spending time with the woman I'd once loved, who was already, if not betrothed, then at least entangled with another man. Instead of wise words and warnings, though, they fell silent, and a smile formed on each of their faces – except Percy's, of course. Our basset hound only ever looked dejected.

"What is it?"

"Nothing, Marius," Mother replied, but she couldn't keep a straight face and had to look at her sister-in-law to avoid bursting.

I turned to my aunt, as she is normally the most sensible of the three. "Auntie Elle, tell me what's so amusing."

Perhaps inevitably, she turned to her husband, who replied with a confident laugh. "There's nothing to worry about, dear boy. We just think that it's important to keep hold of one's past, and we're glad you're finally going home."

Something in his tone gave them away.

"You'd like to come with me, wouldn't you?"

The conspiring pensioners gazed at one another, and I knew that I'd guessed correctly.

"Only if it's no trouble," Mother was quick to respond. "It would be lovely to see the village again, and we really shouldn't have left the house unattended for so long."

"That's right." Uncle Stan couldn't hide how happy he was. "We'll be tidying your old house the whole time. You won't even know we're there."

"Perhaps it's too much to ask." Elle addressed the others. "He'll be busy and there are only two bedrooms anyway."

Before they could get too disappointed, and Percy howled again, I put them out of their misery. "Of course you can come. It will be nice to have your moral support. And Bella said that I could stay with her family in the big house if needed."

Stan clapped his hands together as though all was right with the world. "We won't get in your way for one second, boy. Now tell me all about these letters that someone's been sending. It sounds a ghoulish sort of plot to me. Do you know the gals who received them well?"

His question made me reflect not just on Lucinda but also on her two cousins and all the other young folk I'd known when I lived in Hurtwood.

"Quite well," I replied a little under half truthfully. "I was at school with them. James Heaton was my best friend for a time, and Lucinda and Tilly were close to Bella, even though she's the daughter of the Duke and they're..."

My words trailed off as I didn't feel it was particularly loyal to mention the ill-repute of the Heaton family. I must have fallen to daydreaming, as I felt the mechanical pincer of Auntie Elle's stick on my elbow, and I returned to my chopping.

Stan may not have been much of a scullery maid, but he certainly knew how to cook a roast dinner. It was just what I needed to steel myself for... well, whatever lay before me. When it was over, and I'd come to terms with the fact that I did not have room for another serving of apple crumble, my mother came to see me in my room.

She didn't say anything at first. She just stood in the open doorway, watching me as I sat scribbling some notes for my third novel that was now gestating in my brain.

"I know it won't be easy for you to go back home, Marius," she said when I finally stood to talk to her. "But there's no need to worry."

"Marius Quin, worry? The very idea is absurd." I put my arm around the dear woman to reassure her as I spoke a good deal of nonsense. "I've been through a war and written at least one successful novel. I nearly had my leg blown off and lived to tell the tale. I very much doubt that a small village in Surrey will defeat me, even if there is a lunatic threatening young women there."

She humoured her foolish son with a smile. "I'm certain that you'll get to the bottom of any such nastiness, but there's nothing wrong with being apprehensive."

She'd never addressed my father's disappearance directly. It had been years since she'd said his name and even now, on the eve of our return to our family home, she could only speak of him in abstract terms.

"My wonderful mother." I sighed and placed my cheek against the top of her head. She was a small woman and fitted rather neatly. "I appreciate your compassion, I really do, but I'll be absolutely fine."

I wanted to take her by the shoulders to look into her wise old eyes and ask whether anything had occurred to her in the last decade that might explain what happened to my missing father. I wanted her to solve the mystery that I couldn't, but whenever I tried to broach the subject, the words refused to emerge.

"What about you?" I asked instead. "Are you ready for the trip?"

She tilted her head to see me better. "I'll be fine, my lovely. I always am."

Her messy grey curls seemed to tangle yet more as we both searched for a way to lighten the mood. Life is easy when you pretend everything is fine. I can be perfectly happy for weeks if I don't think about my father or the friends who died in the war. Everything's all "Sir Garnet" when I imagine that I can afford the mortgage on my ridiculous flat and Gilbert Baines doesn't exist.

Whatever sadness Mother carried with her, there was no sign of it the next day when we prepared the cars to leave. She even joined in with one of my uncle's favourite songs.

"Take me away from the streets and houses.
Take me away from the smoke, smoke, smoke.
Take me away from the bricks and mortar.
Take me by land or take me by water."

We had to lift Auntie Elle into Stan's old baker's van, so I didn't have the puff to sing along. Stan was having a wonderful time, though, and I could tell that my mother considered running back into the flat to fetch her accordion.

"Take me away from the cabs and motors.
I want to go for a holiday.
Take me to Kew or Timbuctoo, anywhere will do,
But take, take, take me away."

The three of them broke out in howling laughter, which made a pack of hirsute old fellows who were entering the East India Club next door look very alarmed indeed.

"We're in fine voice this morning," Stan told my mother, though his wife didn't seem to agree.

"What a shame that our destination is only a couple of hours away. I could listen to you singing that song all day." I was fairly sure Auntie Elle didn't mean this.

I placed her wheelchair into the back of the van and went over to my glossy red Invicta. My mother had already settled in the passenger seat, with Percy on her lap. Our dog was overjoyed to be setting out on a journey and licked her face, as his curving tail flapped about like a snake in a trap.

"I can't wait to get going." Her eyes traced out the shape of the black metal steering wheel as I got in beside her.

"Would you like to drive, Mother?" I asked playfully and her face brightened for a moment before she presumably remembered her first and last disastrous spell behind the wheel when she'd managed to tip her brother-in-law's three-wheel van onto its side.

"No, thank you, dear. I'm happy enough as a passenger. I can look at the scenery better that way."

She sounded rather distant as she said this, and I promised myself that I would make the journey as thrilling as possible. To instantly scupper my plans, my uncle had finished cranking the noisy old engine on his baker's van and managed to get away ahead of us. The traffic in London was busy that morning and, whenever I saw the chance to overtake, a bus or knacker's cart would appear from the other direction. I was forced to trundle along at the speed of the van in front of me all the way to Surrey. It was not the first time I'd questioned the logic of owning such a powerful car in a busy city.

We crawled along through Chelsea and Putney before the scenery grew wilder around Richmond Park and Stan went a few miles an hour faster. My mother was as frustrated as I was by the pace we set, and I cursed my good manners for not just honking my horn and making him move aside. Happily, I soon relaxed into the journey. We were in no hurry, after all, and I had some thinking to do before we reached Hurtwood.

I hadn't intentionally lost contact with my old friends, but a lot had changed since the last time I'd seen them. As we got closer to our home town, I began to recognise the lanes and landmarks that I had seen so often as a child. Images of my former companions flooded my brain before memories of my father eclipsed them.

I suddenly pictured our first family car when I was barely big enough to climb aboard on my own. I could still see my father's cheerful face as he showed it off to me and hear his excited laughter as he took us for a spin around the village. I remembered Christmases and birthdays in the old house together and, as the passage of time shuttled me from one memory to the next, I saw him change. It was not just that he got older as I turned from a boy into a man, he seemed to lose his previously unfaltering positivity.

The journey passed quickly and, when we were almost there, I finally overtook Uncle Stan in order to shoot along the narrow lane that led to Hurtwood Village. That isolated spot had always felt otherworldly to me. It was only accessible by a single-lane track through the Hurtwood itself, like a castle in a fairy tale that is hidden in a forest of thorns.

I sped along under the canopy of trees, and I saw my mother tense beside me. She would probably have driven faster had she been the one behind the wheel, but that didn't stop her worrying when I did it. I could tell just how nervous she was without looking and so, when we got to the blind corner just before the town, good sense got the better of me and I slowed the car to a crawl.

I looked in my mirror to see Stan way back at the edge of the forest. He and Elle had never lived in Hurtwood, but they'd been there often enough and knew how to find our old house. Even if they hadn't, it was hard to get lost in such a small place. We emerged from the shadow of the forest to roll along past the pretty cottages on the road towards the centre of town. Hurtwood was essentially made up of three roads, with a pub in the middle, a church on one side, and any number of houses dotted around the edges of the forest. The Duke of Hurtwood's estate was up on the hill and that is the sum total of the village where I was born.

I pulled the car to a stop at the crossroads in front of the Duke's Head public house – or Daddy's Head, as Bella used to call it. The streets were empty as I climbed out of the car, and I felt this was the perfect reintroduction to the old place. I needed a few moments with my thoughts before I had to talk to any of the old gang or deal with a potential crime.

But then, when do I ever get what I need?

"Marius, thank goodness you've come," a voice called, and a young woman with honey-brown eyes and glossy chestnut hair came running from her neat front garden to launch herself into my arms. "I thought I'd die before you got here."

FOUR

It was hard to say what had the bigger impact – seeing all the old sights again, or Lucinda Heaton wrapping herself around me.

The centre of Hurtwood Village was just as picturesque as I remembered. Every other roof was thatched, the walls of the houses were whitewashed and there were roses and ivy creeping up half of them. I can't say that any of that held my attention just then, though.

I looked into Lucinda's much-admired eyes and found it hard to breathe for a moment. In the ten years since I'd last seen her, she'd turned into an adult. She was exactly twelve months younger than me, and I must admit I'd never taken her seriously at school. Of course, a year's difference at eighteen is not the same thing as a year's difference a decade later.

After Heaven knows how long, I managed some feeble response. "I had to come after I'd heard what—"

"Ah, you got here then," Bella strode from Lucinda's house to declare. She had a curious look on her face and bit her lip as she tried to make sense of whatever was happening.

"I was about to..." I began. "Or rather, I was merely helping our friend here with..."

Even as I muttered this nonsense, Lucinda put her head against my chest and squeezed me more tightly. "I can't tell you what it means to have you here. I'm at my wits' end. I really am."

It would have been rude to push the girl away, but Bella's curiosity had turned into disapproval and – lucky old me – as my cheeks turned as red as my car, my aunt and uncle arrived to witness my embarrassment.

"My name's Stan," he said. "I'm Marius's uncle, and this is my wife Eleanor." His voice tentative, he was evidently confused by the scene before him, so he shrugged and drove slowly away.

Mother stayed exactly where she was. It wasn't every day that she got to see a woman throw herself at me, and she was enjoying the spectacle.

"You were helping Lucinda?" Bella asked, to return us to the awkward discussion I had hoped we'd abandoned.

I thought this might make my affectionate assailant release me, but no.

"Helping is possibly a strong word for it," I confessed. "But I'm here now and I'll do whatever I can to..." I failed to think of a synonym for the word "help".

Bella could no longer hide how amused she was by my blushing and clapped her hands together resolutely. "Wonderful. Well, we've just put some water on to make tea, and Tilly and James will be here at any moment." Still grinning, she turned and walked back up the path to Lucinda's house.

The young lady in question had finally found the courage to detach herself and was free to gaze adoringly at me. "How can I ever thank you?"

This was a difficult question to answer. For one thing, I

hadn't done a great deal, but I opted for, "I believe tea was mentioned?"

She looked a touch disappointed and turned away. Mother was still there in my car, apparently enthralled by the entertainment.

"Our house is only a two-minute walk from here," I called over to her. "I'm sure you'll remember the way."

Percy wasn't about to miss out on the attention of a group of strangers, and he jumped from Mother's lap to waddle after me. I say *jumped*, but he was no great athlete, and a better word might be *flopped*. That's it. He flopped through the open door, managed to land on all fours and, evidently pleased with this performance, scampered jauntily off.

"Young Master Quin," a voice I couldn't fail to recognise floated over the neat privet hedge from the house beside Lucinda's. "I heard you were coming back, but I must say that I didn't believe it."

My teacher Mrs Abbot was greyer and rounder than the last time I'd seen her, but there was no mistaking her high, superior tone.

"I'm happy to prove you wrong, miss."

She didn't actually look at me as she clipped at the hedge with a small pair of secateurs. She had done the very same thing when I was at school. Whenever she told off one of her pupils, she would fix her eyes on a point on the wall as though she couldn't bear to look at the offending child before her.

"If I'm being totally honest," she continued, "I really didn't think you'd show your face. Not after... well, you know."

I hadn't a clue what she meant and was frankly a little offended that she could think so poorly of me. "No, miss. I'm afraid I don't. Though I do know that, since the last time I saw you, I fought in the war while you stayed here with your pretty cottage and elegantly presented garden." I hadn't expected to lose my temper, but once I'd started, I couldn't stop. "I almost died on a number of occasions for the sake of this country, and I think it's a little much that—"

She shook her head irritably. "Yes, yes. I'm sure you did a wonderful job in that respect, and all power to you. But I was referring to your studies, Marius. If I remember correctly, which I invariably do, you did not finish your secondary education certificate."

She'd always been a trifle peculiar, but she'd clearly now lost her mind. "That is true, Mrs Abbot. I was unable to finish my final year of schooling as, soon after turning eighteen, I was sent to France to fight. I sincerely apologise for my absence."

She stopped her rhythmic clipping and fixed her eyes on me expectantly.

"Well...?" she finally said when I did not produce the response she required.

"I'm sorry. You'll have to be clearer. I can't for the life of me imagine what you'd like me to say."

Her head tipped back and, with her lips pursed together in a perfectly snooty protrusion, she explained the very simple fact I'd failed to grasp. "Have you considered returning to school to complete your studies? I'm aware that you lived on the continent for some time after the war, but you've been back in Britain long enough to have made a decision about your future. There is a space in my schoolroom should you wish to sit your final exams this year."

I considered telling her that my last book had won the Mid-Surrey Crime Writers' Award for the best debut novel of 1925. I had never made such a petty boast before, but that is the kind of response people like her provoke in me. I thought I might even tell her about the short but complimentary review *A Killer in the Wings* had received in the *London Chronicle*, or the fact it very nearly opened in the theatre in Leicester Square. I could tell that it would do me no good, though, and so I smiled and told her what she wanted to hear.

"To tell you the truth, I really haven't investigated the possibility. I will give it some serious consideration and let you know."

Her stern manner finally softened a little. "Wonderful, Marius. That's wonderful, and it's a real pleasure to see you again after all this time." Her snip snip snipping continued and, as I was about to walk away, she informed me that "No man without a formal educational diploma has ever made anything of his life."

In response, I found myself speaking like a schoolboy. "No, miss. Of course not, miss." In my head, though, I was listing exceptions to her rule as I walked up the path to Lucinda's house.

Michael Faraday, Mark Twain, John Rockefeller, Mary Anning, Jesus Christ. I have no doubt that the list goes on and on.

I wasn't so much shaken by my run-in with our old teacher as reminded of the eccentricity of the place that I'd come to idealise. People like her were the heart of Hurtwood, and we comparative youngsters had yet to put our stamp on the place.

Lucinda's house was immense by Hurtwood's standards, but miniature compared to the castle on the hill. It was only a few decades old and had been built by her rich uncle as a present to her loyal bulldog of a father. It looked like a cottage that had grown too big. It had a simply gigantic thatched roof and matching gabled dormer windows. Two-thirds of the front wall was covered in yellow and green ivy and, underneath, the house itself was all mock-Tudor beams and ornately leaded glass. It was both beautiful and grotesque, and everyone said that the Heaton family had built the overly grand edifice right in the middle of the village to prove just how wealthy they were.

"What's the matter?" Bella asked when I arrived in the neatly appointed living room. She always knew when something was not quite right with me. It was one of the reasons I generally failed to keep secrets from her.

"Did you catch old Abbot's attention in the garden?" Lucinda seemed a little calmer now that she was sitting in a large armchair with Percy on her lap.

"Indeed I did. I don't know how you can live next door to her. I'm twenty-eight now, and I'm still frightened that she'll make me come back at five o'clock to write an essay on Roman Britain."

Bella handed me a cup and saucer in blue and white that matched much of the upholstery and curtains of the room. "We're not in school anymore, Marius," she kindly reminded me. "Mrs Abbot is just a normal person."

Lucinda emitted a sigh, and I felt that, in happier times, this discussion would have forced a laugh. "You are too generous, Bella. You always have been." She turned back to me and, in a perfect approximation of the quirky academic's voice said, "Mrs Abbot is not a normal person. She is something else altogether. In fact, she may not even be human."

I settled down on the sofa to talk of more pressing dangers than whatever Mrs Abbot might present.

"Is that the letter?" I pointed to a folded piece of paper on the table, and Lucinda nodded.

"That's the second one. It came today. The first is on the mantelpiece." The panic was back in her voice. "I don't know what to make of them, Marius. I really don't."

I read the few lines silently and something about the stark black capital letters on the otherwise plain white paper sent a shudder through me.

JUST BECAUSE TIME HAS PASSED, THAT DOESN'T MEAN I'VE FORGOTTEN YOU. 1917 WILL NEVER DIE, BUT YOU WILL.

"1917?" Bella had been reading over my shoulder and asked the question before I could. "What happened in 1917?"

Dressed in silk harem trousers with no socks or shoes, Lucinda pulled her legs a little closer to her body. "To be perfectly honest, I've tried not to think about it. I wouldn't even have opened it if I'd realised what it was. Whoever sent it played a horrible trick on me."

I turned to Bella, as she appeared to know everything that I didn't that week, but she looked just as confused as I was.

"What trick, Cinders?" Bella asked.

Our old friend hesitated before answering. "Look at the envelopes. You'll soon see what I mean."

I lifted my cup to have a sip of tea before realising that it was empty and so, whilst Bella was busy with the detective work, I went around making sure that everyone had refreshments. If she turns out to be a better sleuth than I am, perhaps she'll keep me on as a tea boy.

"How odd!" she remarked.

"Have you looked at the stamps?" Lucinda prompted, and so I put down the teapot and did just that.

The letter I'd just read came in a small cream envelope with three stamps that made up the necessary value, while the original one that Bella held only had one. It was only after I'd recorded this insignificant detail that the most important factor struck me. "The franks are different. They weren't sent from the same place."

I turned to look at mine in the light, and Bella did the same with hers.

"'Barrow-in-Furness'," she read, while the word in the small black ring on mine said, "Canterbury".

Bella was about to seize my envelope, but I grabbed hers before she could. Yes, we may be a little competitive at times.

"That's bizarre," I murmured as I compared the messily written addresses.

"Isn't it just?" Lucinda did not stand up but kept stroking

my contented hound. She had presumably already gone through the same process herself.

"Though one is terribly smudged, the handwriting is the same. And yet they were sent from opposite ends of the country."

Bella's face had turned quite grave, but she still tried to sound positive. "It's not impossible that the first was sent in Canterbury before the sender drove a few hundred miles north-west to the Lake District."

"As long as whoever sent them is still up there, we don't have a problem," I mused. "Sadly, I doubt that's the case."

Lucinda could stand no more of this conversation and closed her eyes tightly, as though she was trying to wish her life back to normal. Bella poked me and pointed at our friend until I understood what she meant.

I hated seeing poor Lucinda suffer so, but it would have been unkind to give her the wrong idea about my intentions. I hope I don't sound conceited, but she evidently still held feelings for me and didn't need heartache on top of everything else that she was enduring.

I'll have to make a correction there as I'm certain I do sound conceited suggesting that the girl would be heartbroken over the smooth-tongued lothario that I am. Either way, not knowing what else I could do, I went to make sure that she was all right.

I crouched down in front of her chair and spoke as softly as I could. "I know things might look bleak, but I've a friend in Scotland Yard who's going to help us. I told him everything on the phone last night, and he said he'll get here as soon as he's available. Bella and I will do all we can to keep you safe until he arrives."

She opened her eyes again, but before she could say anything, a man with a look of pure rage on his face stormed into the room. "We don't need your help, Quin. So crawl back to wherever you've been hiding all this time."

FIVE

The living room at number three, Dovecote Lane, was quickly filling up with figures from my childhood, and some were more welcome than others. James Heaton and I had been friends throughout our childhood. He'd always been a proud, easily angered sort of person, but that wasn't why we'd eventually fallen out.

"How nice to see you, old boy." I somehow managed to sound polite, but James still glared at me as if I'd spat at him.

As adolescents, we'd both been in love with Bella, and when she chose me over James, we barely exchanged another word until I left for war. The fact he never followed in my footsteps – as his father led the town's military service tribunal and made sure he was never put in harm's way – was the seasoning on the top of a perfectly unpalatable dish.

"Who asked you to come back here?" To say he wasn't happy to see me is something of an understatement.

"Calm down, James," Lucinda said, jumping from her chair to intervene. "It was very kind of Bella and Marius to offer their help."

"I just don't think it's a good idea to give a potential

murderer an invitation into your house, that's all. Who's to say
that Quin here isn't the one who wrote those letters?"

My former schoolfriend turned school-foe hadn't changed a
great deal since I'd last seen him. He had the same sharp jaw
and intense stare – the same arrogant manner and booming
voice. The only difference was that he'd grown a foot and a half
to resemble a circus strongman. The fellow was immense. His
body bulged out of the white cotton shirt he was wearing as
though he'd bought the wrong size.

I had no interest in arguing with him and answered without
a hint of aggression. "I haven't come here to antagonise you."

"And I don't need any heroics. Thank you, James." Lucinda
gritted her teeth as though spoiling for a fight. She was good at
everything else she'd tried her hand at, so there was nothing to
say she couldn't have floored the monster. "I've got bigger things
to worry about than your fragile sense of pride."

Though he would no doubt have knocked my lights out if
I'd spoken to him in such a manner, Lucinda had always had a
strange hold over him. He became meeker and smaller, as
though he'd shrunken down to the size of the little boy he was
inside.

Thanks to all the unnecessary bravado – and the sheer
width of him – I hadn't noticed his sister until now. Tilly was
standing in the doorway, gripping the frame as if she didn't have
the strength to support herself.

"Tilly, my dear. It's so nice to see you." Bella had stayed out
of the argument but rushed forward to greet her old friend as
James sank into an armchair.

"That's not the word I would use," she barely whispered in
reply. "If this is the way I finally go, I would say there's nothing
very nice about it at all." The youngest Heaton cousin had
always been a rather frail, ghostlike character. She did not have
the bold personality of her brother or the charm of her older
cousin. She was a grey, mouselike being who, if anyone took the

time to scratch the surface, never seemed to have a great deal underneath.

Perhaps the reason that so many people adored Lucinda Heaton was the simple fact that she was nothing like her cousins whatsoever.

"There's tea made," I said, as I didn't know what else to do to fix the fractured atmosphere. "Although it's probably cold by now. I'll run to the kitchen and make some more."

Bella gave me a pleading look to hurry back but, to be quite honest, I was happy to escape. I remembered the layout of the house from when I was a boy. Nothing had changed, right down to where the now deceased Mrs Heaton had kept the tea leaves. I put water on to boil and found the necessary accoutrements, then stood stock-still for three whole minutes to clear my mind.

When I was on the front line at Amiens, all I could think about was being back home in Hurtwood. It became as idyllic to me as Neverland was to the Darling children. I saw it as a place of harmony and – in the forest that surrounded the village – ancient, earthly magic. As I sat in my muddy, flooded trench on cold days, I forgot all about the busybodies and gossipmongers back home. I ignored how much it rained there in the springtime, and I certainly didn't remember endless schooldays or that brute James Heaton. Hurtwood – and its benevolent queen Bella Montague – was the paradise I wished to visit.

I drifted away on this daydream both in France and there in Lucinda's kitchen. When I came back to myself, the water was boiling over, and some new argument was raging in the living room. I turned off the cooker, filled the teapot and returned to the others, determined to work out who could have sent the threatening letters.

"Here we are," I said cheerily and set about filling the new cups I'd brought. I'm not usually so accommodating, but I had to do something to avoid a fight with the human-horse hybrid who had just stormed the house.

I doubt that the unifying properties of tea can be adequately explained by science. Once we all had a warm cup in our hands, a more tranquil atmosphere descended. My four old friends came together around the sofa to pore over the evidence, and Percy found another comfy spot on Tilly's feet.

"It doesn't make any sense," Bella said after a minute's silence. "Why send so many letters?"

I tried to catch up with the conversation and looked at the various exhibits laid out on the table. Six different envelopes were placed next to one another. In addition to the two we'd already seen, four were addressed to Lucinda's younger cousin.

"Three came to Tilly's house this morning," Bella explained, looking at me with that curious expression of hers. I knew she was enjoying the puzzle, even if she tried to hide it.

We stood behind the two recipients, and James cast a side-long glare at me. Perhaps thanks to my uncharacteristic generosity with the drinks service, he appeared to have begrudgingly accepted my presence there.

"So all four of the letters that came today are identical?" I asked with some surprise as I read the same messy text on each. The messages were printed in ominous capital letters, and there were smudges and ink stains all over them but no other identifying marks.

"That's right," Tilly peered over her shoulder to reply. "I received the first one on Wednesday and the three identical messages arrived today."

There were six letters in total now, with only two different messages. Killer or not, whoever had written them was clearly a madman.

"It doesn't make any sense." The panic had risen once more in Lucinda's voice. "Why would anyone send Tilly and me the same message four times on the same day from different towns across the country?"

I scanned the postmarks and noticed Wellingborough,

Swansea, Exeter and Oxford. I walked back around the sofa to
have a think. "Have you discussed any potential enemies you
might have?"

Lucinda looked at Tilly and shifted away a fraction, as
though she was not sure she wished to be connected to her
joyless cousin any more than she already was. "Obviously
someone doesn't like our family," she concluded. "Our grandparents had few admirers in this village, and our parents only
made things worse."

She was right, of course. Of everyone in her family, she was
the only one with any charm. It was often said of the Heatons
that their one redeeming quality was that they died young. Her
grandparents were long gone by the time we were born, and
both sets of the cousins' parents had perished from various
unpleasant illnesses over the last fifteen years. From what I
remember, their fathers were cold-hearted, belligerent types
who acted as though they were the real lords of Hurtwood just
because they were rich.

I followed up my question with another. "Then why now?"

"You know, Quin." It was about time James said something
rude. "I very much doubt that when some homicidal loon plans
a campaign of intimidation and murder, he wonders to himself,
perhaps the summer would be a better time to go about it."

"Thank you for that considered observation. It was most
helpful." It was becoming increasingly difficult to remain civil.
"I was referring to the time that has passed since your parents
and grandparents had any impact on this town. The last of them
died when I was abroad, isn't that right?"

Lucinda nodded in the same hesitant manner she'd had
since we'd entered the house. "Mother died just after you—"

James broke into her sentence with a voice that was too big
for the room. "Oh, for goodness' sake. This won't have anything
to do with Auntie Deborah succumbing to cancer or our miserly

grandparents. I know what happened that spring when we were idiot children and so does Tilly."

He stared at his sister, who kept her eyes on the table in front of her. When neither of them said anything more, I picked up the baton.

"But 1917 was also the year before I went away to war. The year that Bella—" I couldn't finish that sentence before James crashed his hand down on the back of the chesterfield.

"I'm not here to reminisce on unhappy times." He kept his eyes locked on mine for a few seconds. "And I'm already sick of seeing your ugly face. If anyone needs me, I'll be in the pub." Huffing out a lungful of air, he hurried from the room.

"It's always so nice to see your brother," Lucinda told her remaining cousin. "Do you have any idea what he meant?"

The pallid being on the sofa turned a shade more ghostly. "We got up to all sorts of things that year. It's impossible to know why the monster who's terrorising us would choose 1917 over any other."

She was lying, of course. James was evidently convinced that his sister knew the importance of the date, but I would not be the one to extract the truth from her. In our exciting new enterprise, that was Bella's job.

She came to sit next to Tilly on the sofa. It was something of a tight fit, but Bella was the sort of person for whom people didn't mind making space. Tilly even managed a smile as Bella's hand came to a rest on her sleeve.

"I remember that spring," my friend began. "It was the year we were all in love with someone."

"I was just mad about Marius, if I remember correctly," Lucinda remarked and, as she spoke, those magical eyes shone once more.

I'd often wondered what would have happened if I hadn't been so utterly consumed by Bella that year. Would I have fallen in love with Lucinda and lived a different life? Was it even possible that I'd chosen the wrong girl?

Bella continued to list the ill-fated romances within our circle of friends. "And then there was Dodo and Richard."

"And Richard and Lucinda," Tilly teasingly replied.

"And you and Richard," her cousin bit back. "And you and Ned, and you and that boy who was only here for a couple of months before he was called up."

"Oh yes!" Bella was evidently enjoying the nostalgia and cast her mind back over the years. "What was his name? His father had moved to the area to work, and he was such a lost little fellow – sweet in his own way. Do you remember, Tilly?"

"King..." Lucinda tried. "He had a name like that... No, Kane, I think it was. Surely you remember."

I felt as though this was a conversation to which I would not have been privy when we were younger, and it was no surprise that Tilly blushed and tried to change the topic – this was the first colour I'd seen in her cheeks since she'd arrived.

"We're getting away from the letters now. What could any of that have to do with someone wanting to kill us now? For that matter, why would you and I get them, Cinders, and not James, or any of our friends?"

"Those are interesting questions," I conceded once we'd exhausted ourselves looking pensive. "But all we have for the moment is a long list of doubts. I'm hoping that Inspector Love-brook will have some answers for us. I expect he'll turn up here before long."

"You know, it is possible that the whole thing is just a joke to upset you." Bella was trying to sound positive again. For some reason I couldn't quite define, this sounded just as cruel as the idea that someone really hated the two cousins.

"I could understand if it was just me," Tilly said in a moment of unexpected self-awareness. "But why would anyone do such a thing to Cinders?"

There was a knock on the window, and another familiar face appeared. Richard Fairbanks and Lucinda had been engaged until very recently, and I still hadn't heard an explanation for why she'd called off the wedding. Lazy conclusions formed in my brain, and I identified our first suspect. What if the whole scheme with the letters was her ex-fiancé's idea of revenge? Perhaps he'd sent them to Tilly to cover the truth.

"Go away, Richard." Lucinda got up from the sofa to shout, and Percy followed her with a growl. If there's one thing my dog enjoys, it's the chance to be angry without knowing why. "I've said all I have to say, and I don't want to see you."

Of course, their separation might also explain why Lucinda was so keen to show how fond of me she still was. If Richard had wronged her, she would be only too keen to make him jealous.

Our former classmate had his mouth up to the gap in the open window. "I heard you got another letter, my darling. I'm here to make sure that you're all right."

Her pretty face was creased with anger. "I'm more than all right, Richard. Since I stopped having anything to do with you, the world is a much brighter place."

Just like when we were at school, Richard's slick hair resembled a breaking wave on the top of his head. Unlike back then, however, he now wore a suit that was almost as expensive as my car. He'd always been clever and made a name for himself straight out of school by patenting some special formula for plastic that was far too complicated for me to understand. He was one of those people who, though pleasant to be around, it's impossible to say whether you really like them or not.

"Please, my sweet," he tried one last time. "Please talk to me, Cinders. I can't live without you."

"Then you shouldn't have been carrying on with another girl." Lucinda rushed up to the window. "She wrote you poems,

Richard! Love poems, and you didn't even have the sense to hide them when I came to your house. You're pathetic."

It was just then that James appeared behind our new arrival and grabbed him by the neck. "She said she doesn't want to see you. Or have you lost your grasp of English?"

Richard looked terrified as the hulk pulled him backwards but, once the pair were face to face, he found his courage once more. "I don't want to fight you, James."

"Then remove yourself from my cousin's front lawn. After everything I've done for you, the least you can do is leave her alone."

"You didn't let me finish, old bean." Richard had a smug look as he delivered a neat riposte. "I don't want to fight you, but I will if you get in my way."

James pushed him then. He placed two hands on the man's exquisitely tailored jacket and pushed as hard as he could. The subsequent reaction rather reminded me of a landmine exploding. Richard was propelled backwards into Mrs Abbot's hedge, and it was a good thing our old teacher was no longer around, or she might have issued a detention after all.

"Fine. I'll go," the defeated suitor conceded, before shouting back towards the house, "but I'm close at hand if you need me, my love." He reserved one last furious look for the man who had made a fool of him and, brushing the creases from his jacket, Richard walked off up the road.

SIX

Going back to Hurtwood Village made me feel as if I'd skipped the middle chapters of an extremely dramatic novel. I'd read the opening scenes – which had established the various characters and helped explain the relationships between them – but then the plot jumped ahead ten years, and I could no longer make sense of anything.

At least I knew now why Lucinda had broken off her engagement. I must admit that Richard seemed the type to keep various irons burning. At school, he'd spent most of his time running around after Lucinda but flirted terribly with her cousin (and my good friend Dodo, and practically every other girl at every chance he got).

As for Tilly herself, she refused to explain what James had meant when he claimed she knew the reason for the letters. No matter what we tried, she wouldn't tell us what had happened in 1917. Thus frustrated, Bella and I left the two cousins under Percy's watchful gaze and went off to report to Hurtwood House.

I was surprised to see that Sergeant Rossiter had been despatched to do some work for once and had left his wooden box beside the post office to patrol the street. Our local bobby's philosophy of policing was that anyone under the age of forty was obviously up to no good. He looked at me as though I was the chief suspect in every crime that had taken place in the area in years.

"I'm only here for an hour, you know!" he bellowed as if I'd confronted him on the matter. "Some bigwig from Scotland Yard told me that I have to show my face, but I still plan to have my lunch at twelve noon. My Margaret's making kidney pie. Kidney pie is my favourite!" He spoke in a tone that suggested that his lunch that day was at least of equal importance to whatever the "bigwig from Scotland Yard" asked of him.

"It's wonderful to hear that you're taking your job so seriously," I called in reply.

He was not a worldly man and apparently hadn't come across sarcasm before. "I do a very good job around here. There's hardly any crime in these parts."

I managed to resist telling him that there was hardly any crime in most small villages in Surrey. Bella walked faster to avoid laughing at the ever-bitter officer, and we'd soon made it past the pub and away from the crossroads at the centre of the village.

I had no intention of coming to Hurtwood without seeing Bella's father. A duke by title, he was, to all intents and purposes, the king of that little world within the forest. He'd been a constant presence there in my youth – like a totem up on the hill, watching over us at all times. If there was one person who knew the goings on in Hurtwood Village, it was the Duke, and it felt wrong to have returned without asking his permission first, especially after the stroke he'd suffered a few years earlier.

"You don't love her, do you?" Bella asked very bluntly as we began the walk up the sloping road.

"I don't know how to answer that." I needed a moment to

consider why she would even ask it. "If you wish to know why I chose you over Lucinda, then—"

She shook her head as though I was a fool, which I undoubtedly was when it came to romantic concerns. "No, I mean, you're not enamoured with her as everyone else we know is. You've never seemed to hold her in quite such high regard."

I still had to choose my words carefully. "That might be true, but I've also never thought of sending her a threatening letter. I think there's rather a difference."

"But it's curious, though, don't you think? Most men fall instantly under her spell. She has that kind of charm that leaves people speechless, and yet she was wildly in love with you, and you never looked twice at her... until today, at least."

I enjoyed the flash of mischief in her eyes as she said this. I was glad that my childhood companion hadn't changed too much since I'd first known her.

"Lucinda is kind and beautiful and just perfect in so many ways, but perhaps that was the problem for me. Perfect can become boring after a while."

I thought she might tease me again, but she looked rather serious and said, "It goes to show that we all view different people in different ways."

"So what you're saying is that if someone could fail to love her as I did, then someone else might even hate her?"

"Something like that, yes. I keep trying to imagine that she hides some dark secret and it's finally risen to the surface, but I've never seen even a hint of nastiness in her. She really is as nice as she seems, and it's hard to comprehend what's happening to her."

The road became steeper, and we walked past several establishments that had closed down when I was still living in Hurtwood. There was the Sparrow, a second public house halfway up the hill that had been turned into a private house at some point. The general shop which doubled as a bakery had closed, too. Anyone wanting to buy more than a pint of beer or a stamp would have to drive to a bigger town to do their shopping since the Day family had moved back to Wales.

As we walked past the former pub, I saw a man my age coming out of the front door. I'd never seen him before, so he wasn't a local. He had a scar on the side of his face, and I wondered what horrors he'd seen in the war – or whether he'd just fallen over and hurt his cheek. I smiled as we walked past and, in reply, he gave a solemn nod.

"I must admit," I said, to return us to the conversation, "I've always assumed that the reason Lucinda was so besotted with me was because I was the one man who didn't run after her."

It was hard work going up that hill, and Bella lost her balance a touch and bumped into me as she answered. "You humble thing. It couldn't be that she was head over heels with the dark and delicious Mr Marius Quin? No, of course not. She clearly went wild for your aloof, touch-me-not demeanour."

"I'll pretend you didn't say that." I maintained a straight face and kept my eyes on the tarmac beneath our feet. "But even if I hadn't been smitten with another girl at that moment – I forget who she was – everything came too easily to Lucinda. I could never have been the man for her."

I could tell that she wanted to poke fun at me again, but she stifled her reply and listened.

"Cinders only has to talk to someone, and they instantly fall in love. Forgive me for being picky, but as charming as she is, I never wanted to be bewitched into loving someone."

We were walking past Tilly and James's gigantic house as she responded, and her voice was suddenly quite sincere. "That's a very profound and Marius-esque thing to say, but I have an important question for you."

"Oh, yes?"

"Yes." She peered up the hill and her face brightened. "The

question is, do you still think you can beat me to the gates?" She ran ahead before I could reply.

Much as when we were nine, and she was a foot taller than me and twice as fast, I shouted, "You cheated. That's not fair."

I still beat her to the top, thank goodness. I'd never have lived it down if I hadn't. And once we'd crested the fearful slope, there were the gates of Hurtwood House in all their splendour. The black bars, covered in scrolling vines and foliage, were topped with golden eagles on either side. They would have been quite intimidating if I'd ever had any trouble getting through them but, since I was five years old, I'd been good friends with the guards.

"Good morning, Lady Isabella." Mr Walker staggered out of his little hut as soon as we came into view. "And Marius Quin! Is that really you, sir?" He removed his black and gold guard's hat to reveal a bald head which he proceeded to scratch.

He was a dear old fellow and, once he'd opened the gate rather laboriously, I shook his hand.

"It is indeed, Walker. And may I say you haven't changed one bit. "

His gap-toothed smile brought back memories of my early visits to the house.

"So I look just as old as I ever did? That's awfully kind of you to say." He winked and, had he not been on duty, I'm sure he would have given me a clip around the ear for old times' sake. "I heard that you were expected, but it really is wonderful to have you back. I know that a lot of the staff will be eager to see you."

"Even Caxton?" I joked, as I had been a nemesis to the Montague family's chauffeur since I was old enough to glare back at him. "Maybe some things *have* changed around here after all."

He laughed at this and waved us through. I can't say exactly why, but as I stepped onto the estate, an unusual fizz of electricity travelled over me. Even more than when I'd arrived in the village, it felt as though I was home again.

Hurtwood House was positioned on a plateau above the town. The land had once been part of the Hurtwood itself, but some distant relative of Bella's had cleared the forest to make way for grand gardens, an immense manor and even an ornamental lake on the other side of the property. What I'd always loved most about the luxurious estate, though, was the view as I caught the first glimpse of the house over the lawns. It stood on the horizon like a city in miniature.

Although the manor was one complete building, there were countless different elements to it which sprang up all over the place. A bell tower here, a spire there, muddled in with Tudor arches, steep gables and grand cupolas all joined together with flourishes from the last five hundred years of British architectural design. It was like a fireworks display recreated in brick and stone. Though a little under a century old, it had all the impact of the Elizabethan prodigy houses that had no doubt inspired it.

As I breathed in that refined air and gazed over the drifts of perfect white snowdrops, Bella had a chance to laugh at me again. "Sorry, it's just that I haven't looked at my house in such a way in... well, ever. It's nice to see it differently for a moment."

"You should try to remember how lucky you are," I said, still in awe. "This place is extraordinary – it's like something out of a half-remembered dream."

We continued along the path that, to me as a child, had felt quite infinite – it wasn't, of course, but a mile-long driveway is impressive by most people's standards.

"Dodo has been working up here in the library recently," she explained, and I imagined our bookish friend from school surrounded by dusty tomes. "She found the diary of my ancestor who expanded the old manor that originally stood here. She's done a wonderful job tidying the mess of a century of neglect. Wait until you see it."

We fell silent for some time, which gave me time to ponder a few of the topics I hadn't had the courage to broach since we'd become friends again. In my head, I asked about her father's health and why her mother couldn't do more to help after he'd had his stroke. I enquired ever so politely about what her nice but genuinely lazy brothers had been up to while she cared for their invalid father, and to each imaginary question, she gave a list of possible answers.

"Caxton," Bella called as we approached a large former stable that was now used as a garage. Her pugnacious chauffeur peered out at us, and I wished that all the people in Hurtwood who didn't like me would be less selfish and move away.

"Lady Isabella, how may I be of service this morning?" Even as he delivered this polite entreaty to his employer, he found a way to shoot daggers at me without her noticing.

"You must drive to the village and fetch Marius's bag from the red Invicta in front of Lucinda Heaton's house. He'll be staying with us for a night or two."

"Yes, madam. Of course." He bowed, and I felt just how much he wished that his head had made contact with my own at that moment. The man despised me, and I'd never fully understood why.

Luckily, he was an exception on the estate, and his colleagues took a different view. Bella's maid Agnes had been one of my most ardent fans, even before I was a writer.

"Oh, my boy," she sang as I stepped through the door into the cavernous entrance hall. "Marius, we're all so happy you've come. This house hasn't been the same since you left. It really hasn't."

Agnes had started her life there as the children's nanny and changed jobs every few years, depending on what was required.

"It's lovely to see you, too." I held out my hand to her, but she ignored it to wrap me up in her arms and lift me off the floor.

She was not a big woman, even in her many petticoats and broad skirt, but she was deceptively strong and picked me up like a brewer with a barrel of beer.

"We're calling on Father before lunch." Bella made no sign that she disapproved of the display. "I doubt he'll be up to seeing guests by the time Marius comes home this evening, so I thought it would be best to visit now."

"Well, you don't need my permission to call on His Grace. I'm not the Queen of who knows where." Her pulsating laugh that I remembered so well echoed around the immense space. In any other stately home, such impertinence from staff would have been frowned upon, but Agnes was very much one of the family.

Bella just giggled, and we strolled off towards the main staircase.

"Are any of your brothers here at the moment?" I asked as we reached the gallery on the second floor. The ceiling was covered in ornate hand-painted patterns that, as far as I could remember, had been designed by the original architect but could just as well have been added by Bella and her brothers.

"As far as I know," she replied a little mysteriously before adding an explanation. "It's a big place, Marius. I sometimes go weeks without realising that Jasper is off on a jolly somewhere. Humphry normally locks himself away in the western tower, and as for Kenton—" She cut herself short because, there in front of us, at the far end of the arched corridor, was her youngest brother.

Jasper waved brightly and looked as though he would come to talk to us, then kept walking straight ahead. Bella was evidently embarrassed by her brother's behaviour. In fact, she always had been, but I was used to the whole bizarre bunch of them and would take no offence.

"His Grace is still this way, I imagine?" I suggested and pressed on to our destination. We had to climb a short stone staircase to get to the oaken door, which had been painted an ominous black, as though to warn off visitors in plague times.

"Perhaps I should go first to make certain that he's..." Bella's sentence trailed off as she heaved open the heavy portal and slipped into the darkness beyond.

Ever since she'd come back into my life, I'd noticed an extra characteristic to her that I don't believe had ever existed before. From within this vibrant and exciting person, there was a cautiousness that occasionally peeked out.

When a few seconds had passed, the door swung open, and she stuck her head out to nod at me. I don't think I'd ever been in the Duke's bedchamber when he was inside. I'd run up there to hide from his daughter in our mammoth games of hide and seek when we were very young, but I'd never had permission to enter.

I took a first cautious step into the room and, as my eyes adjusted to the darkness, an inexplicable feeling of fear came over me.

"You took your time."

SEVEN

The Duke still had a deep, resonant voice, but it sounded as though it took more effort to use it than it once would have.

We were in a nineteenth-century manor house styled after sixteenth-century tastes, but the interior of that room looked as though it harked back to a far more ancient time that I would have been hard pressed to name. Although the walls were made of carved stone, they looked strangely natural, as if they had formed in those precise patterns over the millennia. There were carvings of leaf-covered green men in each corner of the room and trailing ivy between them. A standing candelabra, which had been lit and re-lit so many times that there was more wax visible than the metal underneath, offered the only light except for a crack in the thick brocade curtains where a blinding blade of sunlight cut through to us. To sum the place up, I'd say it looked like a wizard's workshop.

I was halfway into the room when I stopped to reply. "Good morning, Your Grace. I only got back to Hurtwood an hour ago. I went to see Lucinda, but we've come straight from there."

Bella urged me onwards and, for the moment, I could make

out nothing of the man I'd come to see except for a large mound beneath a heavy blanket.

"I don't mean today, boy. You've been back in the country for some time, from what I hear."

The scene made me think of my first visit there, when my father had presented me to the family and our parents had encouraged Bella and me to play together.

"Ah, yes, well..." I stuttered out, uncertain what excuse I might summon. "You see..."

My mumbling was interrupted by the sound of hearty laughter, and I moved past that beam of light to see the dear fellow's face more clearly.

"Hello, Marius. I'm glad you're finally here."

"It's been too long, Your Grace."

He laughed again. "It certainly has."

There was a generosity to Bella's father that I had somehow forgotten. I'd always liked the Duke, but I tended to remember just how large and imposing he was rather than this softer side. He attempted to push himself up, and I could see how much of a struggle it was. His right arm refused to do as it was told, so Bella came to help him.

He put a pair of glasses on to look at me. "I want you to know that you are always welcome here, whatever you might feel."

"I never imagined anything else."

"We both know that isn't true, Marius." He wouldn't let me get away with lies of any colour. "You've been in Britain for years, and you've never set foot in Hurtwood in all that time. Not even to collect your belongings or visit your mother."

I took a deep breath as I considered whether I should even try to explain myself. "I sold my first book shortly after I arrived in London, and so she came to live with me. I had plenty of space; it would have been mean not to invite her to stay."

"No, she moved in with you, as she knew you wouldn't visit her here. You can lie to yourself, boy, but not to me."

I took his advice and gave up trying. He appeared to know the workings of my mind better than I did.

Bella was clearly still amused by her father's idiosyncrasies and moved to open the curtains on either side of the bed so that we could see the room more clearly. It was no less mysterious in the daylight and, as with every room I'd passed through to get there, small, individual features chimed with long-neglected memories. There was an alcove with a Roman statue in one corner and a painting of a cheerful old lady in mourning clothes on the wall opposite. Visiting the manor again was like looking through an old box of souvenirs.

"Come along then. Why are you really here? And what took you to the house of the lovely Miss Heaton?"

Bella looked at me across the room, but it was my job to reply. "She's been receiving poison-pen letters. Her cousin Tilly got them, too. They're both quite distressed."

As I sat down in a Louis XVI armchair beside his bed, his joviality faded. "Those poor girls. What did the letters say?"

Bella walked around to us as she answered. "The first was a general threat of violence, and the second that came today mentioned 1917. We were rather hoping you might know something that could explain it."

When he didn't reply, I spoke again. "It's a puzzling case, don't you think?" It was far easier to discuss threats and potential murders than my own life, and I had to wonder what that said about me. "If James was in danger, I might be able to understand it. He's always had a talent for rubbing people up the wrong way, and his sister isn't the easiest person with whom to spend any length of time. But it's hard to imagine what someone could hold against Lucinda?"

Clearing his throat, the Duke reflected on what we'd told him. "Their fathers were real scoundrels. They were known for treating their tenants badly, but I don't remember anything particularly dreadful that they did that year." He sucked in his cheeks to think for a few moments longer. "It could be connected to the war, perhaps. You should look at the boys who were ahead of you in school. If they enlisted in 1917 and had a grievance with the Heatons, that could explain things. James and Tilly's father, Tom, was the one with all the money. His brother Granville was just a bully and had no real power, though they were both on the military service tribunal. Along with a few easily influenced lackeys, they were the ones who put forward young men to fight in the war. I tried to block their more dubious decisions, but I was usually overruled."

This was far too vague, and I pushed him for more. "That's all very interesting, but can you recall any specific rivalries or scandals? You always knew what was going on in the village back then. I imagine you still do."

"There are no secrets from the Duke of Hurtwood." Bella was standing behind me but leaned into the light to speak. "It was terribly infuriating whenever I got into trouble at school."

Even as she was speaking, I could tell that her father's mind was whizzing through memories in search of something that could prove useful.

"Yes, at school..." These words lit a fire under him, and he explained his thinking. "There was a boy who joined your class that year. He wasn't here long before he was called up, but Tilly was very fond of him."

"Yes, Lucinda mentioned him earlier. Kane, wasn't it? I can barely remember him," I replied, and it was my turn to search my memories.

"His father worked at the bank in Guildford, and I used to have some dealings with him. He still lives in the area, in fact."

"Sebastian!" Bella suddenly declared and then, in a softer voice, said, "The boy's name was Sebastian Kane."

"That's right, dear." The Duke lost some of his spark again.

"There was something of a situation between Tilly and Sebastian. Their parents became involved. I never heard the full story, but the boy reacted badly to whatever had happened between them."

"It's strange," I muttered, trying to fit what he'd told us into the context of my last year at school. "I don't remember any of this. I thought Tilly was keen on Richard back then."

The Duke rocked from one side to the other to get more comfortable. "I'm surprised you didn't know, Marius. Sebastian would have been at Aldershot with you during your training."

"Oh, of course: Private Kane! I do remember him there. Shy sort of bloke. Never had much to do with the other conscripts and ended up in a different platoon from mine. I didn't see him again after we went to France." For some reason, I slipped into the youthful speech patterns that were so common in my army days.

Bella thought of something more helpful to say than any of my twittering. "Daddy, do you have any idea what happened to him?"

The Duke's cheerful features changed in the shifting light as a cloud blocked out the sun. "His name is etched on the war memorial in the centre of the village. If I remember correctly, he died at the Battle of the Lys."

"That was in the April of 1918. That poor boy." The news affected me more than I would have expected. "Lys was a bloodbath. Although there were few battles that weren't, of course."

When she spoke again, Bella was similarly muted and finally sat down next to me. "There are thirty-seven names on the war memorial. I walk past it all the time, and yet I hadn't thought of Sebastian since the day he left our class. That's really far too cruel."

I gave her my hand for comfort, and she squeezed it while the silence settled around us.

One of the things I most admired about the Duke was his dedication to the community. When we were at school, he would call by once a week to talk about some fascinating topic that interested him. He knew the name of every child in our class and had been on the parish council. So it hardly surprised me that he remembered more about my classmates than I did, but I still felt guilty.

"There's no reason to think that these letters are connected to Sebastian," he warned us. "Look into what happened if you must, but do so carefully. Tilly has always been a fatalist, and I don't want her thinking that this situation is her fault."

He spoke these words in such a decisive manner that I thought this would be the end of the conversation. His expression lightened, though, and it was clear that he had something else to reveal.

"You know, Marius, I read your book."

"I didn't, but I'm well aware that Bella foisted copies onto everyone in the family." I didn't dare ask what he thought of it, but he told me anyway.

"I couldn't put it down. The whole thing was entirely implausible, of course. People don't act in real life the way they do in mystery novels, but I suppose that you have to take them with a fistful of salt."

"I'm glad you enjoyed it," I replied, still unsure whether he had.

"Oh, yes. I read it in one sitting. But as you can see, my sittings these days can last an awfully long time." He had a good chortle at this. "I like to think that I'm a good judge of character, but you had me bamboozled to the last page."

"Thank you, Your Grace. I'm never sure whether readers feel better when they spot the killer or are entirely confounded."

"I can only speak for myself," he began, and his expression

was so gleeful at that moment, I could have stayed there talking for hours, "but I prefer to be kept in suspense."

"Then you'll have to wait to see what happens in my next book."

"Be away with you, you shameless self-promoter." He laughed at this and batted the air with his hand.

Bella left ahead of me, but I couldn't resist a short, "It's nice to see you, old friend," from the door.

"And you, boy," he replied, looking more serious again. "And please do me the favour of marrying my daughter one day. The calamity of the man she's with now is quite intolerable. I swear he brings me out in a rash."

Bella had thankfully left the room by now, but I still felt my cheeks flush. "I'm afraid that ship has sailed."

"Bah!" He waved his arm once more. I didn't remember him being so very expressive. Perhaps because one side of his body was so limited in movement, he compensated with the other. "Stuff and nonsense. No one blames you for making a mess of things before the war. You were just a child back then."

I bit my lip, wishing that life was as simple as he suggested. "You would have made a wonderful father-in-law, Your Grace. And you can still call me son if it makes you happy."

He let out a glum laugh. "I've got enough sons already, thank you. Although my lack of grandchildren is another matter altogether."

I gave the old devil a salute for some reason and slipped through the door as he grumbled his goodbye.

"Does he really stay up there all day?" I asked his only daughter, who was waiting at the top of the stairs for me.

"Sadly, yes, but he doesn't have to. There's a wheelchair for him, and the staff could bring him up and down whenever he wishes. He may seem a jolly sort of giant, but he's not the man you used to know. He wouldn't show it, but Father is more broken inside than out. It's not his physical care that I stayed here to provide. It's my job to make sure that he doesn't give up on life altogether."

A pool of sympathy welled up within me, and I saw her place there for what it was. "I can imagine why you wouldn't trust anyone else to do it."

"My brothers lend a hand sometimes, but they're not built for conversation." A stoic smile on her face, she turned away to descend the stairs. Her voice travelled back to me over her shoulder, and I knew she would have preferred to change the topic. "They're so devoted to their own interests that it's all they know how to discuss. Jasper has his aeroplanes. Humphry plans to become an inventor, and I'm not sure what's occupying Kenton's time at the moment. He tends to go months between visits, and Mother..."

I drew alongside her at the bottom of the stairs and, as she apparently had no wish to finish that sentence, I thought of something more positive to say. "My Auntie Elle hasn't walked since she was seven years old." I know this might not sound too cheerful, but bear with me. "She lost the use of both legs to polio." Honestly, it's going to get better any second. "And yet she has a more active life than nearly anyone I know." See! "She's read more fine books than most librarians, has a brighter outlook on life than a merry friar and never wants for a hobby or pastime. I constantly praise my lucky stars that I dodged every bomb and hand grenade that came my way in the war, but Elle says that she couldn't have had a better life if she was an Olympic runner."

The sad look on Bella's face told me that it would be no easy thing to comfort her. "Thank you, Marius. You're very sweet, and if you have any ideas to convince my stubborn mule of a father to show his face downstairs, I would be only too willing to hear them."

"I'll put on my thinking cap and let you know."

Her smile was often sad these days. The only time I'd

managed to bring her back to herself was when investigating a crime. Now, I'm not saying that I wanted anyone to be murdered, but it did give her a chance to escape her problems.

"I'll have to go back soon," she told me. "My brothers will be with him this weekend, but I must at least try to get him out of that bed for a while. You can go to the kitchen if you'd like some lunch. The house is as much yours as it ever was."

"So not at all, then," I quipped, and received a roll of the eyes for my trouble.

"You know exactly what I mean." With this, she skipped back up the stairs to her father's lonely cave, and I sauntered off to explore the palace without its princess.

EIGHT

I could have spent days poking about that incredible old building and not grown bored. I sought out the hidey-holes and crevices that I'd known so well as a child, and paid a visit to the staff below stairs, who had overseen much of our mischief (but never admitted it to their employers). Quite the feast was provided, and any number of old faces appeared to say hello. The one person I didn't see on my visit was Bella's mother, which was something I still had to look forward to, or perhaps fear.

I strolled off the Hurtwood House estate, wishing I'd brought Percy with me. He's a good companion, so long as the walk is less than two miles and preferably downhill. My uncle had tried to put the loveable lump on an exercise regimen the previous year, but there was only so much cajoling we could try before accepting that he was incredibly good at ignoring us.

By the time I got to the village, Sergeant Rossiter had retired for lunch. I picked up Percy from Lucinda's house and was happy to know that the two cousins were both still safe. Lucinda was asleep in an upstairs bedroom and Tilly was sitting by the wireless. It felt wrong to leave them, but she promised they would stay together, so that was good... or perhaps spectacularly bad, as they'd both received the death threats and were thus easier to kill off in one go.

A few seasoned drinkers called my name as I walked past the Duke's Head.

"The big fancy mystery novelist is back in town!" Lucinda's other neighbour, Jeb Paignton, raised his glass to me fondly. He had looked seventy-five when I was a child and somehow still looked the same age.

"I'm more of a Carmine Fortescue reader, myself," his companion on a bench in front of the pub declared, and I might have answered rudely, but someone far more interesting caught my attention. Sitting beside the war memorial, with a book open in her lap, was my dear friend Dorothy Lyle.

"Marius?" she practically whispered before yelling, "Marius! It's really you. I felt for certain that you'd never come back. And when I heard you were here, I just..."

Apparently unable to believe her eyes, she threw her arms around me.

"It's lovely to see you, Dodo. I'm sorry it's been so long."

She pulled away to look at me, clearly still unable to comprehend what she was seeing. "It really has. You know I've missed you."

"I can only apologise. I should have invited you to visit me in London before now. I've been so busy for the last few years, but I've often thought of you."

She was dressed just as eccentrically as I remembered, in a cotton polka dot dress with a tightly laced bodice that most women today would find quite inhumane (and rightly so, no doubt). She had long blonde hair in ringlets and a heart-shaped burgundy birthmark on her right cheek. She was every bit the tragic heroine from a Thomas Hardy novel, but she'd always been the cheerful heart of our group of friends, and that did not appear to have changed.

"You didn't think of me," she said and smiled all the more. "You were too busy travelling across Europe and winning prizes for your best-selling novel."

I sniffed at her claim. "Prize, singular. And it was only from the Mid-Surrey Crime Writers' Association. My book wasn't even the best in the whole of Surrey, just the middle of it."

She wouldn't accept this and put her arm through mine to go for a tiny circuit around the island in the middle of the quiet road. Percy followed us the whole way and was evidently not happy to be overlooked.

"I read your book, Marius. It was brilliant. I loved every page and, when I finished reading, I went back to the beginning and started again."

"Was that because Bella gave it to you as a present and you didn't want to seem rude?" Although I knew our mutual friend had bought twenty copies of my debut novel for her friends and family, I hadn't yet worked out who had ended up with them.

Dodo punched me on the arm to keep me in check. "Not at all. I bought it myself, and it was worth every penny."

In the pause between sentences, the old boys from the pub cheered once more. There were calls of "Nice car, Marius!" and, "How about a holiday in London, eh, lads?"

"What about you?" I asked my friend once the noise had died down. "Did you keep writing after school?"

Her cheerful demeanour remained, but I could tell that she would have rather not answered. "I've tried my best, but I found that I didn't have much to inspire me after you boys went off to war."

I did something then that I'd never done before – something which many writers have no doubt gone on to regret. I offered to read her work. "If you'd like me to look at something you've been writing, it would be a pleasure. Who knows, my publishers might be interested in it."

Her jaw fell a good couple of inches. "You don't mean it, Marius! You can't."

"Of course I do." I am an emotional sponge, and her excitement soaked right into me. "I would only be returning the favour. If it weren't for you, I might never have become a writer."

"What do you—" Before she could finish her question, her brother Ned stuck his head out of the post office halfway up the hill and called her in for lunch.

"Dodo, get a move on," the shy postman called down. "Mum says your toad in the hole will get cold."

"I'm sorry, Marius. I have to go. But we'll finish this conversation very soon."

She'd run off before I could agree. It was impossible to avoid anyone in the village, though, and I was sure we'd bump into one another before long. I hadn't paid attention until now but, once she'd disappeared through her front door, I looked up to see that I was standing in front of the war memorial, which stood on a small grassy triangle of land opposite the pub.

I read the names of the thirty-seven men from a town of a few hundred people who had died in the war. I could have written such a list of my own friends and colleagues who'd never made it back to Britain. I found Sebastian Kane, and plenty of the other names were even more familiar. I instantly spotted Montagues and Fairbanks, and Dodo's big brother Malcolm was there, too. Sergeant Rossiter's sons had both died, as had a second cousin of mine who had grown up just around the corner. They put up such memorials so we would never forget the tragedy of war, but there wasn't much chance of that as far as I was concerned.

For the Glory of God and the memory of the men of Hurtwood who gave their lives for their country in 1914–1918, it read, and I took a moment to reflect on their sacrifice.

I could tell that Percy had been well fed by the Heatons

that morning, or else he would have complained that I was standing in a daze when I could have been making lunch. I considered stopping at the pub to listen for gossip, but he would only have been spoilt further if all the characters at the Duke's Head got the chance.

"The problem with you, Percy," I told my loyal hound, "is that you're too good an actor." He wagged his tail and moved his tiny legs at great speed as we took Hawthorn Road towards my childhood home. "That's right, I said it. You're an expert at making everyone think that you're hard done by and that you deserve more food."

He gave a short bark of unashamed agreement, and I increased my pace to get home in time for whatever tasty dish Uncle Stan had prepared for lunch. Well, that was the plan, but Percy had other ideas. A few doors away from number seventeen, he veered off the pavement into a house I'd never had reason to enter before. It had previously belonged to the old Welsh couple who owned the general shop, but it had stood empty for some time after they left. From the fresh paint and smart black Singer Junior 8 parked outside, it was obvious that someone had taken over the old place.

Percy ran right up to the door and sat on the mat there.

"I know you're not familiar with this village, dear pup, but this is not my house."

He looked straight at me but said nothing because Percy is a dog.

"You can sit here all day, if you really want to, but it won't change anything." I am very much used to losing arguments with Percy and thought nothing of this one until he started howling quite insistently. "Don't be like that. All I want is to go home for lunch. I don't care what they're cooking behind that door. I'm going."

And with that, I walked off the property and continued on up the road... for approximately ten steps before waiting to see what he would do. When he didn't appear, I peered through a blackthorn bush to check on him, but he was just sitting in place on the step, waiting for me to return. Now, there's no doubting that he's a clever creature, and he certainly knows how to get what he wants, but this was odd behaviour, even for him.

I soon gave in and walked back up the path to number twelve. "Fine, what is it?"

In reply, he looked terribly sad – which is his usual response to any question – but he still wouldn't come to me.

"Really, Percy. I don't know what more I can—" I was about to pull him away by the collar when I realised the front door was open a fraction and he was a very observant dog indeed. I peered in through the door, and Percy pushed right past me to investigate whatever had caught his nose.

"Hello?" I called ahead of me as I stepped into the bright hallway. It was very modern for Hurtwood, with artistic prints on the walls that were no more than fifty years old – as I said, very modern for Hurtwood. "I'm sorry to bother you, but your door was open, and my dog has wandered through it. I'm just coming to collect him, and then I'll be going."

I knew there would be no answer. There's something about an empty house that tells you you're alone even before you walk inside. My words came back to me too crisply for there to be anyone at home, but I sidled apologetically along the corridor all the same.

Percy had entered the first room to the left. It was a small lounge with a fire smouldering in the grate from that morning. There was a tea tray on the table with a used mug on it and, for a moment, I knew how that hardened housebreaker Goldilocks felt on her first escapade at the bears' cottage.

My dog slipped back out to the corridor and went deeper into the house before I could grab him.

"Come along, Percy. You're not the one who'll be arrested for trespassing. It's time to go."

He made it to the kitchen, but there was no joint of meat in the oven as I had expected. The keen hound was not thinking of his stomach for once, after all. What he did find was the body of a man my age with immensely broad shoulders and a stare that, though now vacant, locked itself onto me from across the room. Even in death, James Heaton had strikingly bright amber eyes.

When I found him there, sprawled out over the round mahogany table, I couldn't help but feel guilty. Not for his murder – there was no obvious way I could have saved his life when I didn't even realise it was at risk. No, what really saddened me was that we had been friends once. Close friends, in fact, but we'd thrown all that away. It was a small detail upon which to concentrate at such a moment, but that was what I was thinking as I walked over to make certain he was really dead.

He had no pulse and wasn't breathing, but there was no blood on the part of the body that was visible. He hadn't turned purple either, as poisoned men tend to in novels, and so I assumed there was a wound on his chest that I couldn't see. A small pool of blood beneath the table seemed to confirm this, but the rest had presumably soaked into his clothes.

His head was twisted at an angle to face the door, and there was something slightly too perfect about him. His brown hair was as neat as ever, his cheeks cleanly shaven that morning. He reminded me of a sculpture of a man, rather than a real one. The room itself was incredibly tidy, too, and the only things that were out of place were an upturned chair, a broken plate and a few red spots on the linoleum by the back door.

I thought of going through his pockets or searching the house for clues, but the police would finally have to take action now, and I didn't want to interfere with any potential evidence. I took Percy by the collar and was just pulling him out of the house when I noticed two letters pushed against the wall on the mat behind the door. They hadn't been opened, but I knew exactly what they were.

NINE

The house that my mother and father had bought when they were first married was at the end of the cul-de-sac. It was a simple white building with no adornment or particularly memorable features, and yet it had a happy face. I know that might sound childish, but it really looked as though it was smiling. Perhaps it was the wide bay windows that peered curiously down the road at me. The door was the slightly surprised mouth, the red-tiled roof the hair and, no, it didn't have a nose. I was pleased to see that it was just as I remembered, and it gave me the strength for what I had to do next.

I used the telephone at home to make the necessary calls while my family fussed over our genius dog. I sometimes forget that bassets are second only to bloodhounds in their sense of smell. Whether he caught the scent of the dead body itself or just had a feeling that something was wrong from the door being open was beyond my knowledge, but it was a nice change for him to use his skills for once.

"He's a marvel," Stan was saying as I got through to the switchboard at Scotland Yard. "I'll give him an egg for his lunch!"

The operator was curt but efficient, and I communicated the situation as rapidly as I could before finishing with, "And please tell Detective Inspector Lovebrook to come to Hurtwood Village as soon as possible."

"He's the best dog in the world. He deserves a medal," my mother said as I listened for the operator's reply.

"No, I've already told the local police. Inspector Lovebrook will want to know what's happened, so please pass on my message."

"I've never known a dog like him." Auntie Elle leaned out of her chair to give Percy a scratch.

"Yes, he's magnificent," I agreed, having hung up the phone on the candlestick holder. I had to wonder why we were still paying for a telephone line when no one had been living in the house for years, but that was not my primary concern just then. "If only he could break the bad news to James's family, he would be the perfect assistant."

We were together in our small, dusty though comfortable breakfast room, and I would have liked to reminisce on old times, but I had told Sergeant Rossiter that I would meet him at the scene of the crime. I'd left a message at Hurtwood House for Bella, too, but the footman who'd taken it was uncertain where she was.

"Mother, I don't suppose you know anything about James Heaton buying a house here?" I asked as I chomped on a pastie and poured a glass of water down my throat.

My mother had spies all over, so it didn't surprise me that she had the answer I needed. "Don't speak with your mouth full, dear." That wasn't the answer I needed, but she soon continued. "Poor James was given the house at number twelve back when you still lived here. He moved in a couple of years ago, and I had it on good authority from the postmistress that he'd made a fortune for himself doing... something. He decided that he was old enough to move out of the family home, leaving his sister alone there."

I was already heading to the door as apparently there would be no time that day to sit down for more than a couple of minutes in one go.

"That's where I found him." I paused to look at myself in the mirror by the door and realised that I must have grown an inch or two since I was eighteen. I was certain I'd never had to stoop to see my curly locks before.

Mother looked pensive for a moment and said, "I don't wish to speak ill of the dead, but he was never an easy child. Even when you were friends, he used to lose his temper like a real devil. I once caught you playing in the garden, and he had his hands around your neck. I thought he was going to kill you and I had to force the pair of you apart. It was quite frightening."

My mother didn't need to say what she was thinking. I said it for her. "So you think someone got even with him for being a bully. It's possible, Mother." I kissed her on the cheek and opened the door. "And if you're the one to crack the case, I will insist that the police give you full credit."

She smiled in that indulgent way that only mothers do. With a call of farewell to Percy and the doting pair in the dining room, I slipped from my house and back down the hill.

"How was your pie, Rossiter?" I asked the skinny officer as he hurried to number twelve.

"Very nice, thank you." He had an officious manner and a self-righteous attitude, which is a poor combination by anyone's standards. "Of course, if I'd known there was going to be a murder, I would have... I would have... Well, I don't know what I would have done."

Even now, he was not admitting any fault. The world had evidently failed to inform him that someone was going to be killed, and so there was nothing he could have done about it. In reality, of course, someone *had* told him that there would be a murder; the murderer himself had written to his targets to say that very thing.

I decided not to start an argument, but gently pushed him towards the realisation that he could have done more for the Heatons. "I saw two envelopes on the mat behind James's door. They must have come this morning when he was out. I can only assume that they're the same kind of letters that his sister and cousin received."

"There'll be no assuming around here, thank you very much, Quin." He came ever so close to me then and jabbed my chest with his bony finger. "If anyone is to do any assuming, it will be the police. I heard about what you got up to at the end of last year, and let me just tell you that we don't need amateurs to do our jobs for us."

"So what will your first step be?" I thought this was a fair question.

"Well... I'm... You see, I'm not totally sure. Old Mrs Gloucester died up in her cottage last year, but I've never handled a murder before. I don't suppose you picked up any clues the last time you were at one of these things?" He talked about the killing as though it were a supper dance or some other polite social occasion.

"From the research I did to prepare my novel, I believe you should survey the scene of the crime and look for clues to determine how the man was killed before any evidence deteriorates."

"Right..." He had incredibly taut skin across his face, and you could make out every feature of his skull. It was almost as though he were a skeleton that had mysteriously come to life. "And how do we go about doing that, then?"

"Alternatively, you could just wait until the officers from Guildford arrive. They should have more experience than us."

"That sounds like something I can do." He sounded very pleased with himself. "I'll stand out here and make sure no one interferes with nothing. Is that what you reckon?"

"I'm sure you're just the man for the job." It was a good thing he didn't understand sarcasm.

He was soon called to action as, from the crossroads at the bottom of the hill, Tilly was running up to us. I wondered at first how she could have found out what had happened, but the furtive look on Rossiter's face told me he'd already blabbed to someone.

Lucinda was just behind her, calling her to stop. Then came Ned the postman and, following him, was every last person who'd been in the pub for lunch. In other words, half the population of the village was about to invade the scene of James's murder.

I looked at the crowd as they approached and could see Lucinda's spurned suitor Richard Fairbanks, a few cheery old drunks, who had been cheery old drunks all my life, and an assortment of the regular characters from the village. The only stranger was the man with the scar I'd seen earlier in the day. Dressed all in black, he watched from the back of the group.

"Oh, heck!" the officer murmured and stretched out his arms to block the doorframe, as if that would be enough to prevent a mob from getting past him. In the end, it wasn't even enough to stop Tilly.

"Don't you dare," he shouted. "Don't you begin to dare to try to get past me, Tilly Heaton!"

All she had to do was duck under his arm to circumvent his defences. She slipped inside the house as Lucinda did the same on the other side. And yet the sergeant's glare told me that, somehow, this was all my fault.

"Well, go after them then!" Rossiter barked, and I had to push past to rescue the crime scene.

I was approximately five seconds too late. Lucinda had pulled James down on top of her and was cradling his neck while Tilly, for some impossible to comprehend reason, had taken hold of the kitchen knife in the dead man's chest and pulled it free as though that would save him.

"Are you both insane? Have you never read a mystery novel or watched a thriller in the cinema?"

Whilst crying profusely, they looked up at me through large, innocent eyes. I felt bad for barracking them at such a moment, but someone had to do it.

"I'm sorry, but if we're to have any chance of stopping whoever wrote you those letters and killed James, then you have to come away from here this second."

"But James didn't get any letters!" Lucinda wailed, and I can only think that Tilly had fallen mute by this point as she peered down at her brother.

"Yes, he did." I spoke more softly now. "They must have come while he was out this morning. There are two similar envelopes behind the front door. I didn't pick them up, but I saw that one was from Edinburgh and the other from Middlesbrough."

"That's not fair. It's just not." Tilly shook her head so fast that her silky hair fanned out around her. "We didn't know about James. We didn't know he needed protecting, or I'd have made him stay with us."

The knife dropped from her hand, splashing tiny droplets of blood over the scene, and I raced forward to help Lucinda to her feet. She didn't want to let go of her cousin. At first, she held on to him for dear life, but there was a moment when she seemed to give up and accept that he wasn't coming back. The two women looked at the body, but we all knew that it wasn't really James anymore. It was just a sculpture of the person he used to be.

TEN

The last dead body I'd encountered had been shot three times in the head. That morbid discovery a few months earlier had brought back memories of the first man I'd seen killed at the front, but as I escorted Lucinda and Tilly from the house where their cousin had been stabbed, it felt more like an escape from an artillery attack. I put an arm around each of them and we ran past the inept sergeant and the heckling locals, much as my companions and I avoided machine-gun fire from enemy biplanes as we dashed for cover. It's not the kind of experience you'd want to live through once, let alone a second time.

I saw them safely through the crowd and asked Dodo to go with them. She was almost as adored as Lucinda in the village, and I knew she'd be better at looking after the two remaining cousins than I would have been. Once I saw they'd safely reached Lucinda's house, I returned to number twelve, Hawthorn Road.

"I imagine that you know what happened," I told the curious rabble. "Did any of you see anything that might reveal who killed James Heaton?"

They fell strangely quiet and glanced at one another to see

who would speak. The answer was *none of them*, so like a teacher with a surly class, I had to nominate respondents.

"Richard, you argued with him this morning—"

The smooth customer was instantly defensive as he fiddled with his painted silk tie. "And that means I'm a killer, does it?" The rising pitch of his voice silenced the scene. "What is happening to this town? You can't breathe here anymore without getting told you've done something dreadful."

"I was going to ask whether you knew where he went afterwards," I replied in a controlled fashion so as not to make the situation any worse.

"He left the Duke's Head at around noon," the slightly pirate-like landlord of the pub informed me. He didn't sound like a pirate. He just wore a lot of stripy clothes and had a big beard.

"Ned?" I asked the postman. "Did you see James any time after midday?"

Ned Lyle was in our class at school, but he was a year younger than Bella and I were. He was rather slow and easily led, and some of the boys were cruel to him as a result, but he knew the village better than anyone.

"I'm afraid not, Marius. I finished my round and went to help Mum in the post office, like always."

"And what about any strangers?" I tried again. "It's easy enough around here to spot them. Did any of you see someone from out of town today?" I was actually praying for the killer to be an outsider, as I knew what James's death would do to the place.

Sadly, all I got in reply were empty looks and a few muttered grunts in the negative.

"Well, thank you. You've all been very helpful." I don't know what it was, but their muted response had upset me more than my initial discovery of the body. "If you could go back to whatever you were doing before and avoid spreading false rumours, that would be very helpful."

They flocked down the hill towards the grassy island in the middle of the road. The Hurtwood sign had been there for centuries, with its pretty ironwork holding the name of the village and three bushy oak trees on either side. I'd always loved the sight of it as a symbol of the place, but as it swung in the breeze, the squeak it made grated, and I lost my temper again.

"It's your job to talk to them, Rossiter," I yelled at the sergeant. "You're supposed to be trained for this sort of thing."

I was lashing out, and I knew it, but it felt good to have someone to blame. It felt good to direct all my anger towards him, knowing that we couldn't do anything more until some real police officers turned up. I sat there wondering whether I'd treated James unfairly both today and back before the war. He was hot-brained and impetuous, and I'd probably never forgiven him for staying behind to fight the battle of his father's living room rather than joining the army, but it was hard to say whether those things had made him unredeemable.

To my genuine surprise, the first officer to arrive had not been dispatched from the nearest big town. It was the inspector I knew from London.

"I'm sorry I didn't get here sooner," Lovebrook said, stopping his car outside number twelve on his way up to the address I'd given him. "Has anything happened in my absence?"

There was too much to tell him in one go, so I gave him a summary and led him along the cobblestone path.

"Sergeant Rossiter," the man guarding the place revealed with an inappropriate salute. "I've kept an eye on the house since the body was found. I'm glad you're here, sir."

Lovebrook was no fool and could sense something wasn't quite true about this statement, so he merely nodded as we passed.

"You know, Marius," he said once he'd donned a pair of

white cotton gloves, "I hope we meet one day without a single corpse present."

"That's generally my preference," I replied. "But for the moment, let's see what we can do to solve this mystery."

"It's certainly a strange case." He stopped as we reached the entrance to the kitchen, and I was curious to see what he would make of the scene. "From the splashes of blood, it looks as though he was stabbed in the chest near the back door and then stumbled over to collapse right there." He pointed to the mess of smudged blood on the table. "For whatever reason, the killer turned him over and placed him on his back on the floor. Judging by the large amount of blood all over his clothes, he then proceeded to remove and reinsert the knife."

"You know, that's very impressive," I had to concede.

He was a smiley fellow, especially for a police officer. "I'm glad you think so."

"Every word you said could be true, but what I didn't tell you was that his sister ran in here after he was killed and removed the knife, thinking it could still save him."

"Does she have a brain?" He had not shown this dry sense of humour during our first encounter, and I rather liked it.

"I believe so. I will put her thoughtless behaviour down to the stress of the moment. Her cousin cradled the poor chap's body, too, and Lucinda was always clever at school."

"Lucinda? So what you're saying is that the other two women who received the letters interfered with the body?"

I considered his point for a moment. "Yes, that is one way of putting it."

There was a gasp behind us, and we turned to see Bella standing a few feet away with shock etched on her pretty features. "My goodness, it's true. I got your message, Marius, but I hoped there was a mistake." She'd evidently had no trouble getting past Sergeant Rossiter.

I went to comfort her, but she wasn't as upset as I had imagined. As James was the second murder victim we'd discovered in the space of a few months, perhaps she was now hardened to such things. Or maybe she was even less forgiving of him than I was.

"We're sorry to disappoint you, Lady Isabella," Lovebrook said rather mournfully before turning to me. "What was the scene before us like when you first found him?"

I needed to think for a moment, but I moved across the kitchen to point at the remaining evidence. "There were drops of blood on the floor over here, along with the broken plate and the fallen chair. So I would imagine you were correct when you said that he was stabbed by the door." I hadn't noticed before that one of the cupboards on the wall was open. "I wonder if he was getting something out of there. Perhaps he turned, and the killer plunged the knife into his chest."

Lovebrook pursed his lips to think. "That would make sense. He was a big strong chap; the killer would have wanted to take him by surprise to avoid a fight."

Bella came forward and sent her careful gaze around the kitchen. "There's bread and butter out on the side. Perhaps he was about to make himself a sandwich. It was almost lunchtime."

"There are two plates," the inspector observed, and we didn't need to ask what this implied. "Perhaps James had a friend here. He took the food out whilst the killer selected a knife."

"Will Scotland Yard send men to look for fingerprints?" Bella enquired.

Lovebrook cleared his throat. "The local lot will. Although, if the killer had any sense, he'd have worn gloves."

"I find it incredible these days that anyone gets caught in such a manner," I had to comment. "Surely criminals read mystery novels like the rest of us, or at least glance at a news-paper from time to time."

Lovebrook was still looking around the kitchen and, having peered under the table, stopped where he was to answer. "There will never be a shortage of idiots in this world. Never underestimate just how naïve, arrogant and short-sighted people can be."

Bella looked surprised by his comment. "What happened since the last time we met you? You were as fresh-faced and innocent as a daffodil. Have a few months at Scotland Yard turned you into an old cynic?"

He shrugged and answered, "Yes."

I bit my lip to stop from smiling. I didn't want Bella to be angry with me, too.

"Right, I think that's all we can do for the moment," the inspector said as he walked towards the hallway. "I would take a look around the house, but it's better to let the fingerprint hunters do that than having the three of us tramping around." Even as he said this, we heard heavy footsteps on the path, and the officers from Guildford appeared.

"So what should we do next?" Bella asked once he'd explained the situation to the new arrivals.

"Well," the inspector needed a moment to consider the question. "I think a swift drink in the pub is in order."

ELEVEN

"Will your father be all right without you this afternoon?" I felt I should ask Bella as we took a table on the terrace in front of the Duke's Head. The weather was perfectly mild, and the occasional bursts of sun through the clouds made me feel more human again.

"He told me to go," she replied as we waited for Lovebrook to return. "He likes to think of me taking on his mantle as the overseer of Hurtwood Village. And besides, the image he has of James Heaton is of a bright little boy who listened keenly to his stories whenever he came into school. He never saw what our friend became."

"What did he become?" Lovebrook asked as he laid down a trio of glasses arranged in a triangle on the table before us. There was one orange juice and two beers and, for a moment, I couldn't imagine whose drink was whose. Bella seized the local bitter, and Lovebrook evidently didn't drink on duty, so that minor mystery was quickly resolved.

We all had a sip before Bella answered him. "He was a brute. There's no other word for him." As an author, I was sure that I could have thought of a few and consulted the thesaurus in my head. "He hadn't always been so cruel, but by the time we were leaving school, there was very little kindness or compassion left in him."

"Marius, you said on the phone last night that, of the three cousins, James was the most likely to incite such hatred. Is there something in particular that he'd done over the years to which people objected?"

I would have answered him, but the people of Hurtwood responded for me.

"James Heaton was a coward," one of the pipe smokers sitting on a bench by the wall of the pub declared.

"He was worse than a coward," Jeb Paignton added. "He was a spoilt brat who got what he wanted his whole life and never did a day's work."

"Have some respect for the dead," I put in, but the pair had some scores to settle and talked straight over me.

"Oh, come on, Marius," the first man continued. "You know that James was a copy of his dad. Not to mention the fact that—"

"Thank you, gentlemen," the inspector interrupted with some authority. "The local police will come to talk to you in good time."

I filled in what they were going to say in a slightly quieter voice so that the old fellows wouldn't bother us again. "James got out of going to the war because his father was on the military service tribunal and had most of the men in the town in his pocket. A lot of people here have never forgotten that."

"Wealthy family, were they?"

"They had money." Bella was there to provide some context. "They weren't aristocrats, but James's grandfather made a tidy sum owning factories in London through the Victorian age. You know the sort of thing. Getting rich off the back of slaving children and near-blind old women."

I might have pointed out that, as members of the English

landed gentry, her own family had got rich on the backs of farm labourers and the sacking of the new world but, as I've already said, I had no wish to upset her.

"It wasn't their wealth which people minded, though. It was what they did with it," I explained instead. "When the grandfather died, James and Tilly's father, Tom Heaton, inherited the bulk of the fortune and tried to buy as much influence as he could around here, which is why James never had to enlist."

Lovebrook took a sip of his juice. "Is that really a reason to kill a man?"

"That would depend on who you ask. All I can say for certain is that James knew what people thought of him, and he became…"

I couldn't find the word and so Bella took up the task. "It made him sensitive and quick to anger. You couldn't say anything without him thinking you were criticising him."

"But he was your friend, at least?" This was a leading question, and I think he knew it.

Bella and I exchanged glances. It was a brief, silent negotiation to decide which of us would have to answer. I lost, of course.

"Not exactly. You see, James was in love with Bella back when we were younger." I managed to say all this without cringing, but there was worse to come.

"And that was a problem because…?" Was he doing it on purpose? Did he wish to see me squirm with embarrassment?

"Bella and I…" I managed this much.

"Marius and I…" Bella didn't get a great deal further.

"Oh, I see." Lovebrook's tone was a little contrite at least. "Lady Isabella and you… Or rather, Marius and you, were…"

You would think, after thousands of years of human history, three adults would be able to talk about a long-terminated romance without blushing.

"That's just it." My ex-love sounded quite enthusiastic

about his summary. "James was in love with me, and he didn't approve of my choice of... Well, he blamed Marius for a lot of his problems even after we stopped being..."

"Sweethearts!" I blurted because, quite frankly, it was becoming ridiculous. "We were sweethearts and James was jealous. But then I was conscripted, and it no longer mattered."

"Thank you," they both mumbled at the same time, before Lovebrook scratched his cheek and said, "So none of this explains what the killer might have had against the victim and his cousins." It was true, of course, and I was considering how to answer this problem when he spoke again. "Wait a moment. If you were sweethearts, why didn't you pick things up where you left off after the—"

"Has Marius told you what we discovered about the letters?" Bella said to change the topic and save us both from more squirming.

I still had to take a good long slug of my beer. "It seems to me," I said when I'd topped up my courage, "that each one was sent by a different person. I've been thinking about it all day, and the only explanation is that the killer made a number of other people send the letters on his behalf. Each one is from a different part of the country. Swansea, Canterbury, Oxford, Wellingborough—"

"Wellingborough?" he replied with a surprised look. "It's a small world. I know Wellingborough well. I used to work for the Northamptonshire Constabulary."

"That was the first letter that Tilly received, but it's not the most significant detail." The interruption had rather broken my concentration, and I had to start again. "What was curious was that she received three identical messages today, all sent from different places."

"Why would anyone want to do that?" He pondered the question that we'd already considered without result.

"We don't know."

"Perhaps it's to distract us." Bella looked pleased with herself as this idea became clearer in her mind. "Perhaps the letters were designed from the beginning to make us ask a lot of unnecessary questions when what we should really be doing is thinking about why James was killed."

"We already tried that, and it didn't get us anywhere." Lovebrook had certainly become blunter since we'd last met him. "I've got an idea, though. I'll call a friend in Wellingborough and get him to ask some locals about the letters. It's not very big compared to the other towns you mentioned. We might be lucky."

"That's a start at least," I conceded. "But our first priority is the girls' safety. The killer clearly has something against the Heaton clan, and we can't just assume that he'll stop now that the police are here."

Lovebrook nodded a few times. "You're right, but the best way to keep them safe is to catch the culprit. So tell me more about them. What did the cousins do for work?"

"Nothing."

"How do you mean?"

I hadn't expected him to ask this. I could imagine it being an odd situation for most police officers, but Lovebrook had a decidedly aristocratic air. He was like a youthful (and much more cheerful) Lord Edgington, which was one of the things that intrigued me about him.

"Their parents all died relatively young," Bella responded. "Each of the cousins has a house of their own, and none of them has ever had to work."

"I don't suppose their parents died in suspicious circumstances? As that would surely provide us with a motive for the crime."

"Far from it, I'm afraid." Bella slowly exhaled. "Lucinda's mother was the last to go, and all four of them were in and out of the hospital for months before they died."

"It could be said that dying runs in the family," I said to sum up the Heatons' poor luck.

He looked more perplexed with each passing minute. "Very well. So we have a victim no one liked and two relatives still at risk. None of them have occupations and we can't be sure why the letters were sent to them. It's hardly a perfect start to the investigation."

"Then I suppose we should wait for one of the girls to be murdered?" Bella's voice was as dry as the desert.

"That's not what I meant at all." Lovebrook looked into the bottom of his empty glass as though he believed he could make a new drink appear. "Perhaps it would help if I knew more about Tilly and Lucinda. It sounds as though James gave everyone plenty of reasons to kill him. What about his sister and cousin?"

"The three of them are three points on a spectrum," I replied. "James was very killable. The best and worst you can say about Tilly is that she's hard to love, and it's impossible to believe that anyone would want to hurt Lucinda in a thousand years."

He became a trifle sterner. "Again, that is very unhelpful."

"We know..." Bella said in an almost apologetic tone. "This isn't the kind of mystery I thought we'd end up investigating. Where's the ancient lord who will leave the killer a fortune? Where's the much younger wife who married for money? We can't even blame this one on the butler."

"We need a plan," Lovebrook said decisively, and they both looked at me.

"Why would I know what to do?"

Lovebrook was a gentleman and kindly let Bella have the floor.

"Because... Well, you must have to sketch your stories out before you write them. I would have thought that being an author has lent you the skills that would come in handy in a murder investigation. You didn't do too badly last time."

This was hardly a vote of confidence and, instead of answering, I tipped the dregs of my beer down my throat and waited for inspiration to strike me.

"I've got it." I clapped my hands together. "Lovebrook, you speak to the officers at James's house. Find out whether anything incriminating was discovered there, check the letters that arrived this morning and get onto your man in Wellingborough. You can report back to us if you discover anything."

"Wonderful stuff." He was clearly motivated by my instructions. "What are you going to do?"

"I'm going to take Bella around the village so that she can ask some questions."

He looked puzzled again. "And why don't you ask them yourself?"

I stood up from the table. "Because I'm not nearly as charming as she is." I walked away without waiting for her response. "Come along, milady. You have work to do."

TWELVE

"As far as I know," I said once we were alone, "in addition to doing no work in their lives, James and Tilly have rarely ever left the village. To me, that suggests someone here knows what caused his death."

"Excellent guesswork, Marius."

"Thank you. I try my best." Her pithy reply had made me laugh – inside, at least. It was not the time to go tittering through the streets.

We'd left Lovebrook behind to fulfil his mission and were walking up the hill once more.

"I do concede that it would be difficult for someone from outside the village to walk around here without being noticed." Bella looked from one side of the street to the other, as if she was the one visiting for the first time in over a decade. "But if the killer had really wanted to conceal his presence, he could have parked a mile away and sneaked in through the forest. There was still a small chance someone might have spotted him, but it's feasible that he could have walked along the path beside your house and made it a little way along the road to number twelve without being seen on a quiet day like today."

"Exactly. So we still can't rule anything out. The question is, where should we go first? Who might be able to help us?"

Bella looked around again, no doubt working her way through the Hurtwood Village address book that we all knew by heart. At number twenty-five, Dovecote Lane, lived an old couple who loved nothing more than to complain about young people. At number twenty-six, on the other side of the road, was a man with a very large collection of ferrets. At number twenty-seven there lived a woman who believed that English people were technically a different species from all the other nationalities – even Welsh, Scottish and Irish. At number twenty-nine... well, I'm sure you get the idea.

"How about the post office?" she suggested cheerfully.

"Why the post office?"

"I would have thought that was perfectly obvious."

The words, *The killer sent lots of letters ran through my head.* "You make a strong point. Let's go."

She led the way to the funny little building where Ned and Dodo's mother ran the village's one remaining shop. If the Heaton dynasty's first house in the centre of the village was an overgrown cottage, the Hurtwood post office looked just like a shrunken one. It was compact and crooked, and over the two hundred or so years since it had been built, the foundations must have crumbled away as the floor had sunk below ground level. This meant that anyone of a reasonable height had to duck under the doorframe, as though we were entering some Lilliputian realm.

Inside the whitewashed building, the post office had a range of stationery and greetings cards. Since the general shop had closed down, there were also a few essential food items on sale that Mrs Lyle kept out of sight in the storeroom. With three people in there, plus Postman Ned leaning against the counter, it felt as though we were crammed into a lift.

"Afternoon, both." Mrs Lyle had a West Country accent

that made her sound as though she'd just stepped off a combine harvester. "Terrible news about James. No one deserves to have their head caved in with a paperweight in the shape of a spaniel."

"He was stabbed through the heart," I found myself admitting in response.

"Was he really? Old Jeb in the pub told me that he'd had his head caved in with a marble cocker spaniel. I thought it were a bit odd, but people do the funniest things these days." She allowed herself a brief laugh before falling silent again. She was a cheerful woman at the worst of times, as she had just proved.

"What other rumours have you heard, Mrs Lyle?" Bella asked, and I didn't blame her for wanting to keep ahead of the gossip.

The postmistress leaned over the counter to whisper for some reason. "Well, now that you ask, I heard tell that James Heaton and the vicar's daughter were besotted with one another, but Reverend Piggins forbade their love. I reckon that the police should pop along to the church to get the full story."

Bella looked more confused. "Reverend Piggins's daughter is nine years old. I very much doubt she'd want to run away with a man whose favourite hobby was sitting in his house feeling sorry for himself."

Mrs Lyle straightened up and looked a little reflective. "S'pose not. You never can trust what people say."

"Mrs Lyle," my friend said to take control of the conversation, "can you tell us whether you've noticed any suspicious behaviour in your shop recently?"

Ned was standing beside his mother, listening intently, but he didn't make a sound.

"Well, that Sergeant Rossiter," she paused then, before continuing in a secretive voice, "he was in here the other day consulting an address in our directories and asked whether we sell hair tonic." She evidently found this most revealing. "You can't see it because of his police helmet, but I reckon he must be going bald under there."

"That is surprising," Bella commented, "but we were more interested in people buying a lot of stamps or sending a suspicious number of letters."

Mrs Lyle was only too happy to help. "You must mean Mrs Abbot."

"Do we?" I was feeling a mite confused by this point.

"She bought twenty 1½d stamps last week and all the paper and envelopes she needed to go with them. She said she had some important work to do, but it struck me as odd that anyone would write so many letters. She came back the next day to send them. She must have been up half the night writing."

Bella was focused now and fired off one question after the next. "When was this?"

"Monday gone."

"And did you notice where the letters were sent?"

"All over, I think. But I try to be discreet in my work. I'm not one for prying or idle gossip."

Bella showed no incredulity to this out-and-out lie. "Did Mrs Abbot tell you to whom she was writing?"

"No, she was very quiet, which isn't like her."

My friend looked at me then. This did sound promising, though it still wouldn't explain how all the Heatons' letters had come from different places unless our old teacher had asked people around the country to send them. Of course, she didn't have many friends in the village where she'd lived for decades. It seemed almost impossible that she'd have such a legion of them scattered across Britain.

I felt that we had learnt all that Mrs Lyle could possibly teach us, and I was about to remind Bella of an imaginary appointment we had to keep when she turned to the postman to ask a question.

"What about you, Ned? You collect the post from the box in town after all. Did you notice anyone sending a lot of letters except for Mrs Abbot?"

He made a long, pensive sound before answering. It went, "Aaaaaa! Not that I recall. But then I don't usually look too carefully at outgoing post. It all goes into a sack and then I drive it to the sorting office in Dorking."

"Thank you, both. You've been very helpful." Bella drifted from the shop then, her mind clearly occupied by what we'd heard. I wondered whether she was weighing up the chances that our bossy teacher had hatched a plan to get even with former students, as that was what I was doing.

Before we could discuss the possibility, Ned ran from the shop to call our names. When we stopped, he ushered us a little way down the road to talk. "There's something I need to say, and I didn't want my mother to hear."

Ned had a soft, slow manner about him. He was a kind-hearted soul, much like his sister, and we'd been friends at school, without ever being close.

"You can tell us anything," Bella reassured him. "What's the matter?"

"It's Lucinda." He stumbled over the word as though he wasn't certain he should be saying it. "There was someone..."

"Don't worry, Ned." I took my turn to gee him on. "Whatever's happened, we won't tell anyone unless you want us to."

"Well, I don't want to get anyone in trouble but, one morning last week, when I was up early on my rounds, I noticed a chap looking in through her hedge."

"What sort of chap?"

He looked down the road for a moment before answering my question. "He was big, like me, but dressed all in black. I chased him off, but I didn't get a good look at him. He'd had his face pressed right up against the hedge and ran off in the opposite direction when he heard me coming. I would have gone after him, but he escaped down a path into the woods."

I studied him more carefully then. I'd never thought of Ned as being particularly big, because he was so calm and unimposing. Richard and James were big men, and they threw their weight around to remind you of the fact. But if Ned was a giant, he was a gentle one. He had a wide, unblemished face, brown eyes as big as any cow's and a timid expression permanently fixed in place.

"Have you seen him again since?" Bella asked.

"No, no. Just that once, but I thought I should mention it."

She smiled to show her appreciation. "You were right to do so, and you should probably tell the police, too."

He clearly didn't like the idea and recoiled a little. "I'm not sure about that." He glanced at Sergeant Rossiter's empty cabin beside the post office.

"You delivered the letters to Lucinda and her cousins, didn't you, Ned?" I asked to change the subject.

"Yes, they've all had a lot this week. Tilly had three today. I noticed because she rarely ever has any. I think James had two, and Lucinda has always got something coming through. She's on so many boards and panels. I know I gave her a letter on Wednesday, but nothing else stood out. Of course, as soon as I heard about the threats they'd been receiving, I tried to remember."

"That's very good. Well done." I sounded terribly patronising, but he didn't seem to mind.

He became hesitant again and, when he spoke, the question was faint. "What about Mrs Abbot? Do you really think she could be to blame for all this?"

"Why, Ned?" Bella was good at reading our witness's reactions. "Do you?"

"No... no, I couldn't say. I mean, she does really scare me." He leaned in closer, and it reminded me of the way his sister used to share her secrets when we were children. "I still have nightmares about those last exams she gave us at the end of school. She was terrifying."

"Well, there's no denying that," I mumbled. "It definitely makes her the killer in my book."

Bella stamped on my foot to keep me quiet. She was not the first woman to use such violence against me. "You've been very helpful, Ned. You should be proud of yourself."

The postman smiled ever so shyly and could no longer look at us. He ran back to his mother's shop, and we continued on to our first real suspect.

We walked in silence for a few seconds, and it was Bella who spoke first. "I know it might sound silly, but there are certain points that suggest that Mrs Abbot could be to blame."

"I was just thinking the same thing."

There was a slight skip in every other step she took. It was sweetly childlike. "For a start, she always comes second to Lucinda in our annual gardening competition in the village. The last time it happened, she got very angry with the judges and told anyone who would listen that it was a conspiracy against her."

"Is that really the word she used? A *conspiracy*?" I shook my head in disbelief. "She is an old-fashioned sort."

Bella kept her mind fixed on the evidence. "Don't forget how she used to treat the Heatons in class, either. She certainly disliked James and Tilly more than the rest of us."

"She was furious when he failed his exams in the penultimate year." A silly thought occurred to me, and I gleefully considered it aloud. "Wouldn't it be funny if our grumpy teacher had turned into an avenging angel and was set on murdering all the students who had failed to live up to their potential."

She looked at me with a terribly unimpressed expression. "No, Marius. No, it wouldn't. But I can't say I'd put it past her."

We'd arrived at the perfect garden in front of Mrs Abbot's house and suddenly lost some of our confidence. It was all very well casting aspersions in private. It was another thing altogether to knock on our old teacher's door and accuse her of murder.

To my surprise, it was Bella who tried to get out of it. "Perhaps we're being silly. How could the old dear be to blame? People don't really murder one another over who has the best garden, or which students were rudest in school."

I couldn't help smiling. "They do in mystery novels, and they might even in real life from time to time. Now come along."

Finding the courage I required, I sped along the stepping-stone path to bang on the front door, then felt guilty for making such a racket.

THIRTEEN

"What do you want?" This was Mrs Abbot's question even before she appeared. When she saw me, her expression changed from one of anger to curiosity. "Oh, it's you again." It was hard to know whether she was pleased by the interruption, but she glanced past me to look at Bella, who still hadn't stepped onto the property.

I wouldn't back down and stated directly, "We'd like to ask you some questions."

She studied the pair of us in turn and there was a moment of indecision before she nodded and stepped aside.

"Are you coming, Lady Isabella?" she called along the path. "I'm not going to stand here all day."

I don't think I'd ever heard Mrs Abbot address Bella as anything other than "Montague" in all the years we were in her school, so it was a little odd to hear her offer such deference now.

I walked ahead of them and was instantly hit by quite how much Mrs Abbot had managed to cram into her miniature dwelling. It looked like the storeroom of a museum. The cases, cabinets and dressers on every wall were stuffed full of curiosities. There was a collection of brass toasting forks and ceramic German shepherds, gas masks, an armadillo's armour, Spode willow dinner sets divided up between the various pieces of furniture and, in a frame all of its own, a photograph of Queen Victoria with a Pomeranian dog.

I'd never been anywhere so cluttered yet harmonious. As hallways go, I found it surprisingly welcoming. Our host directed us into the sitting room and Bella stepped through the door looking less sure of herself than ever. The ghosts of our childhood were haunting us. Back then, the idea of entering our disciplinarian teacher's house would have only occurred to us in nightmares.

The small room was just as busy as the hallway, but there was another feature that I had not expected to find there. Along the far wall was a bed, and in it, laid supine, was a man in his seventies.

I froze as we caught sight of him. It was less than polite, but I for one had always assumed that Mrs Abbot lived alone. I'd never even heard rumours of there being a man in her life. Whoever that man might be.

"Don't worry," she instructed us whilst motioning to two hard wooden chairs beside the fireplace. "That's my husband, Mark. I was just making some tea if you'd like some."

So far in my career as an amateur meddler in other people's lives, I was forever being promised tea and not having the chance to drink it, but I accepted the offer all the same, and she disappeared deeper into the house.

"Did you know she had a husband?" I whispered once I was certain she had gone. "I hadn't a clue."

"Of course I did. Daddy knows everything, and he usually tells me," Bella explained. "And besides, you had a very big clue in her name. She was always Mrs, never Miss."

"I assumed she was a widow. How has no one in town ever mentioned the fact she was caring for a man in here?"

"Why do you think that our families always refer to her as 'poor Mrs Abbot'?"

"I thought they felt bad for her having to look after all of us!" I cast my sympathetic gaze on the man in the narrow bed. "I wonder what happened to him."

"Dementia." Mrs Abbot had evidently caught my question as she returned with a tray of tea things. "Or at least, that's what the doctors believe. It affected him very young. They said he'd probably only last a few years, but here we are decades later." She put the tray down on an occasional table beside a battered armchair and paused to look affectionately at the invalid. "He may outlive us all."

With a smile, she went to wait for the water to boil and reappeared a few minutes later with a hot pot of tea and a small jug of milk. I could rely on Mrs Abbot to provide what she had promised.

"Now, what would you like to discuss?" She was friendlier than I remembered, and I could tell this would be a difficult conversation to conduct.

"Well..." Bella began, as talking was supposed to be her forte.

"You see..." I tried, but I already knew that there was a vast chasm between imagining that a much-maligned teacher was a devil and actually putting such an accusation to her.

"I assume you are here because of the letters that the Heaton girls have received," she said in response to our complete lack of questions. "After all, that was the reason you came back to the village in the first place. Isn't that right, Mr Quin?"

"Yes, that's exactly it."

The tea had been brewing long enough by this point and the always precise woman seized the pot to pour out three servings of amber liquid in three porcelain cups. "Milk?"

"Yes, please." We both nodded, and the inevitable question soon followed.

"Sugar?"

Bella and I did not agree this time but, with the drinks served, we waited for Mrs Abbot to give us permission to speak. It was strange to be so close to her after so long. I'd sat facing the woman in a classroom for all those years, but never looked at her as a person before – let alone a suspect in a murder inquiry. She had dainty features and tiny hands which contrasted with her hard-as-steel personality. Dressed in a mint green woollen skirt and matching jacket with braided yellow lapels, she looked as though she worked on a very colourful cruise ship.

"I suppose you've heard the news about James?" Bella eventually suggested, having blown on her tea and decided it was still too hot.

"I have. Well, I heard the kerfuffle as the pub emptied and that flock of dissolute drinkers thundered up the hill. One of them was shouting about it." This was more like the woman we knew. If she didn't have an opportunity to criticise someone every few minutes, she simply wasn't happy. "I assume his death is linked to the letters."

"We have come to the same conclusion." Bella chose her words carefully. "The police are already at his house."

"So how can I be of help to you, children?"

I don't know whether it was due to fear or smart thinking, but Bella did not put our theories to her directly and found another angle from which to approach the matter. "We were wondering what you knew of James's life here?"

"James Heaton?" She looked up at the ceiling as though trying to recall the man we had only just mentioned, whom she would have seen passing her house every day for almost thirty years. "He was rather an unusual student, but then you'd already know that. He was one of the rare children I have taught who would not accept any kind of authority." She was an intelligent person, and she instantly got to the quick of his character. "It was hard to say whether his problems stemmed from a belief that he knew better than everyone around him, or a realisation that, in fact, he did not."

"Yes, that's very perceptive," Bella agreed. "Even as a child, there was an unhappiness to James. The family's wealth only brought suffering to the Heaton cousins."

"Except Lucinda, perhaps," Mrs Abbot said. "She always seems to rise above the negativity of the others and find the best the world can offer."

Her husband stirred a little at this moment. It was only a small movement as his arm flicked across his chest to land at his side, but his wife responded immediately by taking his hand in hers.

"Everyone loves Lucinda." Bella recited this as if it was the town motto.

"It's hard not to," Mrs Abbot agreed. "She's a charming young lady. As are you, Lady Isabella."

In all the years I had known her, I had never heard the woman attempt such flattery. It was quite unnerving. I had to conclude that, if she really was the killer, she would be too clever for us to catch. With this in mind, I cut short the niceties and presented some evidence.

"We spoke to Mrs Lyle in the post office. She told us that you bought a lot of stamps and writing material last week, before the letters were sent."

Mrs Abbot had a laugh like a wild dog. It sounded all the more peculiar coming in reply to such an observation. "Oh, that's too precious. I called into the post office to buy stationery and now I'm a killer. Is that really what you imagine happened?" Her tone suggested that she felt a little sorry for us.

Bella found her nerve then. She must have fed off the woman's apparent pity. "We're helping an inspector friend of ours from Scotland Yard. He thought that it would be worth confirming such details as we know the village better than he does."

The mention of Scotland Yard had its desired effect and Mrs Abbot sat up higher in the paisley armchair she was occupying. "I see." Her eyes narrowed a fraction before she answered. "Well, if you must know, I was writing letters of complaint."

"Of course you were." If my friend had meant these words critically, she did not let it show. "And about what exactly do you have reason to complain?" It's handy having a well-spoken aristocrat around to pose such snooty questions. If I'd asked such a thing, it would have sounded terribly rude. "The Yorkshire captaincy affair? The recent Thames floods? The Whitehaven pit explosion?"

"The world in general, but as it happens, I've written letters about all those topics over the last few months. You see, I made a New Year's resolution to give back more to my community, and so I started by setting out my thoughts to the London papers. It helped me get a sense of my own feelings."

"That's all it was? You wrote twenty letters to the papers?"

"Yes." Mrs Abbot remained calm throughout this discussion. She was either a completely innocent person, or a perfectly composed criminal mastermind. I knew which was more likely. "I feel that, in each of the cases you mentioned, and many more issues of the day, people deserve our sympathy and support. For their part, the newspapers only wish to divide us and whip up anger."

"Hear, hear!" I found myself saying, and so Bella gave my foot a friendly kick. It was already sore from when she'd stepped on it, so I had some tea to soothe the pain.

Faced with such a resilient opponent, Bella became tougher. "When we spoke of James, you didn't mention how much he upset you in class."

"That's right, I didn't." Mrs Abbot had keen eyes that were

quick to jump between us. It made me think of a cat I'd once known.

"It can't have been easy to have a student who, in your own words, did not accept your authority."

"It wasn't." She was all smiles. "That's why I killed him."

Silence gripped the room. It was as rigid as a block of iron. The only sound was Mr Abbot's soft, steady breathing, but then his wife emitted her howling laugh, and the tension broke.

"My dears, I'm only teasing. The pair of you have always been far too earnest. Of course I didn't kill James Heaton. The boy was an uppity pain in the neck, but the day he left Hurtwood School, he stopped being my problem."

Bella still hadn't recovered her voice, and so I put another empty point to our suspect. "But you can't deny that you have reasons not to like his cousin Lucinda."

"Yes, I can. In fact, I believe I already have. Everyone loves my neighbour. She is a kind, friendly, talented person and, having known her since she was a baby, I have yet to identify a discernible fault in her." When we still looked unconvinced, she added some proof. "You do realise that Lucinda has been volunteering as my assistant at the school for some years? Do you really think I would allow her to do so if I hated her?"

It was one of those moments where Bella and I felt quite out of our depths. The truth was that we were very much amateurs, and not yet fully detectives.

"But the Hurtwood Prettiest Garden Competition—" I tried one last time.

"At which I complained to the judges for coming second?" With a knowing look on her pale face, Mrs Abbot leant forward to place her cup and saucer back on the table. "I objected to her win not on personal grounds, but because my garden was objectively prettier than hers."

"I beg your pardon, but I fail to see the distinction. It must have upset you that Lucinda did you out of the prize."

Her eyes rolled back, and she shook her head as though I were an imbecile. She'd done this hundreds of times when we were at school – and I like to think I was one of her cleverer pupils!

"I was angry at the judges for always kowtowing to the Heaton family, but that's not Lucinda's fault. Even though her bullying father and uncle are long dead, the people of this town are still influenced by them."

It was Bella's turn to be confused. "But the Heaton children themselves aren't the same as their ruthless forebears, wouldn't you agree?"

"I would. And that's one of the things with which I took umbrage. So many people in the village still act as though it's 1895. The original Heatons and their offspring are dead and no longer hold us in their corrupting grip. James, Lucinda and Tilly were never going to follow in their fathers' footsteps, so we should be free to act as we wish around them... and to judge garden competitions fairly."

It was an interesting point. We'd all grown up with the stories of the cruel, self-serving Heaton clan but, though he could undoubtedly be a rotter in other ways, James was nothing like his father.

Before Bella could ask a question, Mrs Abbot spoke again.

"When the Heatons built the house where Lucinda still lives, nobody wanted such a large building in the middle of the town. There had been a small cottage there, much like this one, but instead of buying a large piece of land at the edge of the village to build a monument to their wealth, they wanted everyone passing through the centre of town to see it. And do you know how they achieved their goal?"

I was quite mesmerised by her confident delivery and could only shake my head.

"They bribed, flattered or intimidated anyone who offered resistance to their plans. It was not a nice time to live here." She had to pause to release a deep breath. "You should know all about this, Mr Quin. Your father was the only solicitor in town, and he led the opposition to their building work. No one approved of the Heaton brothers, but they got their own way in the end. And for the last thirty years, my little house has stood in the shadow of their monstrosity."

"That's terrible," Bella replied, forgetting the fact that we had gone there to interrogate a suspect. "Didn't my father do something to stop it?"

"Not even the Duke could defeat the Heaton brothers. Although the fields, forests and hills in the area fall under his family's protection, the Montagues never owned the land upon which the village was built. And that was how the Heatons could buy any property that became available. The old pub up the road, the general shop, the police station and any houses that were sold went to them. It was not just for the money they could make, but the power it gave them. By the time the previous generation of the family died, they were landlords to half the population of Hurtwood Village."

Bella considered the point before replying. "Are you suggesting that this could explain why someone would kill James and threaten the girls? You just conceded that they weren't like their parents. James wouldn't raise rents and throw people out on the street like a Victorian landlord. Tilly has no interest in holding the power her father had amassed over our fellow villagers. And as for Lucinda, her side of the family never had the influence that the other one did. So why would anyone go after them?"

"Because the people of Hurtwood have long memories. Tom and Granville may have died many years ago, but that doesn't mean their cruelty has been forgiven. Perhaps the killer will only stop when every last Heaton is dead."

FOURTEEN

Mrs Abbot's front door shut behind us, and I believe we were both quite drained. It was as though we'd sat through a whole day of school, condensed into a thirty-minute conversation. Our former teacher was certainly a good educator. I'd learnt more in the short time in her house than I had all morning talking to the other inhabitants of Hurtwood Village.

"What do you think?" Bella asked when we reached the village crossroads.

"I think she did a very good job of clearing her name from our list of suspects, which almost makes me suspicious in itself."

"In what sense?"

I tried to put my finger on it. "There was something about her manner. Did you notice it?"

"You mean she was too nice?"

This tickled me, but she was right. "Precisely. She invited us in there without any resistance and did all she could to put us at ease. I wondered whether she wanted us to see her husband and feel sorry for her."

"You cynic, Marius."

"I know, I'm terrible. But this is the woman who once

refused to talk to Ned Lyle for a week after he mispronounced *library*. Why else would she welcome us into her house so readily? It's truly out of character."

There was a bench beside the war memorial, and Bella sat down to think. "Fine, she put on an act to convince us that she's a sweet and innocent person, but that doesn't make her the killer, does it?"

"No... No, you're right. It doesn't. And she gave plenty of good reasons why we were barking up the wrong tree." I huffed out a sigh. "I said before that Lovebrook was at a disadvantage, as he doesn't know this place the way that we do, but I'm beginning to think the opposite might be true."

Instead of responding, she provided a sympathetic look.

I looked about at the cluster of pretty houses around the crossroads. "We have to find a killer, and our first thought was that our witch-like teacher must be to blame. It was juvenile of us, even if she had bought a few stamps." I clapped my hands together as though wishing to forget the whole thing.

"It was still useful to talk to her." Bella found some nuggets of gold in the heap of mud I'd just extracted. "I thought that what she said about the Heatons was interesting. Earlier, when we spoke about the reasons why someone wanted to murder James, we only focused on him and not his wider family. It is quite possible that people in this town would still hold a grudge after the way the Heatons behaved for so long."

I tapped my foot on the tarmac as faint memories pricked my brain. "My parents never talked about the Heaton brothers in front of me. I suppose they didn't want me thinking badly of our classmates, but it's true what Mrs Abbot said. My father was always having to defend Tom Heaton's tenants – often from his thug of a brother. When they wanted to get someone out of one of their properties, Granville would do whatever it took to scare them. Father was the only person that anyone could turn to for help."

"Terence Quin was a very good man." She stood up again and the sympathetic look was back on her face. For a woman who lived in the lap of luxury, she possessed an admirable ability to put herself in the place of those less fortunate. It was what marked her out as different from the Heatons of the world.

"Yes, and I hope that he still is, though that might be wishful thinking on my part." I needed to take a deep breath then. Discussing my long-missing father on top of the murder of our schoolmate was a lot for one afternoon. "The truth is, he's been with me ever since I arrived back here. I see him in every old face I meet and every building in this odd little town. My family were happy to come back, but now that I'm here, I understand why I stayed away for so long."

A shudder passed through her, and I could see the sadness I'd provoked. Instead of being downhearted, though, she offered me some hope. "There's nothing you can do about your father's disappearance right now, but we can solve James's murder." She walked over to the war memorial and pointed at Sebastian's name. "We still have plenty of avenues to explore. We haven't had time to consider anything my father told us. We didn't even ask Mrs Abbot about what happened in 1917."

Before I could reply, we heard someone calling from the direction of my house.

"Marius! Bella!" Lovebrook was running down towards us. He was a lithe fellow and, though I would have said that this was a useful characteristic for a detective to have, most of the officers I had known were on the plump side. "I'm glad that I caught you. My colleagues from Guildford have been through the man's possessions."

This was another reason to feel positive, and I believe I looked a little more cheerful than I had a few moments earlier. "Did they find anything significant?"

"That's the odd thing. There was very little there." Lovebrook put his hands behind his back so that his Burberry raincoat bulged out over his arms. "He owns a big house and yet it's as though no one's ever lived in it. He has no papers, no family photographs. He just has the essentials of daily life and some equipment for exercising. I've never been inside a place that was so free of personality."

"That sounds like James," Bella replied in a cool tone. "His father beat the personality out of him at a young age. The only thing I ever knew him to care about was his perception in the eyes of other people."

"To be fair," I put in, "he cared about you as well, Bella. We've never talked about it, but he changed when he realised you didn't return his feelings. He wasn't nearly so angry or hard done by before then."

I could tell that Lovebrook felt guilty for – to murder two metaphors – waking sleeping dogs with a wasps' nest. "I doubt that his feelings for you will come into his murder, Lady Isabella. His house paints a picture of a very lonely person, which only makes the case more mysterious."

"Were there any fingerprints on the knife or around the scene of the crime?" I asked somewhat hopefully.

"Yes, but only one, so they must belong to the man's sister. It's impossible to say whether there were any on there before she grabbed the knife, but there's nothing to find now."

Bella kept searching for good news. "Was there any progress elsewhere?"

"I called the constable I know in Wellingborough, and he is patrolling the centre of the town, asking questions. I told him to start with the pubs. If anyone knows what's happening in a village, it's the old fellows with nothing better to do than mind other people's business." As he said this, he looked over his shoulder to the spot where we'd previously had our drink. The two aged gentlemen were sipping their pints of ale and once more raised them to the hardworking bobby. Lovebrook waved and asked us a question of his own. "Have you two discovered anything useful?"

I was about to say no, but Bella spoke for the pair of us.

"We haven't had time to consider what it might mean," she began, "but the postman remembers seeing a tall man looking through Lucinda's hedge at some point this week. He thought it could be a lurker of some description."

"And our old teacher helped us see the Heaton family in a context we'd admittedly ignored," I added.

"And that would be?" Lovebrook tilted his head to listen.

"Well, they owned half the houses in this town and the cousins would have inherited all that. She thought that someone could still be angry about the way the previous generations of the family behaved."

"That's more like it," the inspector replied. "I'd take a nice old-fashioned grudge over long-distance poison-pen letters."

Bella had something more practical to contribute. "I think you should assign a man to watch over each girl tonight."

"I agree." Lovebrook nodded sternly. "In fact, I put in a request to the Yard, but they say that they can only spare one man for the whole village. My superior's exact words were that we are the police, not nursemaids."

I'd felt bad about leaving the girls on their own, even in the daylight hours, and offered to make up the shortfall. "Then I'll stay at Lucinda's tonight and your man can focus on Tilly's house."

Bella's face brightened. "Oh really?" She couldn't resist teasing me. "Will it be a terrible hardship to spend the night in the house of the stunningly beautiful girl who's always held you in high esteem and recently broke off her engagement?"

I was glad that Lovebrook reacted to this instead of me. "Gosh, Marius! How many women fall in love with you in an average week?"

I smiled in reply. Even if the job had hardened him, there

was still an innocent core to the inspector that I doubted would ever disappear.

I didn't answer his question but clarified my previous point for Bella's sake. "I'll sleep on the sofa in Lucinda's lounge in case anyone tries to come into the house."

"What a very good idea," she replied, leaving plenty of room for interpretation. I considered stamping on her foot, but I'm not that cruel.

"Excellent. Then it's all arranged." Lovebrook sounded as though he was in a hurry. "I don't know where I'll be tonight. The life of an inspector is an itinerant one. I'll interview Lucinda and Matilda Heaton now, and then I'll probably have to return to London for the night." He had a habit of switching between the personal and the professional. "Strictly speaking, I'm not assigned to this case. My bosses know I'm down here, of course. But there's nothing in the murder itself to attract Scotland Yard's interest. If my man in Wellingborough discovers anything, I'll head up there tomorrow to see about this letter."

"I'll drive you in the Invicta if you like," I suggested, pointing to the car that was still outside Lucinda's house. "Perhaps it will be faster?"

His eyes lit up. "Not if I have to come here to collect you, it won't. But it would still be worth the effort. My father has a Silver Hawk from the same designer and it's an absolute dream. I'll get a message to you if I can come."

The fact that his father owned an incredibly pricy sports car was another reason to make me think that Lovebrook came from substantial wealth. Mumbling excitedly the whole way, he walked towards Lucinda's house without taking his eyes off my car.

"Now what should we do?" I asked Bella once he'd gone.

She tapped my right lapel with the flat of her hand. "I'm sorry to abandon you just as the investigation is gathering steam, but I must go back to the manor. I like to be there for Father's supper when I can. You're welcome to join me."

"That would be my very first choice, but I think I should stay here. There is a killer on the loose, after all."

She tapped my chest once more, then turned to walk off behind the pub. A few moments later, her green Sunbeam motorcar rolled past me with Caxton behind the wheel. He waved sarcastically as he passed and, if Bella hadn't been sitting next to him, I might well have shouted something rude.

FIFTEEN

I considered popping home for some proper lunch, but before I could do any such thing, Dodo appeared from inside Lucinda's house. She'd been with the cousins all afternoon and looked quite defeated by whatever she'd experienced.

"Is everything all right, old friend?" I called to her in an, as it turned out, unintentionally cheery voice.

As she reached me, she burst into tears. "I'm not crying because of James. Please don't think that. He was a brute and a bully, and I don't want anyone to think that I'm crying for him."

I put a hand on either of her shoulders and bent down so that our eyes were at the same level. "Then what can the matter be?"

"I don't know..." She looked away from me, back towards the house. "It's just all so horrible. Tilly is resigned to her imminent death and Lucinda seems to be in shock. It's impossible to talk to either of them."

She started to walk up the road to the post office where she lived with her family, but I pulled on her arm to get her to stay. "Don't go home just yet. Let's walk up to Homestead Hill. Perhaps the sun will come out before it sets."

I looked at the overcast sky a little dubiously, but she didn't notice. Still sniffling, she turned, and we took a path between two houses to dive into the forest that had so often served as our playground when we were children.

"I know it all seems tragic," I told her, "but things are never as black as they appear. The police are here now, and Scotland Yard is keeping an eye on the situation. It's sad that something so evil could happen here in Hurtwood, but we have to hope that the worst is over."

For some reason, this made Dodo cry a little harder.

"No... don't do that." I really should learn how to comfort people. It's difficult to be an amateur sleuth if you can't convince witnesses that you care about their situation.

Before I could think of another reason why she shouldn't be upset, she spoke again. "This place was supposed to be our haven. The forest has always felt so far away from the rest of the world, but now everything's changed."

She hurried on along the winding path through oak and ash trees. No matter how fast I went, she was always a step ahead. I felt that she needed to break free from the village for just a little while, and so we continued on towards the clearing.

She was right about the Hurtwood; it was a sanctuary from the wider world, but that meant it could feel oddly claustrophobic. I hurried after her and, when I saw the light breaking through the line of trees at the edge of the forest, I felt I could breathe more easily again.

We stopped at the crest of the hill, which was like the bald crown at the top of a tonsured monk's head. Although the trees hid the village entirely, the view before us was wide and immense. Dodo rushed forward to the highest point and stood looking out over the landscape like a tourist visiting for the first time.

"It's still beautiful," I had to admit.

There were wood pigeons flying between copses in the

distance and, though the sun still wasn't shining on us, it was a warm day for the end of March. The spring felt as though it would be staying with us for some time.

"There's no shortage of beauty around here." Dodo had a rather old-fashioned manner, and it wasn't just because of her clothes. Her speech and wistful nature reminded me once more of the classic novels I'd read as a child.

We stood with our eyes fixed on the horizon for some minutes without speaking. James and the letters and all the sadness that was floating about the village that day seemed like dreams we'd once had. It made me feel better to know that, even as our classmate lay dead in his house, the world up here continued as before.

"I'm sorry you feel the way you do, but it was nice of you to look after Tilly and Lucinda today."

She looked down at the sandy ground and began to draw with the end of one scuffed shoe. "It's what you're supposed to do for other people, isn't it? You help those in need."

"Did they tell you about the letters?"

She wiped out the figure of eight she had made with her foot and walked a few steps away from me. "Of course. It's all Tilly will talk about. She says that they're being punished for their family's crimes."

"Do you believe that?"

She looked back over her shoulder at me and thought about the answer. "I suppose it could be true. To be honest, I'd half forgotten how hated the Heatons were. I recall James and Tilly's dad being loud and arrogant when we were children, but I didn't know anything about how he made his money."

I perched on the stone pediment at the base of the marker. There'd been a hill fort there once, but whatever was left of it was buried under heather bushes and brambles. The only sign of human intervention was the stone cross that we used to climb in order to say we were the highest people in the whole of England.

We evidently didn't realise that there were much taller mountains out there than Homestead Hill, but the country looked so flat for miles around that it was hard to imagine anything else.

"Why do you think the letters were written if they're not about the family?"

"1917," she replied a little mysteriously.

"I beg your pardon?"

"The letters that the cousins received today mention 1917. I saw them in Lucinda's living room, but when I asked Tilly, she said nothing important happened then."

"It was the last time I spent any time here," I thought aloud, suddenly wondering whether this whole situation was my fault. "You don't think it had something to do with—"

"No, I don't. You egotist!" Even when Dodo was trying to be gloomy, there was something reluctantly positive about her. "I think it's about my friend Sebastian."

It struck me as odd that everyone remembered that boy more than I did. He and Dodo had got on well, so it's not surprising she'd remember him, but even the Duke knew who he was. Whereas I'd had to dig through my memories to even recall what he looked like.

"Why would it have anything to do with him?"

"Because he was the one person who only appeared back then. The letter said '1917 will never die'. He arrived in March and was called up for his training a short time later. The rest of us were here for ages before that, but he was the 1917 boy."

I could see why she would say this, but I couldn't say she was right. "That doesn't mean that the killer would agree with you. Perhaps 1917 was the year when Lucinda's dad Granville evicted some poor family for not paying their rent, or his brother Tom took the old couple who owned the general shop to court for refusing to leave their house when he demanded it."

"Mr and Mrs Day!" Dodo replied, apparently ignoring my

point and focusing on the nostalgia of those names. "They had a little bakery in the corner of the shop. I used to love going there after school to buy butterfly cakes and currant buns." She looked up at me and realised that this was not what we needed to discuss. "Oh, I'm sorry. I got distracted."

"That's all right. It's nice to see you haven't changed."

She turned away again to take in the view. "Fine. The Heatons were a band of villains and they deserved all they got, but that doesn't remove the possibility that the letter was talking about Sebastian."

I was trying to be patient, but I needed her to concentrate for a moment. "You do know that I've come back here to try to solve this case? I don't want anything terrible to happen to our friends, so if you really think that James's murder could be connected to Sebastian Kane, you'll have to provide more evidence than the fact he happened to live here that year."

Instead of giving a straight answer, she turned away and delivered a mild insult. "All these amateur sleuths running about Britain, trying to catch killers – to be quite honest, I find it terribly morbid. Why don't you find a proper hobby, like bird-watching or fly fishing?"

I chose to ignore her shifting mood. "Fine, I'm morbid. Now answer my question."

Dodo was as much a part of the landscape as the moss-covered trees in the forest or the crocuses blooming all over the meadows on the other side of the hill. When we were children, she would chase after butterflies or look for dragonflies around the lake on Bella's estate. It seemed she hadn't changed a great deal, as her eyes were constantly shooting off in search of passing birds.

I could see the effort it took her, but she managed to stay in the human world for long enough to answer my question. "For one thing, if it's Tom and Granville Heaton the killer so despises, why would the notes have said 'you' to the three cousins?"

"I'm sorry?" I'd been apologising a lot recently.

"In the letter that came today, each one said, 'Just because time has passed, that doesn't mean I've forgotten you.' If he was just talking about the family's past, I don't think he would have phrased it like that. This is personal. It has to be."

"I take your point." I did a quick calculation and could see that what she'd said made sense. "But that still doesn't link the letters or James's death to Sebastian."

"What else did the Heatons get up to in 1917?"

This was one question I could answer with ease. "James's father used his connections to make sure his son didn't come to any harm in the war."

"Oh, come along. Why would anyone still care about that? And why go after the girls too, in that case?" She had me this time, and I couldn't summon a response. "Besides, it's obviously Sebastian because of what James and Tilly did to him."

I waited for her to unravel this mystery and, when she didn't, I asked the obvious question. "What *did* they do to him?"

"I've never known for certain, but Tilly does, and she hasn't been herself since the first letter arrived." She took a deep breath and tried to make more of this vague assertion. "Just listen for a moment. As soon as Sebastian arrived in the village, he and I realised that we had a lot in common and became friends. All I know is that, during the one week he spent any time with us outside school, he changed. I asked him what had happened, but he wouldn't speak to me."

I wanted to believe that this was the solution but, whatever happened between Tilly and Sebastian, it simply sounded too juvenile to have led to the death of a man eleven years later.

"Really, Dodo, I don't see it. For one thing, Sebastian died in 1918 at the Battle of the Lys. But even if he hadn't – and all this was connected to the short time he spent here – why would Lucinda have to die? Did she do anything to the boy?"

A note of anger entered her voice then, and she trapped me in her gaze. "Don't talk to me like I'm a fool, Marius. The others have always done it, but not you."

Her words were carried away by the wind, and I didn't know how to respond.

"I wasn't trying to upset you," I eventually tried. "I just meant that you can't solve a murder based on hearsay and imagination."

"I shouldn't have snapped," she said, taking her time to fashion each word. "But I'm tired of people talking down to me as if I'm a child." A shy smile shaped her lips. "You know, I have a job in the Hurtwood House library now. I look after the old books there, and I've been making a record of all the documents they have."

Her cautious positivity picked me back up again, and I shared my own passion for such places. "I love libraries. There's one next to my house in London and I spend half my time there reading and writing. When I was little, I used to hide in that beautiful old treasure trove in Bella's house just to admire all those exquisite books." I doubted this was enough to reassure her, so I kept talking. "And besides, you don't have to prove anything to me. As I tried to tell you this afternoon, your writing when we were younger was one of the things that inspired me to have a go myself."

"Oh, stop it, Marius." Still smiling, she marched away from the viewpoint and entered the forest once more. It took me a few seconds to realise she had really gone, and somewhat longer to catch up with her.

"Dodo, why won't you believe me?" I asked as I scrambled down the hill.

"Because you're talking nonsense. I've never inspired anyone in my life. I'm not that kind of person and you know it."

The last time I'd seen her, she'd been full of dreams and ambitions. I was sorry to see her so worn down by the world. "I may not be able to prove it, but trust me on one thing, Marius. Whoever wrote those letters knows what the Heatons did to Sebastian Kane."

SPRING 1917 – PART ONE

As the men of Britain fought and died in France, and our king and politicians condemned German barbarism all over the continent, eight friends in Hurtwood were enjoying the best year of their young lives. The winter had been as cold as any in the last five decades, and the snow had continued right through to April. So when the weather changed, it felt as though they had upped sticks and moved to another planet.

They had known one another since they were children but, in that very natural way that occurs as time passes and people mature, the ground beneath their feet had gradually shifted. There was love in the air between them. It was a palpable force that never disappeared for a moment. Even in their schoolroom, with thirty other children of all ages in the class, they could no longer return to the way things had been before.

Of the eight, James and Marius were the oldest and so liable to be called up to the army any day. Ned and Richard were a year younger, and then there was the main group of girls in Bella, Lucinda, Tilly and Dodo.

Each had a role to play. Bella was kind, Lucinda exciting, Marius was the leader, and James Heaton railed against the world, because that was the kind of person he was. Tilly was more reserved than her brother, whereas Dodo Lyle spent most of her time reading or writing as life carried on around her. As the youngest, her little brother Ned didn't know how he was supposed to fit in to the lively group, but that didn't stop him wanting to be included in everything. And as for Richard Fairbanks, well, he was too fond of himself to be left until last, but he had a quick mind and the will to change the world. Like the pieces of a jigsaw puzzle, they were all different but clicked neatly together. They loved their life in Hurtwood and never imagined it any other way.

Perhaps it was the arrival of the new boy in town that made the real difference. Sebastian Kane was already old enough to be sent to war when he turned up at their school. He seemed like a quiet, uncomplicated sort of person, but the effects of his presence would be felt for years to come.

"Introduce yourself, boy," Mrs Abbot demanded on Sebastian's first morning, standing him at the front of the classroom so that everyone could get a good look.

It was clear that he wasn't comfortable up there, and a few of the smaller children laughed at his awkwardness.

"Sebastian." He had sandy brown hair and black-framed glasses. His eyes didn't explore the classroom as you might have expected, but he peered down at the students in the front row as though he hadn't worked up the courage to go any further.

"You don't possess a surname?" It was never clear whether our teacher spoke so bluntly for the laughter she could provoke, or simply to show off the power she wielded in her tiny kingdom.

"Kane, miss. My name's Sebastian Kane." He risked a glance at the far corner of the room where the children his age were sitting. "My family and I just moved to the old mill house."

"Your name would have sufficed," the contrary educator chimed. "There's a spare place beside Dorothy Lyle. I'm sure she won't bite you."

That was the moment when the subtle shift could first be

observed. Dodo smiled at her new tablemate, and it set off a ripple around the group. You see, that's the problem with falling in love. It doesn't tend to happen in quite the right way. Lucinda had once professed the belief that the world would be a happier place if we were each assigned our other half at birth, so that there was no arguing and no competition. Had such a reality existed, disaster may well have been averted that year.

Even a simple equation like Bella + Marius, two independent forces who were always likely to combine, could not be isolated from other factors. Although neither of them realised it, Marius's former friend, James, looked at Bella as though she were an angel sent from a higher realm. He suffered in silence, but every muscle in his body burned for Lady Isabella Montague, and Lucinda looked at Marius in just the same way.

In fact, Sebastian was the hand flicking a line of dominos: the final addition atop a house of cards that sent the whole thing cascading. It wasn't his fault. He was just as innocent of the impact he'd had that day as he looked, but that didn't change anything. He was a minor player in this Elizabethan tragedy, but he would set everything else in motion.

There was a week's holiday in May to give the students a chance to catch up on their work before the big push towards the end of the year. Well, that was the idea at least, but now so close to adulthood and all the responsibility that would bring, Marius and his friends were more interested in enjoying themselves. The sun made a rare appearance in the sky over the village and, together, they would while away their time in the Hurtwood or walk up to the ancient fort that looked out across the Surrey Hills.

England looked beautiful from so high. In that singularly green and pleasant part of the country, it was easy to imagine they had been transported back to the time of Robin Hood or King Arthur. The woods there were abundant, the hills plump and rolling, and the sky that week was as blue as Richard Fairbanks's eyes.

Even when Marius and Bella weren't off walking together, they rarely seemed conscious of what anyone else was doing. Dodo and Sebastian spent their time discussing their favourite books and her hopes of becoming a writer – she blushed every time he spoke to her, and it was easy to imagine what she was thinking. Lucinda and Tilly, meanwhile, would sit apart from the others, chattering and giggling about some topic to which the boys could never be party, and James and Richard would have contests to see who could throw stones, sticks or, in one case, snails the furthest.

Sebastian had only been invited because Bella's father told her it would be rude not to include him, but he rarely said much to anyone except Dodo. He was content to observe the interactions of this long-established clique, and no one could imagine what was going through his head.

Their lazy holiday unfolded just as it would have if he hadn't been there, and yet things were different because he was. It was hard to define what had changed but, aside from the largely oblivious love-birds, most in the group noticed it. For one thing, Tilly wasn't her usual distant self. She laughed a lot more than normal and spent her time running her fingers through her hair. It wasn't long before people realised that it was the shy newcomer she was looking at as she did it.

Richard wasn't happy that his girl was looking at someone else. Just to be clear, Richard and Tilly had never discussed their potential romance. They had never kissed or even touched one another in a tender way, but he was of the opinion that, if Lucinda continued playing her games and refusing to walk out with him, Tilly made a perfectly good second option. And, if not, there was always Dodo.

Of course, if Sebastian liked Tilly, that meant he had no time for Dodo, and while Marius was quite in love with Bella, this made him sad for his friend. At the same time, if Richard was looking at Tilly, it meant he couldn't spoil Lucinda with the attention she enjoyed. This confirmed her idea that he wasn't seriously in love with her anyway, which was why she preferred to think of Marius. And so on and so forth the ripples passed through the group until everyone was feeling bad about something, just because Sebastian had come along and disturbed the careful balance that had existed for so long.

Perhaps the fragile peace of the group would have held had it not been for one moment as they sat in a circle on their blankets at the top of the hill, playing a game of questions.

"Where will you be in seven years?" Marius asked Lucinda, and the aim of the game was to answer as quickly as possible and respond in kind.

"Probably right here," the girl replied, then turned to Tilly to change the world. "Who do you love?"

Tilly sought out Sebastian around the circle. It was only for a second, but their eyes clicked onto one another's before Tilly looked away. Sebastian didn't mind. He could still feel her gaze for some time after and would remember that moment for the rest of his short life. He would take it with him wherever he went, just as some men carried photographs of their sweethearts.

"Don't look at my sister like that," James complained, which brought a reaction from everyone but Sebastian. The boys got to their feet, and it was clear the game was over.

"Leave him alone," Bella demanded. She was always the defender of the group – always standing up to injustice.

"Yes, don't be such a bore." Even his sister was tired of him. "Not everything has to be a fight, you know? Sometimes we can just be happy."

To prove her wrong, James smiled a bitter smile and swung his fist at Sebastian. He missed and only bruised his ego, but the sudden hint of violence was enough to break up the party for the day. Marius rushed in to make sure James didn't cause any more trouble. Bella took care of their new friend, and James marched off sullenly down the hill with Dodo following behind, berating him all the way home.

Richard was uncertain how to feel. He and James were always up against one another, but Tilly was the girl he rather liked. He couldn't be sure whether to be angry at Sebastian or the boy who had almost hit him, and so he wandered home feeling quite lost. This wasn't like him. He was used to knowing his own mind and couldn't understand why he would feel so uncertain.

No one but Sebastian stayed at the viewpoint after that. He insisted he was fine and climbed on top of the stone cross at the highest point of the hill to be on his own. Marius and Bella walked off together through the forest and, halfway home, Bella's hand touched his and their fingers became entwined for the first time. They would stop on the path to the village and hold each other for what felt like hours but was probably only seconds. Though they wouldn't tell their friends for some days, this was the moment that they finally knew what it meant to be in love.

In all the drama, no one paid much attention to Tilly. She'd started the trip home with Lucinda but immediately doubled back to the viewpoint when no one was looking. She went all the way to the cross and stood in front of Sebastian. As the sun set over the trees behind her, she climbed up to place a kiss on his lips and whisper five words in his ear.

"Meet me back here tonight."

SIXTEEN

One thing I knew for certain was that my proximity to crimes and criminality was the perfect motivation for me to write. Visiting Hurtwood Village again – and observing the interactions of that tight-knit community which, beneath the pretty façade, was riven with grudges and petty jealousies – provided me with plenty of inspiration.

Perhaps the greatest hazard of being a writer is the terror of forgetting a good idea. So rather than running about, speaking to witness after witness until I'd lost my voice (and any interest in the case), I returned to my childhood bedroom to note down my ideas for a future novel.

Despite my best intentions, when I sat down at my desk with an old exercise book from my school days, I found that I was still focused on James's murder.

I wrote down the sentence...

One way of concealing the real motive of a crime might be to introduce such a vast number of reasons to kill the victim that the reader is quite bamboozled.

Rather than considering how this might be applied to the creation of a new case for my fictional detective, Inspector Rupert L'Estrange, it set me off on a train of thought concerning the man who had been killed that day. It really felt as though we were dealing with far too many threads to the investigation, and we still had plenty more to find. From the initial thought that Lucinda would be the killer's main target it was now clear that the shadow of the previous generation still hung over the village.

The letters hinted at a range of possible explanations. I'd considered jealousy for Lucinda's unparalleled popularity – going so far as to accuse an old teacher of wanting to murder her because of a local gardening competition. The ghost of the boy who had died in the war could be to blame. The only thing that linked Sebastian Kane to James's murder, though, was a date on the poison-pen letters and our friend Dodo's certitude. I thought it highly unlikely that he would be connected to the case, but that didn't mean I could rule out the possibility once and for all.

There was the lurker that Ned had spotted and the anger that people in the village still felt over the Heaton family's dubious business practices. Then there was Lucinda's ex-fiancé, who we'd barely had time to examine as a potential suspect. Richard Fairbanks had been at her house shortly before James was killed. The two men had fought, as well, so why had I over-looked him? Because he'd seemed a nice sort of boy at school, and I didn't think he had it in him? I wouldn't let the sleuth in my books perpetrate such lazy thinking, and I would try my best not to make the same mistake. I pledged to interview Richard at the first possible opportunity... unless he turned out to be busy.

Percy sat on my bed, trying to make me feel guilty for daring to spend the day without him. I soon filled pages of the exercise book with notes, theories and questions, but most of what I wrote was more relevant to the mystery of Hurtwood Village than my paying career.

The afternoon turned to evening and— Fine, I admit it; I had a nap whilst I was up there. And then, as my dear aunt and uncle would be sleeping in my room that night, I had to vacate the premises.

Uncle Stan showed me to the door. "Have a wonderful evening." He was often keen to get rid of me.

"A man has been murdered, and I'm doing my best to help the police find his killer." Percy slipped past me through the open door, and I was too busy talking to object.

"I know all that, but you can still try to enjoy yourself," Stan told me, as his wife and sister-in-law lurked grinningly behind him.

"Why does it feel like you're planning a party without me?"

The trio exchanged guilty looks, and it fell to my mother to answer. "Not a party, dear. You know that people our age aren't allowed to enjoy ourselves. We're working on a plan."

And with that, the door closed in my face, and I realised that Percy was on the same side of it as I was. Looking inordinately pleased with himself, he walked in a circle, flicking his curved tail as he went.

"We're going to the pub," I told him directly, "but the drinks are on you."

Percy did not object because Percy is a dog. Of course, the fact that he did not carry a wallet meant that he would have the last laugh... Not that dogs can laugh, either.

There was a constable walking up and down the road between the two cousins' houses, which made me feel better about my first port of call. I'd decided to go to the pub to discover what the villagers made of the sudden drop in the population, then to Lucinda's to find out how comfortable her sofa was and, if Percy behaved himself, there might even be time for a walk in between.

What I wasn't expecting was for the two elements of my evening to combine. Lucinda and Tilly were there in the Duke's Head when we arrived. Percy didn't see the problem. He knew the moment he saw the young women that they would make a fuss of him again, but I really didn't think it was a good idea for them to be anywhere so public.

Tilly was sitting on a stool at the bar, tipping pints of cider down her neck. I noticed that the newcomer with the scar I had seen in the village that morning was just next to her. He had an aloof manner, and it was hard to know whether he was there with Tilly or not. Sergeant Rossiter was alone at a table, staring angrily into his pint, and Lucinda sat in the opposite corner looking terribly lost and lonely.

"What are you doing here?" I asked as Percy jumped onto her bench in search of affection.

Lucinda acted as though she couldn't quite place who I was, then clicked her fingers and pronounced my name with joy. "Marius! My handsome stranger. Thank goodness you've come."

I took the chair opposite, and instead of fussing over my basset hound, it was my hand she stroked.

"Lucinda, I believe you've had too much to drink."

She lowered her voice but continued pawing me. "Marius, I believe that you're the most exquisite man I've ever set eyes upon. In fact, if you asked me to marry you, I would wake up Reverend Piggins from his slumber and demand that he see us wed at St Mark's this very night."

I carefully moved her glass away from her before responding. "Isn't it a shame that churches aren't open twenty-four hours a day!"

"Why do I like you so much?" She was suddenly more serious, and I could only imagine that she was asking herself this question rather than me. "It's not just that your dark floppy hair makes me want to take up hairdressing to get closer to it, or the fact you have eyes like... like..." She looked around the bar for inspiration. "What's deep and brown and wet?"

"A highly toxic tailing pond beside an abandoned mine?" I suggested, and she clapped her hands together.

"Exactly... wait, no. I don't know what that is. My point is... Actually, what is my point?"

"I believe you were listing my positive attributes."

Percy looked across the table at me then as though to say, *Why tell her, you masochist?* To which, just for a change, I was the one who was unable to answer.

"That's it! You see, it's not just that you're handsome." She supported her heavy head on her fist then, and I felt rather sorry for her. "No, it's not just for your curls and your brooding looks. I like you, Marius Quin because, you're the only man who has never treated me like a golfing trophy."

I failed to see the connection, and so I said, "I'm sorry, but I fail to see the connection. What's golf got to do with anything?"

She noticed that there was a rather sorrowful dog at hand and, as I wouldn't have let her, she gave him a hug instead.

"Oh, do pay attention, man. It's got nothing to do with golf." Though her mind flitted from one point to the next, she somehow managed to make something approaching sense. "I'm saying that the men in this village treat me as though I'm a prize to be won."

I watched her as she waved one hand around and stroked Percy with the other. "Why don't you leave?"

"I beg your pardon?" It was hard to know whether she was offended, or she simply hadn't heard me.

I spoke a little louder all the same. "I said, why don't you leave Hurtwood?"

She laughed. It was not a gentle ladylike titter, but a full-blooded guffaw before she realised I wasn't joking. "Oh, you're serious."

"Of course I am. Why haven't you ever left the village?"

"What a simple way you have of looking at the world." She sighed a troubled sigh.

This time, when she rested her chin on her fist, her eyes closed for a moment, her head slid off her hand and she briefly woke up once more. Despite the scintillating conversation I provided, this process repeated several times until, finally, she fell asleep on the table.

Percy moaned in sympathy, and I thought I should go and get her some water.

In the small bar on the other side of the pub, the place was less busy, but a group of my school friends had assembled there to drink to James's memory.

"This night was supposed to be in your honour, old man," Richard told me as I waited for Hurtwood's alewife to serve me. "I was planning to celebrate your success but, after today, it's turned into a wake." Dressed in a long black coat and matching suit, he looked every bit the mourner.

Ned shyly raised his glass to me, and I could tell that he'd been dragged along there by our boisterous former classmates. There were men I recognised who would have been much younger than me at school, and Dodo was in the corner looking bored. Though, in the city, women largely stayed away from such establishments, the Duke's Head filled various roles in Hurtwood, and men and women alike patronised its services. It functioned as a social centre, restaurant, clinic – so long as all you needed was a talking cure – and debate chamber.

"To James," Richard toasted, and they all drank. "It was hard to like him, harder to love him, but impossible to hate him."

"To James," came the response, and I nodded across the group to Dodo, who looked just as cross as she had when she'd run away from me on Homestead Hill.

I would have tried to speak to her, but Richard grabbed my arm.

"It's good to have you back, Marius, but I wish it were under different circumstances." He had a glass of brandy in his hand and slowly sipped it in abject misery. "The truth is this village has gone to pot. I mean, I know James could be a disaster sometimes, but he was a decent chap. Always willing to help out with a quid or two. A decent chap!"

"It's hard to know what to make of any of it," I replied in almost as bleak a tone. "It seems that James had so little in his life. Do you know anything more about him than the contents of his empty house can tell us?"

He looked at me keenly for a moment, and then a realisation broke. "Oh, yes, of course. You're involved in all that amateur sleuthing business with Bella. Does it pay well?"

Though he could be good company, Richard's main driving interest had always been making money.

I shrugged. "I can't say that it does. Although in my case at least, it has certain perks."

He frowned as though he'd lost interest in the topic and answered my original question. "James and I used to drink and shoot together from time to time. On separate occasions, I mean. We were not in the habit of going out to the woods with bottles of whisky and hunting rifles." He pointed to his glass, and I was tempted to get one of whatever he was drinking.

Instead, I asked him a question. "He was quite aggressive this morning when he removed you from his cousin's garden. Had the pair of you fallen out?"

He looked about the bar then, and I couldn't read his expression. Richard always had more going on in his brain than he wanted anyone to know. I suppose that's often true of clever people.

"No, no. Nothing like that. We may not have seen eye to eye on a few matters, but we were always friends. You remember what we were like at school, don't you? Competitive comrades to the last!"

I recalled the scene that I'd viewed through Lucinda's front window, and a few words that James had uttered came back to me. "He said that, after everything he'd done for you, you could at least leave Lucinda alone. What did he mean?"

Richard's face crumpled at the memory. "He was a great support when I was founding my plastics company, you know? I wouldn't have become the success that I am without James Heaton, and I don't mind who knows it." I don't know whether it was guilt or just sadness that swept over him then. In the brief pause between sentences, a rogue tear escaped his eye, and there were reinforcements at the ready. I could only assume he had consumed more than one drink. "James was one of those people who only came out of his shell in private. You know, he could be a sensitive soul when he tried and I believe that he viewed me as the brother he'd always wanted."

His words reminded me of the James I'd known when we were children – the boy I'd once called my best friend. In fact, I found his tribute quite stirring, but I wasn't about to tell Richard that.

"What about Lucinda? What happened that made her call everything off? The last I heard you were set to walk down the aisle."

He opened his mouth to answer and then changed his mind. "I'm sorry, old thing, but do you mind terribly if I don't?" He had a refined way of speaking for the son of the local plumber. "Not tonight, at least. I'd rather just drink away my sorrows with my pals here and wake up tomorrow morning feeling dreadful."

I did mind, but I'd left Lucinda on her own for long enough, and there was nothing to say that Percy made a competent guard dog.

"Fine, but when you wake up with that swollen head, come and find me, as I still have some questions for you." My water had finally appeared, but before I could order a drink for myself, the woman behind the bar had gone to serve someone else.

"I'll see you soon, Richard," I said and held out my hand for him to shake.

"Don't leave it so long next time. Before you know it, we'll be old men."

I returned to the main bar and was about to sit down again when I realised that something was missing. Percy was there to keep our spot, but there was no sign of Lucinda. I checked the bench in case she'd fallen asleep there, but she'd vanished.

"I can't believe I'm going to do this," I said, cursing under my breath. "Percy, do you happen to know where the young lady who was recently embracing you has gone?"

He immediately dropped to the floor and took a proud lap of the table before following her scent – or perhaps just remembering where the errant potential victim had gone. It was cold outside now, and I wished I'd brought a winter coat with me. The moon was bright behind the thinning clouds, but there was mist low on the marsh behind the pub. Percy led off in that direction and so I followed him, certain that I would get my new leather Oxfords dirty.

There was something rather magical about that spot in the moonlight. The only reason it was there in the middle of the village was because it was no good for building on, but it was a haven for all sorts of animals. Frogs jumped about as I followed the path Lucinda must have taken. Moths and unidentifiable insects flittered about us, and a tawny owl was running reconnaissance missions overhead. I rather admired the boggy plot's resistance against the march of modern life, but then I stepped into a particularly swampy hole, and I suddenly didn't feel so favourable towards it. My left leg was half soaked, and I presumably had some tadpoles making a home in my waterlogged shoe.

Percy led us onwards, and I was glad it hadn't rained in a

while, or I would surely have had to swim. The cold cut through me, and it no longer seemed so magical as a shiver went tingling through my body. I had the sense that someone was following me, but I didn't dare stop and I didn't look back.

"Are you sure you know where you're going, boy?" I asked my companion and, though he managed to respond for once, his howl did little to answer the question.

The moon came out from behind the clouds just as I heard the sound of the reeds rustling behind me and felt the fingers clasp my neck.

What a fool I was. I really should have grabbed a cricket bat from the wall of the pub before walking into a wilderness with a killer on the loose.

SEVENTEEN

My assailant pulled me around by the shoulder and, to my immense surprise, planted a kiss on my lips. For a moment, I assumed it was one of those perverted sorts of killers about whom you occasionally read in the interior pages of the newspaper. You know the kind: men who dress up in bizarre rigouts to attack their victims, or take photographs of the scene of the crime for posterity.

Perhaps even more surprising than this unexpected assault was the fact that I did nothing to stop it.

"Lucinda?" I said when she pulled back to look at me.

"Why don't you love me, Marius?" she asked, as any lovesick adolescent has wondered of her unrequited love.

I had questioned this very same thing only hours earlier but didn't have an answer for her, so I offered a half-hearted compliment instead. "You are a wonderful person."

She gave a low growl of frustration and stormed off along the path I'd already taken. This did beg the question of how she had ended up behind me, but I had other concerns just then.

"Lucinda, wait." I whistled for Percy as I ran after her. "Hold on just one moment, I didn't mean to..." It was at this point that I fell into that watery hole again. "Oh, not the other foot, too!"

By the time we reached the road, I'd managed to catch up with her, and she was not happy.

"I don't know what more I can do. I'm good at everything. You do realise that, don't you? I bake exquisite cakes and have officially the prettiest garden in the village. I'm charming and demure, and people say that I'm quite beautiful. So what more could you want?"

With the moonlight turning her brown hair to liquid silver, she did look quite ravishing. Another Marius – not this idiot, but another one altogether – might have cupped her cheeks in his hands and talked of their future together. A smart, uncomplicated Marius would have got down on one knee and told her that she was empirically the most beautiful and capable woman he had ever met and ask for her hand in marriage.

Of course, this Marius couldn't do anything so sensible as that. Instead of proposing in the moonlight, I said, "Are you sure you're not trying to make Richard jealous? It's only been a few weeks since you ended the engagement."

She groaned this time but had a theory of her own to present. "It's Bella, isn't it? You still love her."

I would rather have turned and just walked away, but I at least tried to answer honestly. "I wouldn't say that. I certainly did love Bella for a long time. But when I saw her with her new boyfriend, something broke off inside me and—"

"For goodness' sake, Marius." Those honey-coloured eyes became even larger as the moon went into hiding once more. "Couldn't you just have said no?"

"Fine, then no. I don't love her. And she doesn't love me. In the decade we spent apart, a lot changed."

She came closer again. "Then love me instead."

Her lips were only centimetres from mine, but I would not

kiss her that night, and Percy came to remind us that he wasn't getting the attention he deserved.

"I'm sorry, Cinders. I can't. We wouldn't even be having this conversation if you hadn't spent the evening drinking."

I was almost relieved when she walked back towards the village.

"I'm staying with you tonight to make certain that nothing bad happens," I explained when we reached her front door, and it dawned on me that I'd left Tilly to fend for herself.

She turned the full force of her gaze on me. "I don't need you, Marius." There were tears in her eyes, and I really wished in that moment that I wouldn't keep making women cry. "I don't need anyone, so just—"

"Hush!" I hissed, as I'd heard a noise on the other side of the hedgerow.

"Oh, that's just charming. First you want nothing to do with me and now..." I believe she kept talking, but it was just the cover I needed to sprint from the garden. As I rounded the bushes at the front of her property, I heard footsteps already pounding away. By the time I'd got to the path that led to the woods, there was nothing to see but a tall figure in dark clothes running off into the night. I wished I'd had something to throw then. I wouldn't have been able to hit him at such a distance, but it might have made me feel a touch less useless.

Once there was definitely no danger of any kind, Percy waddled up to make sure that he hadn't missed out on anything. I thought that these heroics might win Lucinda's gratitude, but she clearly couldn't make sense of what had just happened and looked at me as though I'd lost my mind.

"As I was saying, I'm staying here tonight to make certain that you're all right."

She sighed and waved my words away before Percy and I followed her into the perfectly organised house.

"It's lovely to have house guests," she told me as she lay down on the sofa and fell instantly asleep.

I was confident I could look after Lucinda as long as the doors were locked and the windows secured, and so I stuck my head outside again to call to the police officer on duty.

"Constable!" I shouted up the road to where the policeman was swinging his truncheon under a streetlight. He strolled closer with a dubious air about him, and I spoke in my most authoritative voice. "My name is Marius Quin. I'm a friend of Detective Inspector Lovebrook of Scotland Yard. I have told him that I will stay at this address tonight to look after Lucinda Heaton. However, I've just seen someone lurking in the bushes, and her cousin is currently in the Duke's Head drinking herself senseless. I'd like you to go inside the pub and ask after Tilly Heaton. Please watch to make sure she gets home safely."

He clucked his tongue three times and spoke to me over the privet hedge. "And how do I know you're not saying this to get me away from here so that you can murder the young lady inside?"

"You should be commended, Constable. That is a very good point. First, I have brought a very heavy dog with me." I pointed over my shoulder to where Percy had his muddy paws on a large ottoman. "I can assure you that he would not make a particularly good murderer's accomplice."

"And second?"

"Second..." I hadn't planned on needing a second point, even when I'd introduced the first. "And second, I have just shown you my face. Were it my plan to kill my friend who is asleep on the sofa behind me, I should at least have worn a disguise."

He put one finger to his cheek as he considered the proposition. "How do I know that you really are Marius Quin? Do you have any way of proving it?"

"Well, I'm originally from this village. I'm a writer. I won the Mid-Surrey Crime Writers' Award for my debut novel." It was funny how this fact could serve as both a boast and a point of self-deprecation. It was a very versatile prize to have won.

"Anyone could know that stuff." His expression became more disapproving. "Tell me something that only Marius Quin could know."

"How would you know that it's true?"

He would not be persuaded and grunted, "Just tell me."

"Oh... ummm... all right. Well, I have a debilitating fear of rodents."

"Even beavers?" He sounded quite surprised at the prospect.

"Perhaps not. They seem like useful sorts of creatures."

"What about porcupines?"

"I've never met a porcupine. It's only small rodents in large groups that frighten me – rats in particular." I had never imagined having a night-time conversation with a police officer to discuss my opinion of various animals. "What does any of this have to do with my proving who I am?"

The constable pulled his helmet down a little lower on his head and began to laugh. "I was just pulling your leg, Mr Quin. I saw you this afternoon with the inspector, and he told us to provide you with all the help you require. I will observe Tilly Heaton and watch over her house once I've escorted her home – until someone comes to relieve me at six in the morning, at least."

"Thank you, Constable. I appreciate it."

"You're very welcome, sir. To be honest, I'm quite parched and could do with a glass of something refreshing."

I fished into my pocket for my wallet and threw him a sixpence piece.

He threw it straight back. "Now, now, sir. That could be construed as bribery." He nodded and walked off up the road, laughing as he went.

I popped my head back into the room and locked the window after me. In fact, I took this opportunity to go around the house to ascertain that every point of access was secure and, when I returned, Lucinda had opened her eyes.

"What year is it?"

"Still 1928. Would you care to join me for dinner?"

She didn't sit upright immediately but stared about the place without moving her head. "Coffee!"

I went to her kitchen to make a hot drink for the second time that day. When she'd had a few minutes to reconnect with the waking world, Lucinda came in clutching her stomach with one hand and her head with the other. "Whoever invented alcohol should be arrested."

"I'll tell the constable outside." I placed a cup in front of her and she sat clutching it as though she were freezing cold.

When it had cooled down sufficiently, she took a tiny sip and immediately seemed more collected. "I told you this morning that you would save my life and look where we are."

"I'm glad I could be of service, but I think that a tea lady would have done just as good a job as I have." I decided not to tell her about the man who had been watching her house. She looked nervous enough, now that the alcohol was wearing off.

"I'm so sorry, Marius, for everything I did and said." For a moment, she looked as though she wished to hide behind her cup. "Tilly made me go out to the pub with her, and I'm really not much of a drinker."

I sat opposite her while Percy curled up in a corner and went to sleep. I neither wanted nor required coffee but enjoyed watching the good it did her.

I couldn't suppress my smile entirely. "There's no need to apologise. I've done far worse myself."

"So what should we discuss?" she asked to hide her embarrassment. "Where do you stand on the Yorkshire captaincy affair?"

"It is my long-held opinion that it is not an interesting topic of conversation at this or any other hour. Why do you think your cousin was killed?"

She held her breath for a few moments before replying. "Well that certainly soured the mood."

"Do you miss him?" I was surprisingly cold in my delivery. "Do you really care that he's gone?"

She wrapped her delicate fingers around her cup again. "That's a very hard question to answer. James wasn't like most people. He had no real warmth in him, but he was fiercely loyal. He didn't love so much as not hate, and the number of people he didn't hate was very small. Besides his sister, there was Richard, you – though you hadn't actually spoken for a decade, so that probably helped – and Bella, of course."

I was surprised to hear that James thought so highly of me, but I focused on the others. "He didn't *love* Bella?"

She held her hand to her head to think or perhaps control the pain. "He desired Bella. He wished that she belonged to him, but I can't say that love really came into it." Her speech veered between crystal cut and slurred. "You see, it's impossible to love someone if the only things that concern you are the slights on your character that date back to your childhood. That was all that really motivated James."

"What about your family's name? Did he care about that? I remember when we were at school that he couldn't abide anyone saying the slightest thing about his father. I always assumed that the Heaton brothers were his heroes."

"No, they were rotters, and even James could see that. If it hadn't been for them, he would never have been so tightly wound and easily offended. He probably wouldn't have been stabbed to death in his kitchen."

"So you think that's why he was killed? And that's why you received the letters?"

"What else could it be? Even after all my best efforts, the people here still despise us."

I understood something about her then that had never quite made sense before. "Is that what you've tried to be all your life? Someone different? Something other than a Heaton?"

She took a longer sip this time. "Of course it is. Can you imagine growing up in a family everyone hated? From an early age, I could see that people treated us differently from the other children. Even Mrs Abbot singled us out for punishment."

She sniffed then, as though she'd remembered that she'd recently been crying. "My mother wasn't born a Heaton, of course, but my father did all he could to convert her. One day when I was little, she gave me a piece of advice that I've never forgotten. It was the exact opposite to the philosophy of good old Tom and Granville and my grandfathers before them. I came to her complaining that someone had said something mean and it had upset me. She said that if people treated me badly, then the only solution was to give them a reason to never do it again. My father would have told me to take them to court, or plot my revenge through less legitimate means, but Mummy wanted me to realise that kindness was a better option."

"And you think that, if James had been given such advice, he would have been a different person."

She huffed out a breath so that her perfectly smooth cheeks inflated. "Something like that."

Percy yawned in his sleep, and I allowed the quiet atmosphere to gather around the dining table. It was nice to hear the silence for a moment, but then I broke it to ask her a question she'd failed to answer earlier in the evening.

"If you hate it here so much, why have you never left?"

"No one ever leaves Hurtwood," she replied with a shake of the head. "Except you, of course."

"I'm serious," I persisted. "You complained about the way people here treat you, so why don't you just go?"

"You're very innocent, Marius. I like that about you."

She wouldn't distract me from my question. "I'm serious. Leave."

"Do you really not understand?" she asked with a note of shock in her voice. "Your father must have known about the wills. I assumed he would have told you."

My face explained that this was not the case without my mouth having to produce a word.

"I can't afford to leave. I have just enough money to eat and continue my delightful range of hobbies."

"You're a Heaton. That can't be true."

"It is. My uncle was the one with all the money and he left it to James. My parents left me this house, which is practically worthless. It's so ugly I can't imagine anyone buying it." This was interesting, as it meant that Tilly would now inherit the bulk of the family wealth, but for the moment, I could only think of Lucinda.

"Get a job. Go to university. Marry someone who really loves you. Don't just stay and suffer."

"Oh, but life here is such a dream." Her words came out in a gentle sing-song melody. "It's much easier to continue my stasis in Hurtwood than force myself to make a change."

She drained the last drops of coffee from her cup and her eyes were back to their sparkling best. For a moment, I actually felt sorry for her. She was so admired, so beloved for any number of different reasons, and yet she was clearly quite unhappy.

"Very well, Mr Quin. I will consider leaving this place before it kills me... or I'm killed in it." She stared at me for a few moments longer, then stood up from her chair. "But thank you. You've restored a little of my faith in mankind."

"How did I do that?" I was sincere in my question. I couldn't see what good I'd done her.

She paused with her hands on the door to look back at me. "You're just as good as I always remembered."

"And I like you more when you're being yourself," I called after her, but all I heard in reply was the gentle padding of her feet as she mounted the stairs.

EIGHTEEN

I woke up early the next morning, which was lucky, as Lovebrook had already arrived. Less fortunate was the pain in my neck from a night on Lucinda's sofa.

"Did you actually get any sleep last night?" I asked as the inspector climbed yawning out of his Standard Model S that was almost as old as I was.

"I slept a little on the way here," he told me quite seriously. "I barely remember a moment between Hammersmith and now."

"I hope that's a joke."

He suddenly became more pernickety. "Yes, of course it is. I'm an upstanding police officer and would never drive when incapacitated." It was hard to know whether he was saying this for me or Sergeant Rossiter, who was standing a little way up the road, keeping an eye on the village. "Nothing to report, Sergeant?"

"Nothing to report, Inspector," Rossiter shouted back in his usual angry tone.

When this little show was over, I asked, "Shall we set off? We can discuss our progress on the way."

Lovebrook replied with another yawn, which I took as confirmation.

The sight of the shiny red Invicta did go some way to reviving him. His eyes popped wide open as he admired the sleek lines of the strawberry red chassis and the elegant curve of the glistening black mudguards.

"She's not bad," I said as, for all my claims to have no interest in expensive items these days, I was still a little in love with my car.

"Not bad!" he parroted. "She's a dream made flesh... Well, not flesh, but you know what I mean. Can I drive her?"

"No."

"Well, that answered that."

We climbed inside, and I was about to start the engine when Bella's Sunbeam pulled across my path.

"Thank you, Caxton," she called to her driver.

"You are most welcome, Lady Isabella," the smarmy chauffeur replied, grinning at me the whole time he spoke. "I look forward to your return later today."

"What are you doing?" I asked as her car turned around the Hurtwood Village sign and drove back up the hill.

"I'm coming with you to Nottingham or wherever it was."

"Northampton," Lovebrook grumbled. "Or Wellingborough, to be more precise."

"No, you're not." I had identified a problem with her plan. "This is only a two-seater."

She was typically unfazed. "It must have a dickey seat of some description."

"Well, it has a luggage compartment, but I doubt that—"

Before I could finish, that true gentleman Lovebrook had jumped out of the car to offer her his seat. With the Duke's daughter taking her place beside me, the poor peeler stowed himself away in the tiny space in the back of the car, which was designed for two to three suitcases as opposed to one folded up policeman.

"I'll be fine," he said stoically.

I was about to tell him that we could always take two cars, but he seemed happy to make this sacrifice, and who was I to stop him?

"Perhaps you could swap for the journey home," I suggested to my dear friend in the passenger seat.

"Or perhaps you could let me drive and swap with him yourself?" She had a determined expression on her face and so, instead of arguing, I said, "The inspector will be fine back there. Off we go!"

We plotted a comparatively straight route one hundred miles north, all the way to Northampton, before heading a smidgen east to get to Wellingborough. Lovebrook told me we could make it there in three hours, but we had clear roads all the way, and I'm never afraid to put my foot on the pedal. Apparently, he *was* afraid of such things, and he shouted the occasional complaint from his makeshift seat.

"Ahhhh!" was one of them, and so I asked him a question to keep his mind off things.

"Tell me, Lovebrook, how did a fellow like you find yourself in the police?"

"Well... interesting... ask. As... I was... time... my father... young boy." This was all I heard of his reply, and so I decided that conversation was out of the question.

I would have told Bella everything I had discovered in her absence the previous day, but I knew that I'd only have to repeat myself to the inspector, so I drove with just my thoughts to keep me company. I was turning over a list of essential questions, and though I did not land on any definite answers, I certainly accumulated several more doubts to resolve. So that was good.

I had to stop to fill the tank with petrol halfway through the journey, and we made the most of that time to pool our information.

"So what have you discovered, Lovebrook?" Bella asked as we stood at the side of the road, waiting for the man on duty to see to the car in front of mine.

"I've discovered that luggage compartments are uncomfortable after approximately five minutes of a journey. My legs feel like they're still folded, and I've eaten enough flies to go without lunch today."

I didn't like to mention it, but his usually well coiffured hair was just a fraction... bigger than normal.

"I spent a night on a sofa that was frankly far too small for —" I began, before realising that this would not make him feel any better about the last hour.

Bella took over once more. "I was asking about the case we're investigating, but you've earned a break, so perhaps Marius can start."

I nodded and did just that. I told them about Dodo's belief that the crimes were connected to Sebastian Kane, my time with Lucinda – without mentioning the part about the kiss we'd shared – and the brief sighting of the famous lurker. Best of all, though, I had an actual suspect to present to them.

"Richard Fairbanks?" Bella sounded quite surprised.

"Yes, why couldn't it be him?"

She looked at the inspector as though he might have an opinion. "Well, Richard's always seemed rather pleasant. He's just..." She didn't know how to finish that thought, but I did.

"He's just someone we've known since we were children, and it's hard to suspect him of any such dastardliness?" I waited to see what she would say to this, then continued anyway. "That's the problem we face when investigating a murder in our own village. But if we follow that logic, no one could have done it."

"I suppose you have a point, but it might just as well have

been Dodo, Sergeant Rossiter or my mother. There's nothing to say that Richard is to blame."

"Except that he argued with the victim a short time before the murder. Lucinda cast him off just a few months before they were supposed to wed. Oh, and there was some kind of financial arrangement between Richard and James that I haven't yet uncovered."

Bella looked a trifle taken aback by just how much evidence there was against the man. "Oh, I see."

Taking pity on her, Lovebrook decided to change the subject. "What about you, Lady Isabella? Did you find out anything useful?"

"No." This just made her sadder. "All I did after I left the village yesterday was have dinner, play cards with my father and get a telling-off from Mother for spending so long away from home when I should have been looking after him."

I thought it was better for me not to reveal my opinion of her mother just then. We might never have made it to Wellingborough.

Happily, she found a touch of positivity. "However, the weekend is now upon us, and I am as free as an uncaged bird."

"Jolly good," Lovebrook told us now that he had removed all the dead flies from his mouth. "As for me, I liaised with the Guildford police who had absolutely nothing of any value to tell me. And in my interview with the remaining Heaton cousins, I learnt that Tilly is capable of making any conversation focus solely on her. She was clearly upset by her brother's death, but she talked about nothing but herself for the hour I was in the house. Lucinda barely managed to say a word."

"Brilliant." I let out an exhausted groan. "We just have to cross our fingers that your friend in the north has some information for us."

Lovebrook looked at me as though I was confused.

"Wellingborough is twelve miles east of Northampton. It's not the Scottish Highlands."

"It's still north of Surrey, though, isn't it?"

"The car's ready," Bella informed us, and so we piled inside for the second leg of the journey.

The inspector did not look happy to be going back into the boot and made sure to stretch his legs before climbing aboard. The roads were quiet once we'd made it through London, and I managed to reach our destination in what I could only assume was a record time.

Lovebrook directed me to a square in the centre of town, where a uniformed officer was expecting us.

"Sergeant Meldon," he said with an efficient nod of the head once we'd parked. He was one of those young officers who takes great pride in his uniform and polishes every button on it twice a day before parting his hair with a ruler and compass. "Lovebrook and I joined the police at the same time. Of course, he's better spoken than me, so he got promotions and I'm still here."

He glanced along the high street, and I took in the small, busy market town. It was a perfectly pleasant spot, but I could understand his feelings. It was not the thriving metropolis of London, nor some gangster's haunt. In a few years' time, it would have been just the spot to settle down and start a family, but I could see that, for a young man like the sergeant, it was not the place to inspire him.

"Still," he continued, straightening his back as he considered the excitement we had delivered, "this murder business is interesting. First poison-pen letters, now a dead man. We don't get any of that around here."

"My friend is exaggerating a touch," Lovebrook stepped forward to explain. "It wasn't so long ago that I was in the area investigating a terrible crime under the watchful eye of Lord—"

The sergeant clapped his hands together and turned to

Bella and me. "Should we get started? I'm sure you've had a long drive and would like to know what I've discovered."

"That would be wonderful," I replied. "We're eager to hear all about it."

Bella and Lovebrook walked ahead, and I chatted to the sergeant the whole way there, not knowing that *there* was only a two-minute walk. Meldon took us to a tall, red-brick Edwardian building with a long balcony on the first floor and sash windows all over the front façade.

"He's expecting us," he said without explanation, and we passed through the front door of number one, High Street.

"Ahh, Sergeant Meldon," said a large man with shocking white wavy hair after we'd knocked on the first door off the narrow entrance hall. "I'm glad you're here. I've got the letter ready to show you."

"That's wonderful, Mr Aintree. Perhaps we could come in and you can explain the situation to our guests."

From what I could make out of the building, and the blank-faced receptionist on duty, I believe that we had entered a home for the elderly. It was split up into various flats for the residents to have their own spaces. Mr Aintree's was small, but convenient for a man of his age and needs. The walls were bare except for a few paintings of pastoral landscapes, and there was an easel set up in one corner with an unfinished artwork resting upon it. I didn't ask him whether he was an artist, but it seemed safe to assume that was the case.

"I found Mr Aintree here in the Golden Lion pub last night," the sergeant began.

"I'm not a big drinker, you know," the gent explained, as though afraid we might object. He directed his comment to Bella, who had been rather quiet since we arrived. In fact, he continued to address her through much of the conversation. "I do like the company, though. And there's a fiddler who plays on a Friday night."

"I'm rather partial to a glass of whisky myself," Lovebrook said to set the man's mind at ease. "And if there's music too, that's all the better. You simply can't beat a good public house."

"Quite!" the possible artist replied, still looking at my companion.

The time had come for Sergeant Meldon to explain how we had come to convene there. "On Detective Inspector Lovebrook's instruction, I used my time yesterday evening to go around the pubs in town asking whether anyone knew about a letter that had been sent to Hurtwood Village in Surrey. I asked in the post office first, of course, but they get too many letters each day to be aware of the senders. However, Mr Aintree happened to be seated at the bar of the Lion and was good enough to tell me what he knows."

"That was very kind of you indeed, Mr Aintree," Bella said, apparently realising that she had found an admirer.

"I like to do my bit when I can," he replied, before the patient look on the sergeant's face prompted him to say more. "Oh, yes. Let me tell you what happened."

He motioned for us to sit down in a pair of armchairs on the other side of the small room. As there were only two, Meldon and I remained standing. After what Lovebrook had endured to get there, I felt he deserved a comfy seat.

"I received a letter quite out of the blue," the old man began, "but I'm afraid that I didn't keep the envelope. It didn't have my name on it, just the address and, when the man at reception opened it, he decided it was meant for me due to the class of people with whom I am known to associate." There was a pompousness to everything he said, and yet I found him rather appealing. I evidently wasn't the only one confused by this comment, as he once more rushed to explain himself. "You see, the letter was written by Lady Isabella Montague of Hurtwood House. I'm sure you've heard of her."

"I certainly have," Bella replied with her usual grace.

He turned to a high table behind him and looked affectionately at the letter in question. "I knew the moment I held it in my hands that there was something special about it."

"And what did it say?" Lovebrook asked, leaning forward to get a glimpse.

"It is not just what it said. It is what the good lady included." He deigned to hold up the piece of paper, and I looked at the letterhead.

There was the crest of the Montague family and the address of the manor neatly stamped upon it. The writing underneath was not nearly formal enough to be Bella's and, if anything, looked rather messy.

"Inside the outer envelope was a second one with a stamp already attached. There was also a letter in which Lady Isabella described a game she was playing with her friends. You know the sort of thing youngsters enjoy these days. I've heard all about those Bright Young People in London with their treasure hunts and fancy dress parties, and do you know what I think of them?" He paused to let us wonder, and then his smile somehow grew. "I think they're wonderful. Just wonderful!"

"So the letter invited you to play a game with her?" Bella sounded understandably puzzled, but I had an idea of what he meant.

"Not quite, madam. The letter asked me to post the accompanying pre-stamped envelope to an address in Hurtwood Village. The dear lady had even included a shilling coin for my trouble. And do you know what I thought when I saw that?"

"I can't possibly imagine," I answered, as he clearly didn't consider this a rhetorical question.

"I thought, there are less honest people than me who would take that coin and not even go to the trouble of sending the letter."

"I'm afraid you're right there, Mr Aintree." Lovebrook chose his words carefully so as not to disabuse the man of his belief in the good deed he'd done. "We believe that you weren't the only person to receive such a request, but yours was the only letter that arrived on the first day of the game."

Aintree shook his head sadly. "Now, that is a shame, but I can tell you that I went to the post box *post-haste* to make sure that it reached Lady Isabella's friend at the first possible opportunity. I've never been one to stand in the way of frivolity. In fact, in my own small way, I like to think that I participated in their merriment."

He looked awfully proud of himself then, and Bella turned to me as if to say, *should I really tell him the truth?* She answered the question herself.

"I hope this doesn't upset you, Mr Aintree, but I feel I must say that the letter in your hand was not written by Lady Isabella Montague."

He closed his eyes sagely as he provided the evidence to the contrary. "I looked her up in *Who's Who*, you know. There's no doubt about it. Lady Isabella Montague lives at Hurtwood House in Surrey and wished me to post that letter to her friend in the neighbouring village as a way of hiding who'd really sent it."

"I'm not denying that Lady Isabella is a real person, nor that she lives at the address you mentioned. However, I am quite confident that it was not the lady in question who penned that letter."

He put his hands together beseechingly and, in his most correct and proper voice, said, "I don't wish to contradict you, madam, but how could you possibly know?"

NINETEEN

As it was evident that we would not have the chance to talk on the way home, we decided to stop for lunch before returning to Surrey. Ye Golden Lion did not look like a place for the Lady Isabellas of this world, and so we gave our thanks to Sergeant Meldon – who had more important matters to investigate than cakes and sandwiches – and we found a tea room further along the high street to discuss our findings.

It was a chintzy sort of establishment, with paper doilies under everything, heavily patterned wallpaper and exactly two old ladies apportioned to every table but ours. I rather liked it there.

"It is fascinating, don't you think?" Lovebrook was over the moon at what the old man had told us. "Not only has someone been passing himself off as you, Lady Isabella—"

"Please call me Bella," she insisted. "I feel like we're old friends now, Detective Inspector Lovebrook." It was at this moment that she must have realised we hadn't the faintest idea what our *old friend's* Christian name was.

Either way, the inspector was charmed by her courtesy. "That's most kind of you. What I was about to say was that, not only do we have a case of impersonation, but the killer has gone to the most incredible lengths to hide the origin of the letters."

"Let me see if I've understood it all correctly." Bella made it sound as though there was a chance she was about to get it wrong. She was too clever for that, and also too clever to show just how clever she really was. "The killer wrote several copies of each letter and sent them out to seemingly random addresses across Britain."

I had something to add to this. "No, not random addresses. I bet you a week's pocket money that each address he used was number one, High Street."

"How ever did you fathom that?" Lovebrook was enjoying himself so much that he had to lean forward to get a better look at us, like a little boy on his first trip to the cinema.

"Well, Mr Aintree lived at that address, and I would put ten pounds on the fact that there are more roads in the country called 'High Street' than anything else."

"So what does that prove?"

"It proves," I said, before realising I sounded smug and changing my tone, "that the killer didn't know who lived at any of the places to which he was sending the letters. He wanted to send them to houses all over the country, but phone books only have local addresses and, without making it very obvious in a post office, he wouldn't have been able to check who lived where. The simplest thing was to make up a likely destination and hope for the best. That is also one of the reasons that he sent at least three copies of each letter. If he'd sent one to High Street, Cambridge, for example, I know for a fact it would have gone undelivered as there isn't a High Street in the centre of the city there."

"So you think all the letters were sent to the same address but in different towns?" Bella sounded surprised I'd managed to divine such a thing.

"That's my theory, and it's easy enough to prove. All we

have to do is get the local police to go to number one, High Street, in all the towns from which the Heatons received letters and find out if the people there tell you the same story as our new friend."

Bella added another significant conclusion. "And then, as Mr Aintree said, there would be other people who decided to keep the money and the free stamp and didn't send the letter at all."

"Which explains why there were three copies of some letters sent to each cousin and only one or two of others." Lovebrook devoured a tiny cucumber sandwich in one bite and clicked his fingers.

"And why James didn't receive that first letter at all and assumed he was in the clear." I was rather pleased with this thought, not just because I have a big head, but because the three of us had solved this puzzle together.

The inspector looked pensive for a moment and, raising his finger, asked the question that we hadn't yet addressed. "But why did the killer go to all that trouble? It's not as though he got the people who forwarded the letters to rewrite them so as to hide his own handwriting."

Bella held her teacup, ready to drink, but stopped to have a guess. "To hide the fact that he lives in Hurtwood, I suppose?"

Lovebrook was making a mess of some fruitcake crumbs and waited until his plate was clean before agreeing. "That does seem like the obvious explanation, for all the good it did."

"You do realise that the letter Mr Aintree kept was not in my hand," Bella stated with some urgency.

"Well, obviously." I might have sounded a little patronising.

"No, you're missing my point." She sounded more than a little patronising. "The killer made no attempt to make it appear as though I had written the letter. If he had, it might have told us more than if he'd used his normal style."

I believe that Lovebrook and I both wished to enquire why

this would be the case, but we didn't want to look foolish, so we waited for her to say more.

"I had calligraphy lessons for years as a child. Imagine if he'd done a near perfect imitation of one of my letters, complete with cursive script and elegantly looping ascenders and descenders."

"You have a high opinion of your penmanship," I teased and received a glare for my trouble.

"Oh, stop it, Marius," she replied with a tut. "Imagine that the letter was incredibly neat. It would tell us a lot about the author. We would know more about his education, and perhaps garner some inkling as to his economic and social status. Instead, he simply put the pen in his weaker hand to disguise his writing. It's the same on the envelopes and the messages that the Heatons all received."

We thought this over for a moment and Lovebrook eventually concluded, "It all comes down to arrogance. He thinks he's cleverer than us."

"That's just it," Bella agreed. "He was clearly arrogant enough to trust that everything would come off without a hitch. He wanted us to play this game. That's another reason why he sent the letters in the first place."

I'd inhaled a few sandwiches before moving on to the scones. I cut one open and was just covering it with thick layers of cream and jam when Bella looked disapprovingly at me. I ate it anyway but felt greedy for doing so.

"Now all we have to do is work out how he got hold of headed paper from Hurtwood House." The inspector looked at Bella, who seemed more alarmed by my eating habits than the recent murder.

"I'm sorry?" she said and then, apparently hearing after all, answered the question. "Yes, that is puzzling. I can say quite confidently that the regular staff in the house are unlikely to have done it. None of them are from the local area and, to my knowledge at least, they have no significant connection to the Heaton family."

"The staff live in cottages on the estate," I explained to Lovebrook, who looked puzzled by her comment.

"The only exception is our friend Dorothy Lyle," Bella added somewhat tentatively. "Her mother is the postmistress, if you'd like to question her. It's Saturday, so she won't be at Hurtwood House."

"I shall, thank you." Lovebrook noted down the name in his head. "How easy would it be for the killer to get into Hurtwood House and steal headed notepaper?"

Bella thought for a moment. "Well, we have guards on the gate, and they keep a record of everyone who drives onto the property. Had the killer sneaked in over a fence or what have you, he would have had to know how to get to the library or Father's study without being spotted by anyone. It seems highly unlikely."

"And your family?" Lovebrook continued.

"Father is the only one who had dealings with the Heatons – young or old – and he's housebound. My eldest brother was at school with us, but he isn't at home at the moment."

"So, not the family, then." Lovebrook released a frustrated whistle. "I thought the letters would be the solution to everything. Instead, they appear to have achieved the killer's goal. To confuse the picture, he pretended to be you, but if we can't find out how he got the paper, it doesn't help us."

"Nothing seems to help us," I declared with a hint of anger, though the fact I was licking cream off my fingers slightly reduced the impact.

"Don't be such a defeatist," Bella objected. "The killer claimed that the cousins would be dead a week after the first letter was received; that's not until Wednesday."

"You're hardly filling me with confidence."

Rather than bemoaning the state of the investigation, Love-

brook settled on a plan. "If you don't mind, Lady Bella, when
we get back to Surrey, I'll head up to Hurtwood House to speak
to the housekeeper and butler."

"Of course you must. We should explore every possible
theory."

"And I think it's time to set the letters aside," I added.
"Unless the killer wishes to be caught and is giving us clues to
apprehend him before he kills again, I don't think they have
much more to tell us."

"Precisely." Bella's eyes always shone when she was excited
about something. "We'll have to go back to the core of the case.
We've barely had a word of sense out of Tilly, so we'll speak to
her on her own this time."

"That sounds like a wise plan all round," Lovebrook
declared, and Bella pretended to curtsey while sitting down.
She looked just as graceful as the daughter of a duke should.

Pleased with this burst of decisiveness, we enjoyed another
pot of tea and the last of the food before walking back to the car.
I could see that Lovebrook was dreading the return journey, and
I felt a little sorry for him.

"Do you know what, Lovebrook?" I said as I opened the
door for Bella and loosened the latch on the luggage compartment. "It can't have been nice for you on the way, so I'll tell you
what."

He looked ever so hopeful.

"I'll stop every hour on the way home for you to stretch your
legs."

Bella came to swat me around the back of the head.

"I'm joking!" I reassured her. "I'm only joking. You can
drive, Inspector." I handed him the keys and that singularly
cheerful chap looked happier than I'd ever seen him.

TWENTY

There was something strange about being back in Hurtwood Village. It was not merely that the drive home had been just as bad as Lovebrook had described, and the wind had nearly knocked my head off. It was the fact that everything seemed so... normal.

My first return visit had (to me at least) felt quite momentous, but now that the novelty had vanished, it was as though I'd never gone away – as if I'd spent the last ten years there after all. It was oddly unnerving.

The inspector dropped us off by his car, and we climbed out of the Invicta for Bella to glide in her satin frock and me to stumble up the road to the biggest of all houses that the Heaton family owned. As we walked, I wondered how many of the buildings there now belonged to Tilly. It occurred to me that we'd have to ask who would inherit their estate if – heaven forbid – both of them should fall prey to the killer. I thought to leave this question to Bella as there was no way I would have known how to phrase it without making someone cry.

Sergeant Rossiter was standing in his little wooden box near the post office. One of the cottages there had once been the police station, but the Heatons had done a deal with the former owner and Rossiter had been consigned to a space the size of a telephone box. He was never a particularly cheerful man but looked even more morose than usual as he tipped his helmet to Bella, and we walked up the drive to Heaton Manor.

No one in the village called it by that name, of course. It was normally known as "the monstrosity" or, occasionally, "the eyesore" though I'd always thought it fairly elegant compared to the blot on the village which Lucinda called home. It's true that their fake manor was far too big, but it was built in a rather pretty style with a red-tiled roof, ivy growing up the wall beside the sandstone porch, and almost as many windows set into its façade as the Great Palm House at Kew.

This was where Tilly and James had grown up with their father Tom and their mother... I don't actually remember her name. She was a shy, browbeaten woman who rarely spoke, least of all in her husband's presence.

"I'll let you do the talking," I told my partner as I grabbed the bellpull and awaited admission.

"No, you won't. You'll let me start talking but soon inter-fere." She sounded vexed at first, then smiled. "That's what works best for us, don't you think?"

Tilly opened the door before I could agree, so then I had to look sad again for her sake.

"You're just as well to come inside," she said listlessly. "No one else has visited me today. I must be cursed in the eyes of the village. A sentence hangs over my head. The sword of Damocles is—"

"It's nice to see you too, Tilly," Bella brightly cut her off before she could complain any more.

If anything, I believe that Tilly Heaton was in her element. She had the perfect reason to feel melancholy and complain about her existence. Just as some people love cycling and others are train aficionados, this was the very thing that Moaning

Matilda had been keen on since we were children. Everyone in town knew that she was suffering, and there was a subtle undercurrent to everything she said that told me she was enjoying herself – as much as a truly miserable person can.

"Follow me," she suggested, and we trailed after her across the chequerboard floor of the spacious entrance hall.

Number twenty-eight, Dovecote Lane had been built with the spoils of the Heaton brothers' thuggery, and the interior was as showy as my car. A sweeping staircase cut into the hall, and the salon to which Tilly now led us was plushly appointed with immense, powder-puff sofas and floor-length blue velvet curtains on every window. There were tall vases in the corners of the room that looked as though they'd been stolen from a Chinese temple – which, to be honest, sounds like something Tilly's father would have done.

Tilly landed on the sofa and brought her knees up to her chin. There was a handkerchief crushed in a ball beside her but no sign that she'd been engaged in any particular activity before we arrived. There was no book open beside her, nor newspaper to peruse. The poor little brotherless orphan had been sitting all alone, feeling sorry for herself. Thankfully, we'd saved her from that ordeal, and she could now sit feeling sorry for herself with us beside her.

"You know that I'm just waiting for the killer to come for me?" she said to get things started.

I'm really very sorry for being unkind. I should have had more compassion for her, and I genuinely did regret James's death, no matter the differences between us. But Tilly was one of those people who are so hungry for sympathy that it's hard to muster any.

"There was a constable on duty outside your house all night. I imagine you saw him at the pub?"

"Oh, that was a police officer?" she sounded surprised. "I did wonder why a tall dark stranger kept watching me."

"He had his uniform—" I began, but Bella would not allow us to follow such a pointless line of discussion.

"We've come to talk to you today because we believe that you might know something that will help us identify the killer."

She huffed, then slumped despondently sideways onto a cushion. "I spoke to that inspector chappy. He didn't seem to think I was very helpful, but that's been the story of my life."

I'm fairly certain that A.A. Milne must have met Tilly before thinking up the character of Eeyore in *Winnie-the-Pooh*.

"Yes, but we know you better. We know this village better, and it seems to us that whoever is targeting your family must have a grudge against you three Heatons."

Tilly didn't reply then, but made a face to say, *My goodness! You must be a genius.*

It was enough to knock the confidence from my sleuthing partner and, when she next spoke, her voice was fainter. "We know... Well, we know that your father and your uncle were not always the most popular people in Hurtwood."

"That's right. It's a trait that runs in the family."

"Yes..." Each time Tilly broke the flow of Bella's thoughts, it was hard for her to start again. "And so we were wondering whether there was something that could be linked to all three of you, which could explain the hatred the killer feels."

Tilly did not look impressed. "There are a hundred people who might want to get rid of us. That old man in the pub... The one who's always sitting out in front shouting things to passers-by."

"Jeb Paignton?"

"That's the chap. Well, Lucinda's dad threw old Mr Paignton's mother out on the street because she couldn't pay her rent. I don't mean that metaphorically, either. On the first day of the month, Uncle Granville walked into her house, carried every last thing she owned outside, and then went back for her."

"He really was a very sweet man." This wasn't necessary, but I felt a lot better saying it.

"And then there was Mrs Abbot. The dispute over the house where Lucinda lives went on for years."

"Yes, we've spoken to her," I replied so that Bella could have a short break. "But did she ever threaten to kill anyone as a result?"

Tilly looked less sure of herself. "No, but that doesn't mean she didn't want to. And you didn't let me finish. Father once called Ned Lyle a jabbering idiot. Sergeant Rossiter hates every last one of us after we evicted him just months after his two sons had died in the war. Richard Fairbanks borrowed money from James to set up his plastics company on stupidly uneven terms that meant we essentially owned every part of it – he's an employee of his own business, which must still rankle to this day. Oh, and Mrs Clarke, who lives up on the hill, always accused my auntie's dog of fouling her lawn. Are those enough reasons to explain why someone might want us all dead?"

"Yes and no." Before this point, Bella had sounded like an estate agent showing someone around a house. She'd been calm and considered in every word she spoke, but things had changed now. She leaned forward and looked piercingly at Tilly, as though she was about to attack. "You've provided plenty of reasons for why people didn't like the Heatons, but we've already considered those. What I want to know about is some-thing personal to the three of you."

Tilly was presumably disappointed that we hadn't believed every word she said and showered her with pity. "I don't know what it could be. Don't you think I've tried to work out what's happening myself?"

In some ways, our time in Hurtwood had been leading up to this moment. From the moment that Ned the postman handed the first letter to Lucinda, we were set on a path to this very spot, even if Tilly had tried to avoid it.

Bella breathed in slowly and asked, "What happened in 1917?"

Our witness became more nervous. "I was still basically a child back then. How could I possibly remember?"

Bella's response was short and direct. "Think."

Tilly squirmed in her seat and looked to me for help. "I don't know. I really don't. Why are you talking to me like this when my brother's been murdered? As you sit here chattering, someone is plotting to kill me!"

"We're trying to save your life."

"Fine... 1917." Her hands flopped down in front of her as though she was drained of energy. "Well, we were still at school." Had I not been so focused on not making anyone cry, I would have told her to stop telling us things we already knew. "I would have been sixteen. James turned eighteen."

"We know this, Tilly, we were there." Oops.

She did at least speak a little faster. "That was the year that Mr and Mrs Day's lease on the general shop was cancelled. Dad only did it because he didn't like them. They sold their house to us, and he gave it to James as though it were an old book that he didn't think he'd read again." I found this hard to understand as, what sort of person gives away old books? "Do you think perhaps they could have killed my brother?"

Tilly looked truly innocent at that moment, but I knew she was still trying to distract us.

Bella is far more patient than I am and responded with the poise required. "I very much doubt that Mr and Mrs Day were responsible for your brother's death, Tilly. For one thing, they moved to Wales a decade ago, and for another, they were nearly ninety when they left." Her irritation was just peeping above the surface, but it was a masterful effort. "So perhaps you can stop pretending and tell us what really happened that year."

Her mouth hung open for a few moments, but she held to the same line. "I'm telling the honest truth. Why would I lie?"

"Why did James say otherwise?" This is what I like to call a necessary comment. "He said that you both knew exactly what happened in the spring that year and, if you'd like to stay alive, I think you should tell us."

"Sebastian Kane," she practically shouted, then blanched so much that she looked quite transparent. "The boy who came to our school for one term."

"What about him, Tilly?" Bella moved from our oversized sofa to our friend's. "I remember him being in our class, but we still don't know what happened between you."

"It was horrible," she replied, and I wondered whether we would get anything more out of her as she trapped her lips in her mouth as if to avoid speaking again.

"We don't want to make you relive anything uncomfortable, Tilly." My friend spoke even more slowly than before. She sounded like she was addressing a traumatised child. "But you must tell us what happened. Or you could speak to the police again if you prefer."

"No, not the police. I don't want them here in the house." She was shaking now. She held her hand in front of her as though reaching out to catch a fly.

"Just take it slowly and tell us every last detail you can remember." Bella creased her brow as she looked at the poor girl in front of us.

Whatever was in Tilly's head at that moment was eating through her. "I did know. I worked it out as soon as I read the letter. It's not as if I haven't thought about what happened ever since. I've never felt so guilty about anything in my life."

It was clearly Bella's instinct to comfort the girl, but she restrained herself and waited for the story to continue.

"It was the week off we had before our exams, and we all went up to the fort at the top of Homestead Hill. The whole lot of us were there. We girls were being coy and trying to get the boys' attention. You boys were ignoring us entirely, but there was one there who didn't. He was ever so shy, but he looked straight at me, and I felt... special, I suppose. It was a new feeling – different to anything else. All the other boys were crazy about Bella and Lucinda. I was just in the background, making up the numbers, but not to Sebastian."

She fell quiet then, and so Bella filled in a part of the story in a soft voice. "I hadn't thought of him for years until yesterday, but he seemed a nice boy. He was bookish like Dodo and apparently more comfortable with you, me and Lucinda than James and the others."

"That's right." Tilly picked a spot in the middle distance as though she could see him there. "He was ever so sensitive. I realised that he must like me, and so when the rest of you had gone, I told him to meet me back there at sunset. We spent the night talking. He knew all about books and science, and he was interested in a hundred different topics I'd never even thought about before. But the best thing about him was that he talked to me as if I knew just as much as him.

"Since I was a child, I've been 'that blasted Heaton girl' to anyone who hated my family and 'silly old Tilly' to my friends. No one cares who I really am. No one cares about my interests or hobbies or what I think about the world. You know, I loved football when my dad used to take us, and I have written a diary every day since I was eight years old. No one cares about any of that, but Sebastian was fascinated by me. We sat on the hill fort with the sun setting on the horizon and the sky ablaze with colours as though it were putting on a show for us alone. We could see for miles with no one in sight and, for just a little while, I imagined what my life might be like if we could spend it together."

She was right about one thing; it was easy to overlook Tilly Heaton. She wasn't charming or obviously pretty like her cousin. Nor was she loud and forceful as James had been. She was always somewhere in the middle, and I didn't blame her for feeling ignored. I was captivated by the way she told her tale and had to accept that there really was more to her than we'd all assumed.

She looked at her limp hands as she spoke. "I knew my fantasy had to end, of course. I just didn't think it would happen so soon. Sebastian would have grown bored when he realised I was no great thinker and that I didn't know much about anything. But if I could have just enjoyed it for a little longer – a few weeks maybe, or even a month or two – perhaps it wouldn't have been so bad to lose him."

She came to a halt then, as it was clearly painful to discuss. Part of her must have realised the good it was doing to unburden herself, though, as she took a deep breath and continued. "My idiot brother came out of the woods and found us lying on the ground together. He was in a foul mood as usual and immediately yelled at poor Sebastian that he was defiling his little sister. The only good thing is that he didn't—"

Tilly's words were overwhelmed by deep, tear-racked sobs. She looked across the room at me, and I felt awful never to have been nicer to her. Like most people, I hadn't been outright cruel, but what hurts more, attracting the wrong kind of attention or none at all?

"You can trust us, Tilly." It was my turn to show some compassion. "No one will think badly of you for something that happened when you were so young."

She took a slow, cautious breath and looked back at that imaginary point in front of her. This time, it offered no comfort and whatever she saw there was too much for her to bear.

"I'm sorry," she murmured as she pulled her knees back up to her chest. "I can't tell you what I did. It's lived with me ever since, but I can't find the words. All I know is that I deserve whatever punishment he decides to give me."

"My goodness, what do you mean?" Bella's voice took on a

frightened tone, and she stretched her hand out to touch our tortured friend's arm.

When Tilly could finally speak again, she was oddly serene. She looked at Bella as though she was happy for what would come next.

"Sebastian, of course. He's already killed James, and I'll surely be next."

TWENTY-ONE

"I know you think I'm crazy, but I'm not." Tilly got up from the sofa to cross the room. "I know that everyone says he died in the war, but it's not impossible that the wrong name was recorded, or he intentionally set out to confuse things."

"Be serious for a moment, Tilly." Bella was about to start a no doubt rational explanation for why this whole idea was absurd when I interrupted.

"I don't think you're crazy."

My former love looked at me then as though I was the one who needed a head doctor. Her lips parted, and I believe that she was debating whether to disagree with me or deliver a short, sharp slap to see whether that would reposition the screw that had evidently come loose.

"I honestly don't," I continued, and got up to join Tilly by the window. "Since I arrived yesterday, there's been something odd about this whole case. Nobody loved James, but it would be ridiculous to blame him for his forebears' failings. He was a pain, and he could be a real bully sometimes, but we all knew why that was. He lived with the guilt of being a Heaton far more than you and Lucinda ever did. But rather than go out of his way to prove that he was a good person as your cousin has, he felt sorry for himself. From what I can tell, over the last decade, he's done nothing but drink in the pub and sit in his empty house feeling empty. Nothing we've discovered offered a good enough reason for someone to kill him, but this could explain it."

Complaining under her breath all the way, Bella came to argue with us. "That doesn't mean a man has returned from the dead. The next thing you'll be telling me is that you believe in ghosts."

Tilly tilted her head to one side as if to suggest, *Well, you never know!* But she responded in a surprisingly composed voice. "I'm not saying he's back from the dead. I'm saying that he never died. I'm saying that he wanted revenge on us, so he made sure to be listed as dead in the war records and bided his time until he could kill us and still get away with it."

"If he wanted to get away with it, why would he have sent letters explaining that the murders were connected to 1917?" Bella sounded bewildered by what she was hearing, but Tilly had more to say.

"So that I would stand here now feeling this way. The torture I am going through at this very moment is worse than the knowledge I will soon be dead." She paused to let her words sink in. "He killed James first so that I knew what was coming."

"Then what about Lucinda?" Bella asked, as though this was the point that would blow apart the fiction Tilly had created.

"Lucinda's always known what happened. She wasn't there that night, but I told her the next day. She could have made things better if she really wanted. Perhaps Sebastian thinks he can wipe us all out in one go to prevent anyone else having to put up with us. Can you really blame him?"

"But, Tilly, you don't..." Bella looked at me again in the hope that I would change my mind and convince our friend she was wrong. I wished that I could take her side, but I didn't think we could dismiss the idea out of hand.

Tilly suddenly became more animated. "I haven't even told you the biggest thing yet." She rushed across the room and disappeared through the door. When she returned, she had two letters in her hand, and she held them out to us with a surprising urgency.

I recognised the first one as the letter the cousins had received the previous day. The second was entirely new though. In the same block capital letters and thick black ink, all it said was...

I WILL NEVER FORGIVE YOU.

"Did that come today?" Bella asked as her eyes flicked between the two.

"No." Tilly held us in suspense for a moment before delivering her secret. "It arrived in April 1918. It was sent from France."

"That was the month he was supposed to have died at the Battle of the Lys," I said. "Bella's father told us when we went to visit him yesterday."

There was a nobility to Tilly's expression. In some odd, terrible way, it was almost as if she was proud to die at Sebastian's hand. "He hates us for what we did to him, and he's finally taking his revenge."

"The lurker," I said, putting the pieces together to make Tilly's fantasy a fraction more realistic. "Ned Lyle saw a man lurking about the town recently, and I caught sight of him again last night. He was looking in through Lucinda's garden, but perhaps that wasn't all he was doing here."

"Marius, stop encouraging her."

"Bella, face the facts." I realised that I was getting carried away then and altered this statement. "I mean, you should at least consider the possibility that what Tilly believes is true."

"I'll do whatever I can to keep our friends safe, but I'm not going to indulge her in this fairy tale."

Tilly stood back and suddenly this was my battle to fight.

"How do we even know that Sebastian is dead? Just because your father heard third- or fourth-hand information, that doesn't make it true. Think about it, Bella. We only knew him for a couple of months. Would we really recognise him all this time later?" I could see that her resolve was weakening, so I kept talking. "He could be living here amongst us, and we'd never know. It's incredible what a long beard and a change of name can do to the way people perceive you. There's a huge difference between introducing yourself as plain old Bob Smith and the esteemed Mr Barrington Fitzgerald-St Clair."

My oldest friend pursed her lips, and I think she realised that there was no sense in arguing anymore. "Very well. But if I was going to entertain the possibility – and I'm not saying that I am – how would we go about finding a ghost?"

"We can't." I allowed myself a moment to think. "But our friend the inspector might be able to help."

Instead of responding to my simple plan, Bella turned to Tilly with an ultimatum. "Before we do anything else, you have to tell us what happened when James found you and Sebastian together."

I'd been wondering this myself. There had to be more to the story than she'd revealed, or Sebastian wouldn't have needed to murder anyone.

She walked a few steps away to where three golden-haired dolls stood on a box-shaped window seat. Rather than answering, she sat down and picked up one of the tiny porcelain figures. She looked at it so intently that I had to wonder what she was thinking. How did the cheery simulacrum before her chime with her thoughts of a lost boy she had wronged?

"James found us together and decided that Sebastian had forced himself upon me. He savaged the poor boy." She stared off through the window as if reliving that moment on a cinema screen. "I can't begin to describe the fury I saw in his eyes. It was horrifying."

"But Sebastian was still in class for a time after the holiday, and we never saw any bruises or wounds."

"My brother left his face untouched, but he made sure that he suffered. I wouldn't be surprised if Sebastian's ribs were broken. He could barely climb to his feet after James had tired of his cruelty."

"Then why blame yourself?" I watched as the answer played around her brain and she eventually found the strength to answer.

"Because it wouldn't have happened if it weren't for me." I could hear a click in her throat as the emotion rose up from within her. "I should have at least come between them, but I couldn't move. As James beat Sebastian, he looked just like Daddy. My brother was doing the same thing that our father had done to him so many times, and I was helpless to stop him."

Her sad account deserved the silence that followed it. I still had questions to put to her and gaps to fill, but I had no wish to make her suffer more than she already had.

"I'm sorry," Bella told her as she went to put her arm around the poor girl. "I'm so sorry you had to bear that secret for so long."

Tilly rested her head on her old friend's shoulder and, not knowing what else I could do to make her feel better, I went to make some tea.

TWENTY-TWO

By the time we left her house that afternoon, Tilly looked oddly cheerful. I don't know that her face had ever developed the necessary muscles for a full smile, but she was definitely less forlorn than when we'd arrived. Bella said that we would do everything we could to rule out the possibility that Sebastian Kane was the killer, and we left promising that we'd send someone to stay with her that night. Short of sitting there being miserable together, I didn't see what else we could do to protect her.

"Do you think she really believes he's alive?" Bella asked as we walked past the post office and back towards the pub.

"Of course she does. Not only is it a plausible theory in a particularly confusing case, it gives her a sense of an ending to a story that never quite finished."

Bella looked down at her closed-toe sandals. They weren't so very different from the shoes she'd worn to school twenty years before. "And do you believe it?"

I'd been waiting for this. "I wouldn't go that far, but I still think we have to make sure. There were plenty of men during the war who were reported dead but turned up later, right as rain. Perhaps Kane chose to swap identities with a dead man. We lost over a hundred thousand men at the Battle of the Lys. If he'd been in a unit that suffered heavy casualties, he could have taken a new name and transferred elsewhere without anyone realising the difference. He might even have deserted and come back here under an alias."

"It all sounds so far-fetched."

"But that's just it; the truth is often hard to believe." I knew this more than most. "When I was ten years old, I would never have imagined that a war would break out across half the globe, and I would have to cross the sea to fight in another country. Or that I would then wander about the continent for a few years before writing a mystery novel, bumping into you on a frozen pavement and, merry as a cricket, deciding to become detectives together. I'd say that was all pretty far-fetched, wouldn't you?"

"Yes, it's truly abysmal writing."

She had a talent for making me laugh, even at the darkest moments, and I was happy that the world had sent me on such a curious and meandering journey.

"I forgot to tell you," Bella began. "My mother is upset that you haven't been to see her yet. You will come by this evening, won't you? She'll be terribly sore if you don't visit."

Yes, but I'll be terribly sore if I do, I thought but didn't say.

Bella's mother was the one member of her family that I'd never quite managed to convince of my worth. She was a hedge-hoggy sort of person with a truly impenetrable mind. In short, she scared me.

What I wanted to say was, *No, I don't want to visit your mother. We have a murder to solve.* What I said was, "Of course, I'll visit your mother. I can't think of anything more pleasant." I grinned inanely and added a small caveat. "Wind, weather and dead bodies permitting."

"I appreciate it." I believe that she really meant this. The

Duchess of Hurtwood was a hard woman to please, even for the golden child of the family.

We had come to a stop in front of the pub, and Bella was glancing around the group of locals who were sitting in the sunshine on that relatively warm afternoon. "While Lovebrook is still up at the house, I think we should find Lucinda's former suitor."

"Richard, you mean?"

"Yes, his name keeps popping up. I know that he's not a dead soldier who's come back to life, but he could still be involved in the case. What do you think?"

"I think you are a very wise woman, and I'm thirsty."

I shot off ahead of her before she could tell me that Richard wouldn't be in the pub at that time of day or that he hunted on Saturdays or whatever excuse she could find for me not to have a glass of beer. Happily, she followed me in there and we soon found our suspect standing at the bar. He wasn't alone. In fact, there were all the regulars I would expect to find on a Saturday afternoon, plus the new man with the scar, who was sitting at a table with Mrs Abbot, of all people. Oh, and Uncle Stan was at the piano with our dog beside him singing "Where Did You Get That Hat?" Obviously, Stan was the one singing, but Percy did his best to join in at opportune moments.

"Now how I came to get this hat is very strange and funny.
Grandfather died and left to me his property and money,
And when the will it was read out, they told me straight and flat,
If I would have his money, I must always wear his hat."

There was a roar of appreciation as Stan shouted, "All together now," and the crowd broke into song.

"'Where did you get that hat? Where did you get that tile?

Isn't it a nobby one and just the proper style?
I should like to have one just the same as that.'
Wherever I go, they shout, 'Hello, where did you get that hat?"'

Percy howled as the song came to its conclusion, and the crowd of singers all applauded. I was about to ask my uncle what he, my mother and aunt were doing in the pub at that time of day, when he rushed across to tell me.

"My boy, we're celebrating!"

"I can tell that," I responded with little surprise in my voice.

"Yes, yes. But you don't know why."

My mother wheeled my aunt over to us and Percy stayed behind on the piano stool as if waiting for the next musician who might accompany him.

"We have some news, Marius," my dear aunt announced. "We went to see Major Walker, the estate agent in Dorking, to enquire about the old general shop. It's been empty for years and is available at an affordable price, so we've decided to take up the lease."

"I'm going to bake again!" Uncle Stan proclaimed with a hoot and began to dance about the place. "A baker who doesn't bake is like a fisherman who doesn't fish!" While this was undoubtedly true, I wasn't sure it conveyed any great wisdom.

Mother said nothing but watched to see how I would react.

"Why here, though?" I was more than a little flabbergasted. "The village may look quaint, but haven't you heard that it's a hotbed of violent crime?"

"It's time for a change," Stan told me between hops and jumps. "We've been under your feet for long enough. It was never meant to be permanent, so we are moving on to greener pastures."

I wasn't sure how to take this. "I thought that my pasture was fairly green."

"Aye, but it doesn't have a bread oven on the premises." He

grabbed hold of Bella, who had been patiently standing next to me this whole time and danced off with her around the bar.

My aunt was a little more diplomatic. "We're sorry not to have told you before, Marius. Stan has always wanted to open another shop, and it's too good an opportunity to miss."

I couldn't bear to see her worry about me, and so I stopped acting like a child and gave her my blessing. "It's wonderful news, Auntie Elle. I'll miss you, of course, but I'm sure that everything will work out just as it should."

She patted me on the back just as Stan returned to swap my partner for his.

"It's lovely to see you again, Bella," my mother told her, then planted a kiss on my cheek and whispered, "Don't worry, boy, I'm not going anywhere just yet." Which I considered both highly presumptuous – to think that I would be upset that my eccentric relatives would finally be leaving my stylish London flat – but also deeply comforting.

"Thank you, Mother. Enjoy your celebration while Bella and I try to solve this murder."

She placed both hands on my cheeks and wouldn't let go of me. "You're just like your father," she said. "He was always rushing off to save the world, too."

She let go of me just as I realised that this was the first time in years that I'd heard her talk of him directly. Her gaze stayed on me for a moment longer than expected, and it was clear then that we both knew that we both knew.

"Richard's over by the bar," Bella told me, and I snapped back into detective mode – more or less.

"I'm sorry if that whole scene was too bizarre. I'd like to find the words to explain my family to you, but I'm afraid they don't exist."

"Don't be silly, Marius. Mine is far stranger than most people's."

I pursed my lips. "It's not a competition, Bella. But, fine, you win."

Richard was chatting away to one of the old gents who kept the Duke's Head in business and looked to be enjoying himself. His mourning attire was forgotten, and he was not dressed in one of his sharp suits for once, but he cut a fine figure in hunting tweeds. I must say that he really did fit the part of a country gent, though I also knew the humble background from which he sprang.

"Bella! Marius!" he cooed on noticing us. "It's lovely to see the pair of you together."

"You're no longer mourning James then?" I couldn't resist observing.

He didn't see any problem with this and hugged the tankard of whatever frothy beverage he was drinking. "No, that was last night. As your uncle keeps telling everyone, this is a celebration. No more having to drive to Dorking just to buy some milk. I haven't been so happy in years."

I turned my head to one side, much as Percy does when he's thinking really hard... or possibly just tired... or possibly both. "You're happy despite the fact that your fiancée left you, you don't own the company you created, and one of your best friends in the world was recently murdered?"

Bella deftly delivered the decisive blow. "It's time for us to have a conversation, Richard. Don't you think?"

TWENTY-THREE

He led us into the small bar, which was deserted at that time of day. There was little to speak of in the way of decoration except for a few old rowing oars attached to one wall and an outdated photograph of King Edward in a frame on the wall. In fact, the rest of the pub was much the same. The most elaborate decoration there was the sign attached to the front of the building with a very literal depiction of its name.

"Now what's all this about?" Richard asked in a pompous voice, as though we were taking up his time unnecessarily.

"We'd like to know what happened between you and Lucinda for a start." Over the initial phase of our fledgling hobby, Bella had learnt to deploy a steelier tone for our steelier opponents.

"I'm not sure that's anyone else's business."

She became a little sweeter even as she goaded him. "Come along, Richard. You can trust us. We certainly don't wish to cause you any harm. We just want to catch the killer."

He glanced at me for a moment, but evidently decided he was happier talking to Bella after all. "Very well. I'll answer your questions."

Bella cleared her throat meaningfully and began. "Until recently, you were engaged to Lucinda Heaton. From what I saw, the two of you were perfectly happy together and you'd even sent out invitations for the wedding this July. Three weeks ago, everyone in the village was told that your engagement was off, but nobody seems to know why. Except for a passing mention of the poems you received, even Lucinda hasn't revealed any details. So perhaps you can tell us what happened."

"It's all a terrible misunderstanding. I've tried to convince her of my innocence." He pulled at the cotton undershirt beneath his Norfolk jacket. It wasn't hot in there, and he had no excuse.

"Well, now you can try to convince us," I contributed. I don't think he appreciated it.

"Right... yes." Though a year younger than Bella and I, Richard had deep lines on his forehead, as if he'd spent much of his life worrying. They creased together as he considered what to say. "You see, she got it into her head that I was..." He sought a polite term and, as there really wasn't one, went with, "... carrying on with some strumpet."

I looked at Bella then to see whether she would be able to keep a straight face. So this was another point to her.

"Did she have any particular *strumpet* in mind?" she asked as politely as she could.

"Did you?" I added, less graciously.

"No names were mentioned, but she implied that she knew who it was." This was all becoming extremely cryptic, and I was grateful when he went on to explain. "You see, I'd received a number of letters."

"Letters?" Bella asked with a note of excitement.

Richard shook his head. "No, no. Not that kind of letter. They weren't threatening. They were poems... To be perfectly honest, they were love poems."

"Sonnets?" I asked for no other reason than the fact I liked such poetry.

"In some cases, yes."

"Were they any good?" I wouldn't get away with this one, and he looked at me rather sniffily.

"I didn't pay too much attention to their literary merit, but the rhyme structure was clean and the author—" He stopped himself and did my job for me by keeping the conversation focused on more significant issues. "I'm sorry, but was it a recommendation for a good poet you wanted or information that could lead to the killer?"

Rather than admitting that I can get carried away with my love of the written word, I lied. "For detectives, it's surprising how often a tiny detail may turn out to be of the utmost importance."

"The poetry was fine. It was good even, and the sender had clearly taken some time over them. But I swear that I did not have anything to do with any woman other than Lucinda. She found one of them in my hallway one day and saw red. She claimed that I had gone behind her back to seduce another woman. I tried to convince her that it must have been sent to the wrong address, but she wouldn't listen."

It was about time that Bella asked a question, and a relevant one at that. "Was there anything in particular that made her think the poem was meant for you?"

He squirmed and writhed and looked terribly uncomfortable. "Well, yes, actually. One of the lines was something like, 'O, Richard, the light of a summer's sky, Burns within your blessed eyes.'"

"It's remarkable that she could misconstrue the meaning so wildly."

I received an elbow to the ribs from my dear partner.

"And what happened after that?"

Richard removed a handkerchief from his top pocket and

proceeded to dab his brow. Again, I must state that it wasn't hot in the bar, and he had no excuse. "She hit me, as it happens."

"Lucinda hit you?" I doubt Bella's comment was any more necessary than mine, but it certainly put Richard in his place.

"That's right. You see, she was furious and said she could never trust me again. So for some silly reason, I showed her the other poems I'd received, as though that would prove my innocence."

"And it didn't work?"

"No, it made things worse, and that was when she hit me. She beat my chest with both hands and said that I'd always wanted to sow my wild oats, even when we were younger. I wasn't expecting another attack, and she got me right on the jaw with her fist. It's true what they say, Lucinda is good at every-thing – even fighting."

He became quite dispirited then and let out a moan. "That's one of the things I love most about her. She's just so capable. Not to mention beautiful, warm-hearted, and friendly to children and old people."

"Then why did you carry on with this poet?" I thought I'd try to catch him unprepared, but it didn't quite work.

"I wouldn't say... Marius, you're twisting things. I've already told you that I had nothing to do with whoever wrote those poems. I couldn't betray Lucinda like that. When I think of the suffering that she has already endured, I feel quite heartsick."

"You poor thing." Bella's softness hadn't been entirely eradi-cated, but I felt confident that a few more corpses would do the trick.

So then it was my turn to be the serious detective while she mooned over the dear man's broken heart. "Very well. If you had nothing to do with the woman who wrote the poems, have you come to any kind of understanding as to why they were sent to you?"

Turning to Bella once more, he adopted a solemn tone. "I

would say that was obvious. Someone evidently wrote them to come between Lucinda and myself. I believe that the sender was unhappy at the idea of our marrying and decided to do something about it."

"That is a possibility," Bella began. "But isn't it just as likely that someone really was in love with you?" She surely only said this because he was a handsome, nattily dressed devil.

"I really couldn't say." To be fair to him, Richard at least feigned modesty in response. "All I know is that Lucinda has had nothing more to do with me since the day she found out about my supposed admirer."

"Did you continue to receive any poems after that?" This was good thinking on Bella's part and might well have told us whether the person who had been writing them was in his immediate circle.

"The last arrived approximately a week later. I believe it was the day after Lucinda told everyone that the wedding had been cancelled."

"That is interesting." Bella walked over to the unlit fireplace and stood holding the mantelpiece for a moment. I must admit that there is no better place to have a good think. "That does fit with the idea that the sender's goal was to interfere with the wedding."

"Did you study the envelopes to see from where they'd been sent?" I asked.

"I did." Richard stood up straighter, apparently proud of his own detective work. "The postmark showed they were from Dorking, which doesn't particularly help us as it's only seven miles from here. Anyone in the village could have sent them."

"What about enemies?"

"What about them?" He sounded quite perplexed.

A hint of exhaustion entered my voice. "Do you have any?"

"No, of course I don't. The only person with whom I've

ever come to blows besides Cinders was James, and he's..." I
don't know whether he broke off this sentence to spare a
thought for our murdered friend or because he was questioning
our dead friend's role in sending the poems.

"That is an interesting point," I said, plumping for the
second option. "We would have to assume that the person who
wrote to you was a woman because of the language and subject
matter, but it might well have been a man stirring the pot.
Perhaps James didn't approve of your union with his cousin."

Richard did not take kindly to the suggestion. "Now wait
just one moment."

"Yes, I think this makes a lot of sense. James knew that
Lucinda wouldn't listen to him if he told her not to marry you,
and so he set about sabotaging the engagement." A narrative
had formed in my head, and I found it rather intriguing.

Richard was apparently less impressed. "I very much doubt
that James ever thought about anyone but himself. Lucinda and
I were engaged for several months, and he never spoke out
against me. And besides, can you really imagine him sitting in
his lonely house, writing fake poems to me?"

"It's possible. The two of you were always very competitive
when I knew you." I had apparently taken over the interview as
Bella stood by the hearth staring pensively at a painting of a
storm for some reason.

"Competitive, yes. Enemies, I don't think so." He was reso-
lute in this, at least. "I told you last night, James and I were
friends. We enjoyed a healthy rivalry, but we always got along."

"So you didn't blame him for the fact his family became
even richer from the company you established together?"

He narrowed his eyes to object to this. "No, I did not. And
do you know why?"

It would have been rude not to wait for the answer.

"Because I was born with nothing, and no matter how much

money I made the Heatons, I would have remained penniless if they hadn't helped me. It wasn't Tom or Granville who invested in my business, it was James himself. I could have had all the grand ideas in the world, but without the trust he placed in me, the company would never have existed."

"You also said last night that James was good for a quid or two when you were short. Did you owe him a lot of money?"

"Yes: a quid or two!" he replied in exasperation. "You see, the difference between us was that I actually enjoyed spending the money I made. I never imagined I would become as wealthy as the Heatons, but I have enough to enjoy the finer things in life and, whenever I didn't, James would give me a small loan that I would pay back at the end of each month. I can show you the receipts to prove it." He turned the discussion back on me then. "You drive the red Invicta I've seen parked in front of Lucinda's house, isn't that right?"

"It is."

"Well, it's very nice, but I have a Bentley Speed Six. It has a six and a half litre engine and, let me tell you, that extra half litre makes all the difference." As it was clear he was going to blather on like this for some time, I sat down on a stool to wait. "My suits are from Savile Row. My top hats are made by Lock and Co. – hatters to countless kings, politicians and presidents. The furniture in my house was specially made for me by—"

"Yes, that's wonderful, but you still live in Hurtwood for some reason."

"How dare you! I stayed to be close to my family and Lucinda, whom I love most ardently." He shook his head, as if trying to comprehend my insolence. "Allow me to reiterate. I would never have murdered her cousin nor strayed with another woman, no matter the quality of her poetry."

We could have bickered like this all day, and I'm sure I would have enjoyed it, but Bella finally returned to us with a question of her own.

"Where are the poems now?"

He hesitated this time, and I thought I saw a touch of fear in his eyes. "I burnt them. I couldn't bear to have them in my house a moment longer." He leant against the bar for support. "I must confess that, after Lucinda broke off our engagement, I went through a dark period that I would not wish upon my worst enemy."

"The same worst enemy who doesn't exist?" I was just being cheeky now, but he didn't seem to notice.

"That's right. The burden of Lucinda's mistrust in me was not easy to shake, and my spirits are only now recovering."

Bella chose her words carefully. "That must have been dreadful. I can only imagine how you have suffered. You have our deepest sympathies, Richard."

"Does he?"

"Thank you, Bella. I appreciate your consideration and only wish this conversation could have been avoided. Since James's death, the sorrow I bear has only multiplied. If Lucinda never takes me back, I don't know what I'll do."

He looked at me then as if I was the architect of his misfortune. Bella directed a similarly judgemental glare in my direction, and I realised I'd gone too far. "I'm sorry, old thing. It seems I have treated you poorly."

He was presumably still coming to terms with some of my more lurid accusations and did not reply.

"I know what we must do, Richard." I was too kind for my own good. "Someone should be with Lucinda tonight and, as the Duchess of Hurtwood has requested my presence at the manor, it should probably be you."

"She'll never allow it." He stepped forward and I could see on his face just how much he liked the plan, regardless.

"I'll make certain that she does, but I do have one piece of advice for you."

He already sounded more chipper. "Oh, yes?"

"Yes, bring one of your no doubt expensive pillows from home. Her sofa is fine for sitting, but not the most comfortable place to sleep. I've still got a crick in my neck."

TWENTY-FOUR

We left Richard to dream of his reunion with Lucinda. I wasn't sure that my plan would work, but if the pair of them were destined to be together, I could but lend their overworked cupid a helping hand.

Out in the main bar, Stan was back at the piano and the crowd had grown – though I have a feeling many of them were there to marvel at the singing dog. It would have been nice to stay with my family to celebrate their news, but we had work still to do.

First, we found Dodo at her house and asked her to spend the night at Tilly's, as there was no guarantee that the police would keep sending officers on the off-chance that someone else was murdered. Dodo was only too happy to help, but that was the easy part. Next, we had to speak to Lucinda.

"I'm truly sorry, Lucinda." I knelt before her usual spot on the armchair to show just how deeply I meant this. "I can't be here tonight because we have to investigate something up at Hurtwood House. I don't want to take the risk of coming back late and leaving you here alone, so I've had to find someone else to look after you."

She showed no emotion then, though I could see that, behind her tough façade, she was still afraid. "Who will it be?"

Bella had chosen to stay out of this discussion entirely and hovered by the door, probably laughing at me. I suppose it was my fault for being so hard on our old friend, but I was trying to be a good detective. This was easier said than done when the only examples I had to follow were the characters from any number of poorly written sevenpennies I'd read.

"Richard," I told Lucinda as quickly as I could, in the hope she wouldn't explode with anger.

Oddly, the opposite occurred. She fell deathly quiet, and her breathing became a little more rapid. "You do know what he did, don't you? He was seeing another woman behind my back." She looked deep into my eyes, so then I felt bad for her too. It's really not easy being nice to people.

I placed my hand on hers. "I'm not trying to push you back together, Lucinda." That was part of the plan, but I wasn't about to tell her that. "I just want to keep you safe and, unless you think that Richard is behind James's death, I believe he'd be a good choice to stay here tonight."

Bella finally spoke from across the room. "Do you think he could be the killer, Cinders?"

She glanced over and, holding her breath for a few seconds as she considered the possibility, said, "No, I don't think it could be him. Richard just isn't the kind of person who would go to all that trouble with the letters. I still don't understand what the point of them was, but I know that he is far more practical." She nodded to herself as she spoke, as though gaining in confidence. "If he wanted to kill anyone, he'd make sure it happened when he was several miles away and there were plenty of witnesses. He's too wily for whatever nonsense has been going on this week."

Bella responded with an optimistic smile. "So we can tell him to come?"

"He can come." Lucinda nodded again, but this time she was less positive. "But I'll be locked in my room the whole time he's here, and he'll have to sleep on the sofa."

"Of course," I said, and squeezed her hand tighter.

She looked just as jumpy as she had since I'd returned to Hurtwood, but I felt better knowing that there would be someone with her that night while I fulfilled my social obligations to an aristocrat who didn't particularly like me.

When we left Lucinda's ugly house, Mrs Abbot was in her yard clipping the same hedge as the day before. She still appeared suspicious of me for some reason, even as I waved hello.

Bella, on the other hand, seemed rather proud. "You know, you're very nice when you try." She elbowed me in the side as we stopped at the crossroads.

"Nice but potentially stupid," I said. "I'm a little worried that we've just arranged for a murderer to look after one of his chosen victims. But think of it like this; either Richard is innocent, and he'll be there to protect her."

"Or?"

"Or he's the killer and he can no longer murder Lucinda because we'd know he was responsible. It's a perfect solution."

She no longer looked so proud. "Yes, a perfect situation." In fact, she was studying me rather critically. "On another topic, do you think you might wish to change before meeting my mother?"

I decided not to give an honest answer.

"That is a very good idea." I glanced down at the crumpled suit I'd been wearing since the night before. "I would hate to make a bad impression."

"Time's short if you're to speak to her before dinner, too. So perhaps we should take your car." She was already walking towards the Invicta.

I've never been one to upset Bella – except for that time

when I failed to ask her to marry me, leading to years of heartache. Agreeing to change into smarter clothes to visit the woman who would not be my mother-in-law was the least I could do.

We drove in silence up the hill, and Mr Walker waved us through the gate with his usual benevolent air. In the evening light, Hurtwood House looked even more impressive and its creamy, Ancaster stone façade turned pink as the sun dropped ever closer to the horizon.

"I'll meet you for dinner in the orangery if you like," Bella told me as we parked my car in the garage beside her Sunbeam. "It's a shade more intimate than the Great Hall."

Caxton was there cleaning the family's fleet of Bentleys and Daimlers.

"Oh my goodness!" I said in a sharp tone as something significant occurred to me. "I know who the killer is!"

"Do you really mean it?"

"Yes, your chauffeur must have done it. I've rarely met such a disagreeable chap."

"Very funny, Marius." She punched me then; she literally punched me! Fine, it was only on the arm, but I still disagree with such violence, especially when it's directed at me. "I thought you were serious for a moment."

"I was... for a moment."

She punched me once more for luck and then hurried off into the house.

"Shown your face again, have you?" Caxton growled as I exited my car.

"Urrmmm, yes. It certainly appears that way."

"Well, I'm watching you, Quin. I never liked you and I still don't."

It was hard to know how to respond to such a comment, but I gave it a go. "I appreciate your honesty. And for my part, I will do all that I can to win your good opinion."

The hulking chauffeur with his gigantic head and, I can only imagine, tiny brain, was not the most intelligent cove I'd ever come across and could merely grunt in reply. I didn't mean a word of what I'd said, but I could tell that politeness annoyed him far more than my anger would have.

"Have a lovely evening, Caxton. And if you've nothing else to do, my car could use a clean." I gave him a wink and sauntered off to the main building.

I had brought my best suit and, though I couldn't quite match Richard for the labels within it or the price I'd paid, I thought the end result was really rather good. It is an undeniable fact that black three-piece suits are mysteriously powerful things. It's surprising that their use is not controlled more tightly by the government. I was not convinced that I could make the Duchess love me so easily, but my white-gold cufflinks and gleaming leather shoes certainly wouldn't hurt.

When I was a child, she could normally be found in her sitting room in the eastern tower. I think she liked to imagine that she was a queen from days gone by. Of course, based on her title, home and immense estate, this wasn't so far from the truth.

"Lady Montague?" I asked as I knocked on the half-open door.

There was no answer at first, and an uneasy feeling came over me. Don't worry. I wasn't about to find another body. I simply hadn't spoken loudly enough.

"Hello, is there someone there?" she called.

I pushed the door wider, and there she was at her desk, just as I remembered.

"I'm sorry to disturb you, Your Grace. Bella told me that you wanted to see me."

"Marius Quin?" She looked impressed. I'm fairly certain this was down to the suit. "Come in, young man. Let me see how you've changed."

I did as requested, and she certainly did have a look at me. I felt quite self-conscious for a moment, and I was reminded of my induction into the army when we were checked over by a superior to ensure that we wouldn't collapse when loaded with a knapsack and rifle. One boy I knew had barely enough strength to support his helmet, so it was probably a good idea to make such inspections.

"You're an adult now," she said, as though this came as a surprise. "I know that may sound like a trite observation, but the picture I had in my head was of a spotty adolescent."

I considered telling her that I'd always had a perfectly acceptable complexion, but this was not the moment for such smart talk.

"For your part, madam, you haven't changed a bit." This was bordering on the sycophantic but also quite true. Though in her sixties, she was a youthful woman. Sadly, her unfeeling manner belied the soft features of her face that she had passed down to her daughter.

"That's kind of you to say."

A few awkward seconds passed in which I was uncertain whether to stand or sit, talk or wait. To be perfectly honest, I hadn't a clue why she'd summoned me there.

"Please, sit down." She pointed to the heavy wooden chair across the table from her and I tried to see what dusty tome she'd been reading. At least as old as Hurtwood House, it was probably something dry and worthy that most people gave up reading a century or so earlier.

When she said no more, I decided to ramble. "It's so strange to be visiting again. I held on to images of the place all the time I'd been away, and it is quite uncanny to compare them to the real thing. As I've walked around the village and up here on your estate, the world before me keeps filling in gaps in my memory."

"I can imagine that would be unsettling." Her voice was flat, as though she were reading her words from a script. "Life often presents us with situations we could never have predicted, like your return here after so long."

I felt she wanted me to ask why I was there, but I sat and waited for her to take the conversation wherever she wanted it to go.

"I asked you here in order to explain that, if you do anything to upset my daughter, I will show you no mercy." After what felt like hours of ambiguity, her words were as direct as a knife to the heart. "I don't trust you, Marius. I haven't since the very first time you set foot in this house."

I couldn't hold back my response. "I was only five years old."

"That's right, and you were charming. Your father brought you up here to play with my Isabella, and I'd never seen such a handsome child. You made my boys look like ogres, and I could already see the trouble you would cause her. That is why I am happy for Bella to be with a charmless boor like Gilbert Baines." She seemed to squint as though looking at me through a sheet of ice. "We live in a time when one's offspring are afforded great autonomy and any number of worthless freedoms. And so, sadly, I cannot forbid you from seeing her, but I wish that I could."

"What a shame," I replied in an unflustered tone. "I was rather hoping you called me here to explain some fascinating insight into the death of James Heaton."

I sat back in the uncomfortable chair. Now that I knew where I stood with her, I actually felt more confident. It was the doubt that had so unnerved me.

She continued in that same gently hostile manner. "Your inspector was here poking around, but I don't think he found anything significant. And as for the Heatons, I have no interest in any of them. The two brothers, in particular, were despicable people who seemed to possess the belief that they could outdo my family."

"You're not the first to share such a view. I suppose it's lucky that their children turned out far better. James was no hero. In fact, he did everything he could to get out of fighting in the war, but he was never so cruel as his father or uncle."

"That is not a recommendation." She sat staring at me for a few moments and, for all her harsh words, I felt that she must have admired me just a little. "However, I would have thought that you would know all there is to about the Heatons. Your father worked for them in that last year before he left Hurtwood." She made it sound as though he had moved away, or retired to the coast somewhere, as opposed to disappearing without a trace and never contacting his family thereafter.

"What do you mean? Father never worked for the Heatons. He opposed them at every turn."

She smiled the smile of a wicked queen. "That's true, my boy. But even the ever-principled Terence Quin had to work with them eventually. I imagined you already knew that."

I could see no reason for her to say this other than out of a desire to upset me, and it had worked. Now an adult and no longer trapped within her sphere of influence, I had assumed myself invulnerable, but she knew just how to wound me.

"Well, it's been lovely seeing you again," I lied, as I rose from my seat without waiting for her permission.

"You don't mean that." Her voice was as cold as a winter's day in the Himalayas.

"You're right, I don't. But it is a pleasure to leave you." I gritted my teeth so hard I'm surprised they didn't crumble. "Goodbye, Sylvia." And yes, I intentionally used her Christian name. In my experience, duchesses hate that.

I rushed down the spiral staircase and all the way to the orangery, where Bella was not yet waiting. Instead, the Hurtwood family butler was overseeing the preparation of a small table. He was pot-bellied, had a superior attitude and rather liked me for some reason.

"Mr Quin, I hear you will be dining with Lady Isabella tonight."

"That's right, Pullman, but take your time. I'll stand here looking furious, if you don't mind."

"Very good, sir." He went about his work in a whisper as various footmen rushed in with candelabras, wine glasses and silver chargers to make the room perfect for a party of two.

I, meanwhile, did just as I'd promised and looked out of the curved glass at the Hurtwood House lake. Dark clouds had rolled over the estate to match my mood, and I didn't think anything would push them away again, but then Bella arrived.

"You're early," she said from the doorway, and I turned to see a portrait come to life.

TWENTY-FIVE

Bella was dressed in a turquoise silk gown that floated an inch above the floor. It was loose at the bottom and tight at the top and, in describing it, I am once again reminded how little I know about women's clothing. All I can say is that, as she moved into the candlelight, I was quite speechless... for a few seconds, at least.

"If I'd known you were getting dressed up, I would have made more of an effort."

"Very funny, Marius. You should be on the stage with jokes like that."

I would have said something pithy in reply, but I was in awe of her again. She was beautiful, and she was more than beautiful. She was Bella.

"I thought you would prefer this to a family meal. I'm sure that Mother has scared you enough already without giving her the opportunity to do so in front of the staff."

In the fog of my bad mood, I had failed to notice that the small round table was now laid with everything we could need.

"That was kind of you." Like a waiter in the Parisian cafés I had once frequented, I nipped around the table to pull out her seat for her. It was a little excessive, but she smiled and took her place. I sat down opposite her, feeling every bit as smooth as when I was fourteen, and I finally noticed how pretty she was.

"The truth is that my family rarely dine as one. In fact, I don't remember the last time we were all in the same room together. My parents aren't..."

I could tell this was not something she wished to discuss, so I mumbled a swift, "This is much nicer than a big do," and she changed the topic.

"I believe we just missed Lovebrook when we arrived here," she said and I could only hum my agreement, though it soon turned into a tune and that tune soon turned into "Knees Up Mother Brown" which really isn't the thing to accompany a sophisticated dinner, or any smart occasion for that matter.

"It must be strange for you to be back here." She peered about the place as if she hadn't seen it in some time.

I suddenly realised that I was oddly slow in replying. I'd been distracted by the fact that the colour of her dress made her eyes shine more brightly, which made me nervous that I would now say something inappropriate.

"Strange? Why strange?" I asked, a little strangely considering the fact that I had just told her mother how strange it was for me to be back there... which was strange.

"Seeing all these old faces again and walking through a village that you haven't visited in ten years."

"No, that's perfectly normal."

"Really?"

"Oh, yes. Perfectly normal. There's nothing unusual about that in the slightest." I crossed my legs at the ankle and leaned back in my chair. It turned out that it was not a sturdy piece and would have tipped backwards if I hadn't slammed my hands down on the table. She must have thought I was clowning about like Harold Lloyd.

To save me from my idiocy, she laughed, and I instantly felt better. "You are funny, Marius. I believe I'd forgotten that about you."

I leaned forwards instead and, should the front legs of the antique beneath me prove to be just as weak, I at least had the table there for support.

"I've never understood why we remember some things and forget others. I have memories from my childhood of completely insignificant moments but ask me to draw a picture of my father and I wouldn't know how to begin." My voice faded out for a moment, and she evidently didn't know what to say to this, so I continued. "It had quite gone from my mind what a good singer you were, but when I heard you on New Year's Eve, I was amazed."

Her smile became a touch wickeder. "Then I have a confession to make. I had a terrible voice when I was a child, but I had singing lessons while you were away." Her cheeks flushed, and she tried to change the subject. She'd always hated talking about herself. "Lucinda is the singer. Do you remember her in the school play when we were ten years old?"

"I do now." A button was pressed, and the memory came hurtling to the front of my mind. "Dodo wrote it. You were the narrator, James and I had to fight to the death for some reason and Lucinda sang every song. It wasn't so much a play as an opportunity for everyone to bask in her brilliance."

We both fell quiet, and I can't imagine what occupied Bella's mind just then, but I know what was in mine. I was thinking about the war and everything it had changed. It wasn't just the people who died and the people who loved them, but all those whose lives were interrupted, paused and put on hold.

Bella obviously wasn't thinking the same thing as, looking at me across the candle flame, with that warm smile on her face and her delicate hands resting on the tablecloth in front of her, she said, "It's amazing to think that someone we have known all our lives is probably responsible for James's murder."

This sudden switch in the conversation was almost as bad as my inappropriate humming.

"As I see it," she continued with no thought for the previous atmosphere we had enjoyed, "there are two likely reasons for why James was killed. Whatever the circumstances of his death, it seems to me that everything comes back to love or money."

"Isn't that always true?"

Instead of her beauty, or her elegant gown, I had the chance to marvel at her phenomenal brain now. I believe it was even more exhilarating.

"Perhaps, but that was particularly the case with our friends, don't you think?" I didn't know what to think, so she continued. "James and Richard wanted to be as rich as my father, and the rest of us wanted to fall in love and talked of little else."

"You don't think James and Richard wanted love?"

She considered my question. "In their own way, I suppose they did. But I always had the impression that, for them, love was a symbol of success instead of a goal in its own right."

"You're quite right. Before the war at least, James and Richard were terribly ambitious. However, I think that Lucinda and Tilly shared some of their characteristics. It's not just men who wish to rule the realm. Perhaps even Dodo and I were driven in our own way."

"No, you were creative. That's different."

I had a stab at looking thoughtful for a moment. "I see. So we have the romantics, the creative types and the aspirant millionaires. I wonder if there was also a homicidal maniac amongst our ranks."

"That is what we still have to discover."

Silence fell as Pullman returned to serve the first course. The food barely registered with me that night. I know it must have been delicious because it had been produced by the Hurtwood House kitchen. And I'm sure that I enjoyed it, because at no point during the meal did I notice what I was eating.

We discussed crimes and criminals. We thought over the suspects we'd encountered and the ones we might have overlooked. We went through every person we could think of in the village, from the regulars in the pub to the man who came from Dorking twice a week to sweep the streets. We listed the evidence we'd amassed, starting with the letters themselves through to the headed notepaper, Lucinda's lurker and the poems that Richard had received in the post.

"Do you believe his story?" I asked, as I still couldn't make up my mind.

"I'm not sure. He's an excellent actor if he's lying. He described the poems in detail and could even recite a line from them. And yet the fact he burnt them struck me as suspicious."

"I believe there was another line which read, 'Richard, how I dream of you! Say, please say, your heart is true.'"

She almost choked on her... whatever she was eating. "Gosh, was there really? I didn't hear him say anything about it."

"No, Bella. No, there wasn't. I just made it up to prove how easy it would be."

I half expected to receive a kick under the table, but it never came.

"Fine, he could have thought of a rhyming couplet on the spot, but that doesn't mean he did. And now that I think of it, why would he have? It's easy enough to ask Lucinda about the poems she saw."

"True." I took a mouthful of... something. "What's more interesting to consider is whether the person who wrote those poems also wrote the letters."

"It would certainly be wrong to conflate the two things without evidence. Maybe there's no connection between them, and Richard sent the poems to himself in order to make

Lucinda break off the engagement. Perhaps he realised that marrying into the Heaton family wasn't all he'd been hoping."

"How interesting." I paused to give it some thought. "I would have never imagined that."

"Anything is possible." Her smile straightened itself out, and she gazed into the waving flame. "Our problem is that we have to take everything at face value. We can ask the inspector to check a few facts for us from time to time, but we have to rely on our ability to judge people to know whether they're lying or not."

I was about to question this when she spoke again. "Richard could have told us a pack of lies and we'd never know it. Did he resent James for making the most money from his business? Did he owe him far more than he admitted and wish to erase his debt in the most drastic way possible? If so, threatening not just James, but Tilly and Lucinda too, was a good way to distance himself from the crime."

"You're absolutely right. Everyone would assume that the killer started his campaign of terror but got scared away by all the police hanging around."

Our ideas bounced off one another's and each new thought we had led to more.

Bella was so excited by the possibilities, and I was happy to see her come alive. "We'd never think that all those letters – all that talk of 1917 and revenge – had been a way for Richard to distract from the fact that he couldn't pay back his debts."

I raised my glass of... the drink I was drinking to toast this smart observation. "We should ask Lovebrook to investigate Richard's financial situation to see whether he has more skeletons hidden away somewhere."

"Perhaps, but I doubt it will lead to anything."

I enjoyed her confidence. "Oh, really, and why not?"

"Because this crime must have been planned well in advance. The killer sent letters informing his potential victims and James wasn't murdered until two days after the first was received."

"Your point being...?"

"Well, if he's gone to all that trouble, he's unlikely to be condemned by such an obvious motive as outstanding bank debts. I think that whoever is doing this believes he can get away with it."

I paused to think this over and returned to a theory that I didn't want to believe but couldn't help admiring. "That's what appeals to me about the idea of Sebastian coming back here for revenge. No police officer would ever suspect him. To be frank, if one suggested such a solution, he'd be laughed out of Scotland Yard."

"There we go then. It's the only sensible option. James was murdered by a dead man."

We smiled across the table, happy in one another's company, just as two footmen brought in plates that were piled high with delicious selections of... something.

TWENTY-SIX

I was up with the sun the next morning. A pale light broke over the estate, and I felt indescribably serene. It was as though the pieces of my life were finally fitting together. Of course, it's at just such moments that I should know to expect the very worst. It may sound pessimistic but, in murder investigations at least, optimism can be a fatal flaw.

I strolled out of my bedroom in Hurtwood House, waving at every maid and footman I passed and issuing hellos and good mornings left, right and behind me. I drove across the estate and past the drowsy guard in his sentry box, who reluctantly jumped out to unlock the gate. The village was shrouded in fog, and I found it rather beautiful. When one's head is full of pleasant thoughts, even bad weather can seem charming. I stopped on the crest of the hill to admire the sight of St Mark's spire, which pierced the layer of soft white cloud.

I let my car roll down into town as the sun emerged to burn off the fog. Such was my lightness of spirit I decided to pop home to see whether Uncle Stan had been practising his baking – which of course he had. With my hunger satiated, I strolled over to see whether Lovebrook had slept in his car –

which of course he had. You should have seen the smile on his face when I tapped on the window with a plate of buttered muffins.

"You're a saint." He spoke with a full mouth, but I'm fairly certain these were his words. "An actual saint."

"You loon, why didn't you call at the manor and ask for a room for the night?" We sat on Lucinda's garden wall, eating the sweet and doughy delights.

He certainly had his quirks and looked nonplussed by the question. "You know, I didn't think of that. I considered bunking in with one of the victims, but I thought it might have looked unprofessional. The car was my only resort."

I looked at his old brown box on wheels and shrugged. "It isn't the kind of resort I'd ever wish to visit."

"You may have a point."

"You could have driven home to London, too. It's not as if you're actually assigned to this case. We've abducted you from your other duties."

"That may be true. But I haven't been given many interesting cases since I moved to London. I thought my days would be filled with gangsters and cunning murderers, but I tend to spend more time filing reports about missing old ladies who we soon discover have gone to the seaside without telling anyone."

"That doesn't sound like the work of a detective," I told him. "Is someone pulling your leg?"

"No, the chief inspector says that I have to prove my worth, but it's taking longer than I'd hoped. I did get to do some surveillance work, and even met Lord—" He interrupted himself then as he had just taken another bite of his muffin. "These are just delicious. You must send my compliments to your uncle."

I was about to ask more about his background – and perhaps what his first name was – when we heard a scream from further up the hill, and we sped off in that direction. We followed the sound to Tilly's sparkling white house. Sergeant Rossiter was already there, banging on the front door.

"There's no answer," he told us in a weak voice. "I've been out here all night. I don't understand what could've happened." To be fair to the man, he sounded quite distressed. He was breathing hard as he continued to knock.

"Let's try the back door," I told Lovebrook, and we darted around the house to look for another entrance. We saw shards of glass as soon as we rounded the bend. It was everywhere, as though whoever had broken the window had thrown pieces of it out of his way.

There were observations we could have made, conclusions to form, but I remained silent, and Lovebrook moved ahead of me to pass through the half-open door. I followed him, with the feeling that there would be nothing good to find inside.

Tilly was lying face down in a perfect oval pool of blood. She wasn't the one who had screamed, though. Dodo was crouching on the floor nearby in a silent trance. I had to assume that she was in shock, as she stared at her friend's body without looking up at us.

"Are you all right, miss?" Lovebrook began, going through the process he would have learnt in his training. "Do you know if the killer is in the house?"

She couldn't speak, but managed a nervous shake of the head, and I went to put my arms around her. I had to fall to my knees to do so, but it seemed to soothe her as the inspector searched the neighbouring rooms.

"I don't understand," Dodo finally said. "I didn't hear anything. Why didn't I hear anything? I was upstairs all night."

Lovebrook was back now, and I got the sense he knew the answer to her question but wasn't going to say it there in front of her. The blood had already developed a tacky sheen. I knew from writing such a scene in my second novel that this suggested she'd been lying there for some time. I didn't want to look at her. It was just too sad, but I forced myself to look at the gaping wound on her neck.

Having had no luck at the front of the house, Rossiter poked his head through the door and Lovebrook gave an order. "Take the young lady outside, please. If any neighbours come to gawk, ask them to take her into their house and give her a cup of something hot."

I'd never seen the typically arrogant sergeant look so distraught. He kept his eyes on the corpse even as he answered. "Yes, sir. Of course, sir."

I must say, it pained me to see Dodo follow him then. She looked so fragile, so alone, and I would have gone with her, but it was evident that Lovebrook had something to tell me.

"It's my layman's guess that she died in the early morning." He knelt down to look at the wound. "I'm no pathologist, but I imagine she was killed between two and four." He evidently didn't think this was good enough, but I was impressed. "She didn't have time to scream – that's why your friend didn't hear her. The victim's windpipe was cut before she could make a sound."

I had to crouch down myself then. The thought of what my friend must have gone through – not just Tilly, but Dodo too – was just so distressing. All the bodies on the Western Front couldn't prepare me for the sight of an innocent girl I'd known for twenty-five years, lying murdered on her kitchen floor.

"There's no sign of the murder weapon." Lovebrook's troubled expression wouldn't leave him for some time. "I was up till midnight with the constable on duty – that's when Rossiter took over. All the lights in this house turned off around eleven, so she was presumably in bed by the time the killer arrived. She must have been tempted down here somehow." He went to look at the broken glass that was sprinkled around the door into the kitchen. "It looks as though she was facing away from the killer, and her throat was slashed from behind."

I didn't want to think of such things just yet, but I knew there was no time to waste if we had any hope of catching him. "So someone must have broken into the house, taken the knife upstairs to threaten Tilly and forced her to come down here in order to..."

"What?" Lovebrook asked. "In order to what? Avoid a stain on the carpets?"

A half-decent answer eventually came to me. "To stop from waking up Dodo, I suppose. He brought her down here to avoid having to deal with anyone else."

"It doesn't fit together." Lovebrook walked back to me, the various theories clearly battling for space in his mind. "Tilly was just as likely to scream when she woke up and saw the knife as when she had her throat slit. Perhaps even more so if the killing was done swiftly." He pursed his lips as he made a decision. "There's one thing that's no longer in doubt, though. This is now a case for Scotland Yard."

TWENTY-SEVEN

Extra officers were called from Guildford, and Lovebrook spoke to his superiors back in London. A pack of constables soon arrived in Hurtwood to comb the gardens around Tilly's house for clues. Another man was stationed outside Lucinda's door to prevent the killer from finishing his plan.

I found myself wishing that Bella was there. She wouldn't have been able to bring Tilly back to life, of course, but just having her around made everything feel easier. I didn't have it in me to call her but was certain the Hurtwood Village rumour-mongers would already be winging the terrible news to the Duke.

In the meantime, I went to talk to Dodo. The sergeant had taken her home, and she was curled up like a cat on a sofa in her living room. Her mother and brother were there to look after her, and Rossiter was on duty outside to ensure that she came to no harm, but there was nothing anyone could say to make the world seem less terrifying.

"I didn't stop it," she complained. "I was supposed to look after her, and I failed."

I squashed myself into the tiny space next to her. Sitting

across the room would have felt too impersonal. "What could you have done, Dodo? If anyone is at fault, it's me for not insisting that the police station an officer with you. I really didn't believe the killer would take the risk of breaking into Tilly's house with you there."

"I'm sorry, Marius. I really am." Tears came to her eyes. It was a tragic sight, and I felt quite useless for failing to comfort her.

"She's had a hard time," Ned told me in his usual under-stated manner, while their mother hung passively in the corner.

In the end, I realised that the best thing to do was find out anything that might help solve the case. The police were busy searching the village for clues, but I knew my old friend well and hoped to get more out of her than they could.

"I'm sorry to come here like this, Dodo. But I have to ask you some questions. The killer could still be in the village, and we must try to stop him before he hurts anyone else."

She looked up at me, and though she wouldn't say a word yet, she nodded her consent.

"Thank you." I took my time choosing my first question. "Can you tell me what happened before you went to bed last night?"

She glanced out of the window to where the police were milling about in the street. It would take her a moment to find her voice, but she managed to answer my question in a hollow whisper. "Tilly and I talked for a long time. It scared me because she seemed so resigned to her fate. She kept saying that he was coming for her, and it should have already happened long before. I asked who she meant, but she just smiled as if it wasn't her secret to share. I told her there was no need to worry, but she didn't believe me. It turns out she was right not to."

"What time was that?"

"We got ready for bed at half past ten, and I read until almost eleven. I fell asleep on my book." For half a second, she almost looked happy. This was just what I'd expect from her, and we both knew it.

"Where was your room in relation to Tilly's?"

"They were right next to one another." She still looked muddled, and I had to conclude she was working through the same puzzle as when we'd found her in the kitchen. I wasn't going to tell her that her friend's throat had been slit to keep her from making a sound. I could be indiscreet at times, but I wasn't entirely insensitive.

"Did you hear anything in the night? Even the slightest sound?"

Each answer came a little quicker than the last. "I did. I heard her get up and go downstairs. She sounded as though she was whispering to herself, but I was only half awake."

"And that was all you heard?"

"No, sometime later, she came back up. I was only awake for a few seconds, but I'm sure that's what happened."

"Do you know what time it was?"

She looked at her family for support and her mother responded with a cautious smile.

"It's hard to say. It didn't feel as though I'd been asleep long. It was definitely still dark out, but there was no clock in the room."

"That's good, Dodo. Thank you."

I didn't see that there was much else I could ask her. I knew the state that Tilly had been in when we'd spoken to her the day before, and it chimed with what Dodo had said. She was waiting for death, and it came in the night.

There was one other person who might be able to help, and I addressed Dodo's brother. "What about you, Ned? Did you see anything?"

He became unexpectedly nervous and gripped the side of the open door. "Me? Why are you asking me? What could I have seen?"

"On your round, I mean. When you were out delivering letters. Did you notice anything unusual about Tilly's house or see anyone on the street?"

He seemed to hold his breath for a moment and then, releasing it slowly, he said, "It's Sunday, Marius. There's no post on a Sunday."

"Of course not. How silly of me."

Mrs Lyle came to sit next to her daughter, and I moved towards the door.

"You've all been very helpful. I'm afraid the police will need to ask you some similar questions, but maybe that will jog your memory. One thing you don't have to worry about is the killer coming back. This village will be the safest place in England until he's caught. There'll be a policeman on every corner. Have no doubt about it."

Outside their house, there were officers everywhere. I could see them rifling through flowerbeds in gardens up and down the road, searching herbaceous borders and hydrangea bushes. As I stepped out of the small grey door at the side of the post office, I noticed Sergeant Rossiter sitting on the garden wall in front of his cabin.

"This has got nothing to do with me, you know," he said without taking his eyes off the fake manor across the road. "I know that's what you must be thinking, what with everything that went on with the Heatons after my boys died, but it wasn't me."

I struggled to summon a response as he laid out the evidence against himself.

"I know I was the one on duty last night, and I'm not going to deny that I hated every last one of them Heatons. They threw me out o' my home after my boys were killed in the war and then they had the cheek to sell off the police station, so I was out in the cold every day. It makes my blood boil to think o' them, but I would never murder no one – not even my worst enemies."

The truth was, I hadn't considered his involvement for a second, but perhaps I should have. He stared into the middle distance, and I wanted to reassure him, but a shout went up to distract me. I watched as several of the constables ran to the garden next door to Tilly's to see what had been found.

"It's the knife, guv," one of the officers said rather proudly as Lovebrook appeared from the house. "It was dumped just the other side of the fence from the kitchen door."

"That's good work, Constable," the inspector replied. "Make sure that it's wrapped up safely so it can be checked for fingerprints. Not that I'd expect our killer to be so careless, but you never know."

Lovebrook didn't call over when he saw me there, and so I continued on down the road. I passed the pub, which was silent at that time on a Sunday morning, and carried on to Lucinda's house, which was no livelier.

Peering in through the living-room window, I could see Richard in the spot I'd occupied the night before. His head was on a pillow, so he'd evidently taken my advice. I almost felt guilty for waking him, but there was no other choice.

"What are you thinking, man?" He was not happy to have been disturbed. "You don't wake people up on a Sunday morning. It's the first rule of a civil society." He ranted like this for no short time. "I believe it says it in the Bible somewhere. On the seventh day, God rested, and no one came along to bother him until he was back to his absolute best."

"Were you up late, then?" I snapped back at him, whilst pointing to the front door to let me in.

I had to wait there for a few seconds but, rousing himself, he eventually did as I'd asked.

"It took me a long time and even more energy to convince Lucinda that I was only here for her safety and that I had no intention of trying to convince her to marry me."

"And did she? Accept your presence, I mean."

He became coy, which wasn't like him. "No, she didn't. Once the shouting had subsided, she went up to her bedroom and locked the door."

Despite this, I could hear the sound of sizzling coming from the kitchen and followed the smell of bacon. It was intoxicating, and I would have followed it for miles if there was the guarantee of an English breakfast at the end of it.

Lucinda was standing in front of the cooker in a long silk robe. Tending to the sausages, eggs and what have you, she turned to smile when she saw me there, but I must have given away more than I'd planned as her face soon fell.

"Why are you...?" She couldn't finish her question, and I decided that the best thing to do was tell the truth straight out.

"I don't know how to say this, Lucinda, but Tilly was killed in the night."

The spatula she was holding seemed to drop in slow motion. It fell from her hand to bounce off the hob and onto the floor. I was expecting wails of anguish, but her sorrow manifested itself in a near silent scream.

She collapsed to the floor, and I ran over as Richard joined us. I held on to her as best I could, but her body was limp. It was as though she wished to sink into the cellar and out of sight. All I could do was put my hand on her cheek and whisper empty words.

"It will be all right," I tried and, when even I realised this was nonsense, I added, "It was over quickly. She wouldn't have suffered for long."

Her face was bright red as she tensed every muscle in her body and lay with one cheek against the cold kitchen tiles. Richard came to talk to her, and I hoped he would have more luck than I had, but I couldn't imagine it.

"I'm here, Cinders," was all he would say. It was hard to know whether we'd helped, but her tears finally came. She sobbed long and hard and sat up to be held.

I waited for the pain to subside just a little. I stroked her long hair and hoped that she would recover in time. And then, when she'd recovered enough to walk to the living room, I left her with Richard and their slightly overcooked breakfast.

It seemed that everyone in the village already knew what had happened. The streets were lined with people watching the officers work as Lovebrook strode down the hill, his black mackintosh billowing behind him.

"Have you discovered anything useful?" he asked when he reached me.

"I can't be sure. Dodo says that Tilly got up in the night to go downstairs. She didn't hear the murder, but the house is gigantic, so it's hardly surprising. What was interesting is that she thought she heard her go upstairs again, which makes our understanding of the crime scene even more muddled. At least Lucinda is safe, though she's understandably both heartbroken and half terrified."

He released a sigh that told me all I needed to know. "I spoke to the local sergeant again. He didn't hear anything until we did. There were no night-time visitors to either of the houses – no trouble in the streets. The killer must have entered the back garden through the woods. There's a fence, but anyone could have found a way over it."

"It's a disaster," I said, our moods apparently matching.

"You don't need to tell me. I feel we should have done more, but I don't know what."

I stopped listening to him for a moment, as something caught my eye. Hanging from the stone cross at the top of the war memorial was a large white envelope secured with a piece of string.

"How did that get there with an officer on patrol all night?" I ran to see the thick black letters that were scrawled upon it. "'Spring 1917'," I read aloud and, having taken my driving gloves from the car, I pulled it free of its purchase. "How did this get here, Lovebrook?"

He came to stand alongside me, his eyes on the document I now extracted. "It's the angle of the road. This spot is just out of sight of Tilly's house. If the killer waited until the sergeant passed on his round, he would have had a minute or two to hang it without being caught."

I flicked through the first few typewritten pages. I saw Sebastian Kane's name there over and over and knew what I was holding. It was an account of his time in Hurtwood. I could see no claim to authorship, but an idea entered my head, and I needed to be certain I was wrong.

I handed Lovebrook the envelope and its contents and ran as fast as I could to the house at the top of the hill that had once been a pub. The young man with the scar that I'd seen just about everywhere in the village that weekend was standing with a young woman of a similar age. I went up to him to stare into his eyes for some sign of familiarity.

He appeared a little frightened by the madman in front of him, but then he relaxed and looked straight back at me.

"Is it you?" I yelled. "Are you Sebastian? Did you do this?"

I must have been making quite a scene as the neighbours on either side began to chatter, and I heard footsteps behind me.

"Marius, calm down." It was Postman Ned, of all people. He put his hand on my shoulder to pull me away and, when I wouldn't move, he spoke again. "This is Mrs Abbot's nephew, Peter. He moved here last year."

The woman standing next to the stranger I'd just confronted came a little closer. "Peter, do you know this man?"

"Not personally," he replied in a remarkably deep voice that I was sure I'd never heard before.

"I'm sorry," I said, feeling like the prize fool that I was. "My mind's all muddled. I made a mistake."

"That's fine, Mr Quin." The chap with the scar evidently

knew who I was, even if I'd never heard of him. "It's been a trying week for everyone."

He put his hand out to me, and I shook it without feeling. There was a police van arriving, and Bella's Sunbeam appeared in front of the pub, but nothing quite sank in for me then. What I wished most of all was that I could go back to London with my family, not just geographically, but chronologically. I wished that I could travel back to the beginning of the week when I knew nothing of the threats against the Heatons or the corruption of my beautiful village in the woods.

"Marius?" I could hear Bella's voice but I was barely aware of where it came from. "Marius, are you alright?"

I took the document from Lovebrook and the two of them followed me to the nearest bench.

SPRING 1917 - PART TWO

Dodo was a romantic without anyone to love until Sebastian arrived. Her friends all had their prospective other halves – Richard even had a few candidates lined up – but none of the boys at school were right for Dorothy 'Dodo' Lyle.

Dodo was a butterfly who flew about the village, going where she wished without fear or any great design. She was a swift in the summertime, looping and diving about her natural playground, never worried about what those around her might think.

Of course, that was until Sebastian Kane arrived and spoilt everything. When he stood at the front of the class with Mrs Abbot, Dodo knew that her life had changed. He pronounced his name ever so hesitantly, and everything became clear.

This was the boy she would marry, not James, whose skin was so thin he lived in fear of anyone directing the slightest insult his way. Not even Richard, who was so fond of himself he saw the people around him as mirrors to reflect back his brilliance. Sebastian was different. He liked books and knew how to form sentences, even if they were spoken very quietly.

From his first day there, the pair of them were drawn together. It was not so much magnetic – that was far too dramatic a word for it – but natural. Like all that Dodo did, she gravitated toward Sebastian in a slow, natural manner.

And they talked about everything. From films that they'd seen to music, the theatre and, most of all, books. Dodo's dream was to be a writer, and she already penned sketches of her friends each week in two hundred words or less. Marius was the only one she trusted to read them, of course, but Marius wasn't like the other boys. She viewed him as a kindly brother, much like her real brother, in fact, who might have been allowed a glance at her compositions if he hadn't viewed reading as one great laborious effort.

Dodo and Sebastian met up each day in the woods after school. They had their own spot in a circular clearing with immense stones dotted about the place like living room furniture. To Dodo, at least, it felt just like home. It was impossible to say how Sebastian felt about it as, though the conversations they shared could stretch on for hours, his feelings – his real feelings, not just his opinions on the various art forms he enjoyed – were rarely mentioned.

When the holiday arrived and Bella invited Sebastian to spend his free days lazing about with the rest of the group, Dodo was happy. This would be her chance to show everyone how close they had become. They would have the same conversations as always, only now with an audience. Dodo wasn't the kind of girl to tell everyone about the boy she adored, but now they would have the chance to see it for themselves.

There was only one thing for which she hadn't accounted, and that thing was Matilda Heaton. Tilly was supposed to be in love with Richard… or was it Marius? Or perhaps her heart was for Ivor Novello alone, of whom she cut out every picture she could find in the news-papers to fix to her bedroom wall. Tilly wasn't interested in reading or nature. She wasn't sensitive or softly spoken like Sebastian. She was the female embodiment of a wild boar, with the wit and charm to match. She was *wildly boring*!

As Dodo and Sebastian walked up the hill for the first time, they looked at one another in that shy, furtive manner which Dodo was certain could only mean one thing. But once the others arrived, he didn't look at her anymore. It was Tilly he watched through the corners of his eyes whenever he thought no one was looking. It was Tilly whose pathetic jokes made him laugh so hard he had to clutch his side. And it was Tilly who looked back at him as she once had at Richard.

As that week wore on, Dodo's very being felt as though it were twisting and coiling around itself. When James lost his temper at Sebastian and almost hit him, those twists became a knot, but there was nothing she could do to help him. She ran over to comfort him, but he wouldn't look at her at all now, and she walked home feeling like the world would be better if she'd never been born.

She spent the afternoon playing the worst scenes from that week over and over again in her head. Each time she did, she recalled different things that she hadn't taken notice of before. She remembered how James had looked at Marius and Bella a few minutes before the fight. She saw Richard, not arrogant or confident for once, but truly uncertain as Sebastian jumped back from the punch. But most of all, she remembered the look on Tilly's face when they arrived back in the village. It was a look of pure mischief, and Dodo thought she knew what had happened after everyone else had left.

As the sun set over Hurtwood Village, she slipped out of the house as quietly as she could and slunk off into the woods behind her house. She could get anywhere from there. The whole village was connected by the lines of trees that grew right up to the backs of the houses, almost merging with the long, neat lawns that fathers across the valley tended to every Saturday morning with their mowers.

It wasn't the village that concerned her just then, though. It was the clearing on top of the hill where Sebastian Kane was sitting with Tilly Heaton. She crept up there and spied on them as they kissed for the second time – not that she knew about the first until much later, when Tilly confessed everything one teary afternoon after school.

Their embrace was so tender that it was Dodo who felt as though she were doing something wrong by watching them. She pulled back beyond the treeline, afraid that they would see her, even though she had gone there to confront them – to tell Sebastian that she was the one he should love as, if any two people were meant to be together, it was them.

Instead, she just watched. She watched her Sebastian stroke Tilly's face as if they had been together for years. She watched the look of excitement as they kissed, and Tilly opened her eyes to check that it really was happening. Dodo watched as James appeared and came to stand over them.

Tilly's brother looked like a monster then – like some ancient mythical beast. He was a cyclops – a giant there to bite off Sebastian's head and throw his body from the cliffs. Dodo had never seen a person look so frightened as Sebastian did at that moment. He was on his back as James landed the first blow.

"Leave him alone," Tilly shouted, but her brother wouldn't listen.

His fists flew through the air, like rockets crashing into the boy's chest. James could have closed his eyes and done just as much damage. He seemed to be controlled by his instincts, as Sebastian cried out in agony. It was hard to say how long it lasted – a minute, perhaps, or maybe even less – but by the end of it, none of them could speak.

James grabbed his sister's arm and pulled her to her feet. Sebastian wasn't so lucky. He couldn't just stand back up again. He was too bruised and broken for that. His eyes held loosely onto Tilly, as if he was waiting for her to come to him and say the same sweet things she'd been saying all evening.

But Tilly wasn't the kind of girl to make trouble. She allowed herself to be half led, half dragged down the hill, and it fell to Dodo to come to the aid of her savaged love. The ethereal girl sped from the trees to kneel by Sebastian's side, just as the others disappeared into the forest.

It would take a long time to get him home. For the first twenty minutes, he could barely breathe, let alone talk. Dodo had seen every-thing, and she couldn't be angry with Sebastian after what James Heaton had done. So, when he was ready to stand up, she put her arm under his and helped him walk.

Dodo was light and wiry, she wasn't built for carrying a near-grown man down a hillside, but she found the strength that she needed. Step by step and ever so slowly, they made it back to the mill house at the bottom of the valley, where Sebastian lived with his parents. He wouldn't let her come inside, and so she left him on the doorstep and watched from the distance as, still clutching his ribs, he passed through the door.

He didn't appear in the village for the rest of the holiday. No one knew how his parents reacted or whether he'd even told them of the fight. It was only when they were back at school that Tilly had a sense of what might happen next. He wouldn't look at her – that was the hardest part. She tried to catch his gaze in class, but he wouldn't look back.

It was later that afternoon that Sebastian's father came to speak to Mrs Abbot. They talked in whispers outside the door, but it was obvious why he was there. The teacher returned to the class and made a short announcement that, to anyone who hadn't been on the hillside the previous Friday night, would have seemed quite insignificant.

"James, Tilly and Sebastian, you'll have to stay behind after school today." That was all their teacher said, and the majority of her students thought nothing of it. Well, there were a few whistles and calls from the little ones at the front of the class who assumed their much older classmates were in trouble, but that happened whenever such an announcement was made, and Mrs Abbot was quick to restore calm.

At the end of the day, all but three students filed out to make the most of the warm spring afternoon. Some of them would go pond dipping or try to catch frogs in the boggy marsh behind the Duke's

Head, some would studiously complete their homework before having any fun, and some of the naughtier pupils, who really should have known better, would find a quiet spot in the forest and smoke a packet of cigarettes that Martin Darby had stolen from his father's coat pocket.

When the others had all left, James, Tilly and Sebastian remained in their seats as first Sebastian's father then James and Tilly's arrived to stand next to Mrs Abbot. Tom Heaton was a big man who walked with an instantly apparent sense of his own importance. Tom wasn't afraid of anyone, but his children were. Just the sight of him there sent waves of fear through the room. Most people in Hurtwood had experienced that before, but now Sebastian felt it, too. Tilly watched as Sebastian made himself smaller, sinking down into his seat so that he could barely see above the level of the desk.

"Children, your fathers have come here to discuss a sensitive matter," Mrs Abbot began, with none of her usual fire. It was almost as if she felt sorry for them.

Mr Kane took over then. He'd only been living in the village for a short time and the other children had never heard him talk before.

"This boy attacked my Sebastian. He's lucky his ribs weren't broken." With his tentative manner, he really wasn't the man to take on Tom Heaton. "I want to know what you're going to do about it." The words were suitably confrontational, but he had a soft, almost squeaky voice, and his opposite number just laughed.

"That's not how I heard it." Tom Heaton never stayed still. He swayed from one side to the other at all moments, like an animal waiting to pounce, or a boxer in the ring hoping to land the first punch. "James told me about it as soon as he come home. He says that your boy was asking for a beating."

Mr Kane looked just like his son as he pushed his glasses up his nose. "No one asks for a beating."

"Oh, yeah?" Heaton seemed to grow taller as the meeting continued. "I'd say you're asking for one right now if you keep talking to me like that."

The only person in Hurtwood who was braver than Tom and Granville Heaton was Mrs Marjorie Abbot, and even she looked apprehensive as she stepped between the two men to take control of the situation.

"Very well, gentlemen. We're not going to get anywhere by arguing, so why don't we ask the children what really happened?"

Still dancing and shuffling about, Heaton retreated to his corner, evidently celebrating a points victory for the first round.

Mrs Abbot waited until he had settled before speaking again. "James, would you like to tell us why you hurt Sebastian?"

James attempted to adopt his father's infinitely confident expression, but it just made him look like the little boy that he was inside. "I hit him because he's a reprobate and it's what he deserved."

"How dare you speak that way about my son." Mr Kane stepped forward again, but the teacher was quicker and stepped straight in front of him.

"If he's such a good boy, ask him what he was doing with my sister." James knew that words could be as dangerous as any weapon. He chose each one to do the most possible damage.

"What exactly are you suggesting?" Mrs Abbot's voice faltered a touch as though she wasn't sure she wished to know the answer.

James was cockier now. He could see that he had the loudest voice, and that Sebastian and Tilly weren't going to stand up to him. He could say whatever he liked, and he knew he would get away with it because his father was there, and everyone was afraid of Tom Heaton.

"I'm suggesting that he got her alone at the top of Homestead Hill and touched her in a way that gentlemen should not touch young girls like Tilly." He added a touch of innocence just to sell the act. "I realised that it was late and that my sister hadn't come home, so I went up there looking for her. I saw the whole thing with my own eyes. She told him to stop, and he wouldn't."

Tilly couldn't watch anymore. She turned to Sebastian instead and at least the tears that came to his eyes were real. He wasn't like her, and she should never have gone anywhere near him. Heatons didn't deserve to be in the same universe as good people like him, and she wanted to tell him how sorry she was, but she no longer had a voice.

"Tilly?" Mrs Abbot's tone changed within a single word. "We need to know what really happened. Is your brother telling the truth?"

She looked at her father and knew there was only one answer. A lie could save her, but the truth would only make things worse. The one sacrifice she made was that she looked at Sebastian as she confirmed the story. She deserved that pain. It was not enough of a punishment, but she would remember it for the rest of her life and, just like Sebastian, she would never forgive herself.

With a nod of the head, it was done.

"It's your kid who needs punishing, Kane," Tom Heaton yelled as soon as the result was announced. "It's despicable the way boys like him behave. You'd better give him a hiding, or someone else will."

He escorted his son outside with a victorious grin on his face. He was clearly proud of James for giving the little runt the thrashing he deserved. He paid no attention to Tilly. He didn't see the sadness on her face or even particularly care what had happened to her. He'd done what he set out to achieve, and to a man like Tom Heaton, nothing else mattered.

Sebastian and his family remained in Hurtwood, but he didn't see the other children from his class outside of school anymore, and he didn't talk to Tilly or even Dodo as he previously had. A few weeks later, he got the letter from the army telling him that he would go for training at Aldershot. By the end of the year, he was sent to the front line, and no one saw him again.

His time in Hurtwood Village was short but dramatic and the events of that spring would be felt for a decade after. The only other contact that anyone had with Sebastian Kane was in the month his death was reported at the Battle of the Lys. It was in the April of 1918 when two letters passed through the post office in the village. One was for Dodo, apologising for everything that had gone wrong, and the other was to the girl Sebastian had kissed.

Tilly's letter was only five words long. It was written in thick black capital letters on an otherwise plain white piece of paper, and it confirmed to her just what she feared. Sebastian blamed her for everything.

TWENTY-EIGHT

Lovebrook, Bella and I read the long document in front of the Duke's Head pub, which had been taken over by the police as a place to take refreshments and rest. Men from Scotland Yard had recently turned up and, as a junior inspector, Lovebrook was now required to report to them. Of course, we didn't tell anyone what we were reading until we'd finished it. We sat three to the bench, and Bella was in the middle holding the twenty-page pamphlet. She'd always been a faster reader than I was, and I had to keep asking her to wait before turning the page. She must have been anxious to get to the end, and she wasn't the only one.

When it was over, we looked at one another, uncertain what to say. The inspector was apparently shaken by what he'd read, so you can imagine what it had done to us. We'd found a parallel history to the one we'd lived that year. The only part of it I remembered was falling in love with Bella. I could still almost feel that thrilling intoxication, which explains why all the other details went ignored.

"The good news is that Tilly will be the last victim," I said, staring at the heavy type on the pages in Bella's hands.

"We can trace the typewriter," Lovebrook replied. "If we're lucky, there'll be something distinctive about the way it jams on certain letters or is fainter on others."

"There's no need," I told him. "I know who wrote it."

I stood up from the bench to move a little. I needed to stretch my legs and think about that long-past spring and how the events of 1917 related to the present day. The one thing of which I was certain was who had killed James and Tilly, but the rest was still hazy and poorly defined. I couldn't quite believe that any of it was possible, but there was only one solution that made sense.

"We have to find Dodo," Bella said before I could, and the three of us left the pub to walk up the road one last time. The post office was closed on a Sunday, but the side door to the part of the building where the Lyle family lived was standing open.

"Where's Dorothy?" I asked her mother, who was hovering in the shadows, as though she'd been waiting for us to arrive.

"She went up to the library at Hurtwood House." She'd been crying again since I'd left her, as even in the dark kitchen, I could see her bloodshot eyes. "She said she couldn't stand to be down here doing nothing after what she'd seen."

"Thank you, Mrs Lyle," Bella replied, as she is infinitely more polite than I am.

I nodded to Dodo's mother and stepped back outside so as not to be overheard. "Lovebrook, you must find her immediately. Send men up to Bella's house and have someone search the wood, too. She may not have told her mother the truth when she left the house."

"Of course. I'll do it at once." He ran to the largest concentration of officers on the opposite side of the road and spoke to one of his superiors who issued instructions to the men.

I was about to walk away when I realised that we were missing one final ingredient. "There's something we have to do." Poor Bella didn't know which way to turn but followed me across the road to speak to Lovebrook. "Inspector, do I have your permission to look around the dead woman's bedroom?"

"I suppose so. If you don't mind my observing you. And it would be nice if you could fill me in on what you've worked out. I've guessed some of it from the story we read, but I'm sure there are plenty of gaps in my knowledge."

"I will tell you just as soon as we've examined Tilly Heaton's bedroom. Do we have a deal?"

"That sounds fair." He looked serious for a moment, and I realised how glad I was to have him on our side. "There's something I have to tell you, too, Marius. Scotland Yard has received word from various officers who went to number one, High Street, in towns and cities around the country. The occupants reported receiving a letter from Lady Isabella Montague, each of which included a sealed envelope that they subsequently posted. From the dates that they arrived, it's clear the killer staggered the letters and sent them in batches two days apart."

Bella's response was the spoken equivalent of a shrug of the shoulders. "But that's just as we suspected."

Lovebrook had more to say. "From what I've heard, each letter was the same as the one that the old man we visited in Wellingborough showed us. However, a lady in Swansea kept the envelope in which it came." He paused then, as though hoping to impress us. "It was sent from right here in Hurtwood."

"Which only confirms our beliefs," she replied. "It doesn't shed any light on why the killer went to such trouble."

"Actually, it might," I mumbled and was about to explain a new theory when I remembered a more pressing task. "Though that will have to wait."

I motioned for Lovebrook to go ahead, so that he could wave us past the police officers who were still scouring Tilly's house for clues. We stopped to take our shoes off at the door and don thin cotton gloves. It turns out that interfering with the scene of the crime is something that the police worry about these days. Bella had blue leather boots on to match her navy skirt and jacket. They had laces from the ankle to the calf and it took her an age to loosen them, but then we were free to enter. I must admit that I was eager to find out whether my prediction would turn out to be true and raced up that grand staircase in the entrance hall as fast as my legs would motor.

Tilly's bedroom was where it had been when we were children, and just above her immense, puffy bed was a bookshelf with any number of romantic novels and very little else. Her diaries would have been her biggest secret when she was younger, so I had no doubt that she would have kept them carefully hidden.

The others watched me as I gazed about the rather simple room. There was very little furniture beyond a chest of drawers and the bed itself, and there was nothing in, under or behind any of them.

"Marius," Bella began, "if you told us why you've brought us here, perhaps we could help you."

I didn't answer because I was trying to imagine where an adolescent girl would have hidden her prize possessions. The entire floor was covered in a thick white carpet and there was a brown bearskin rug on top of it. I whipped it away, but that didn't help, and so I looked through a large chest beside the window while Lovebrook speculatively poked around under the bed. I really should have told them what I was doing, but I had one more idea and checked the corners of the room. Walking over to a spot diagonally opposite the door, I noticed that the edges of the carpet looked a little frayed and there was a small space in front of the wall where Tilly could have pushed her fingers through to get to the floorboards.

I pulled back the carpet, and Bella pointed out my stupidity. "Oh, her diaries." She was distinctly unimpressed by my find. "Why didn't you tell me what you wanted? I knew exactly where she kept them."

"My apologies. It's hard for writers not to get carried away with the dramatic voice in our heads. The narration of our heroic adventures can be very entertaining, but it means that I don't always pay enough attention to real life." With this confession made, I turned back to discover that there was a large piece of floorboard that could be lifted away. In between the joists, there was a line of approximately twenty diaries dating back to 1908. Well, there weren't quite twenty, as I was fairly sure that one was missing.

"Still, it was clever of you to think of them," Lovebrook said with his usual good cheer.

"Tilly told us yesterday that she'd been writing a diary for years. I have no memory of her doing so when we were children, but then I was never her confidante."

"Yes, but I was," Bella conceded, "and it didn't enter my mind that they would be of any value. She was ever so proud of her diaries when we were younger, but we were sworn to secrecy if we wished to see them. Whenever we came to the house, Tilly would read out excerpts as if they were quotes from a newspaper column. I'm sure she never told me about Sebastian, though. She really must have been ashamed of what she did."

I ran my gloved finger along the spines of the books to determine which one was missing. To no one's amazement, there was a space between 1916 and 1918.

"Guv?" a voice called up from downstairs and we could hear the clumping feet of a fellow officer who soon appeared in the doorway. "Sergeant Rossiter just received a call from Hurtwood House. They've found Dorothy Lyle."

TWENTY-NINE

I explained the few elements that Lovebrook hadn't been able to work out for himself, and then he drove to join his officers up at the only real manor in Hurtwood. As Bella and I walked down to Lucinda's house to break the news, all the regular characters from the village were standing on their doorsteps. It was the most excitement the place had seen since the end of the war, and even my family had come to the crossroads to discover what was happening.

I must confess that the closer I got to the giant cottage the Heatons had squeezed into that small plot of land in the centre of the village, the heavier my legs became. We'd witnessed so much unnecessary suffering, but it was finally over.

There was a constable on duty in Lucinda's front garden. I explained why we'd come, and he stood aside to let Bella ring the bell. It's hard to know whether my heart or head stung more as we waited for the door to open, but I certainly wasn't at my best.

Richard opened the door and looked at us without saying anything.

"We've got news for Cinders," I told him. Bella should probably have said this, but it had all got too much for her. With little doubt left over what had really happened, I could tell that she was trying her hardest not to cry, and I wondered how long she would manage it.

"Lucinda," I said in my softest voice when we followed Richard into the living room, to find her curled up in the armchair. "Everything's all right now. You're safe."

It would be a little while before I could explain what had happened. Lucinda naturally burst into tears, and Richard went to comfort her. Bella stood there looking competent, and so I decided it would be a good idea to make tea – seeing as that was my main role in the investigation. By the time it was brewed, and I'd assembled the necessary paraphernalia on a tray, everyone was in place in the living room. For some reason, my dog Percy had popped by to sit on Lucinda's lap, too, or perhaps he'd stayed overnight to play guard dog and no one had informed me.

"I can't promise this will be easy to hear," I told them once I'd handed out steaming cups of tea. "I'm struggling to make sense of it myself but every scrap of evidence we've found this weekend points to the fact that Dodo killed your cousins."

"It can't be," Richard replied, and I could see that it was just as difficult for him to comprehend as it was for Bella and me.

"It all comes back to Sebastian Kane," Bella explained. She was tougher than I realised and had fought off her sorrow to assist with our sad task. "That was the name of the boy who lived here for a few months before he and Marius were called up."

"Yes, Lucinda's been telling me about him." Richard paused then and looked at the distraught young woman in the chair next to him. Perhaps he felt he wasn't the one who should be talking, but Lucinda still wouldn't look at us. She stroked Percy over and over and, in time, I continued.

"It seems that Dodo was in love with Sebastian, and Tilly

stole his affection away." Now that the time had come to detail the evidence against her, I didn't know where to start. Everything that had happened since I'd arrived back in my home town had been layered in complexity. Every clue we'd discovered had been disguised as something else and, though I knew why she had to be the killer, it was hard to put it into words.

"Tilly and Sebastian kissed one night on Homestead Hill. James found them together and beat the daylights out of the poor boy. When their parents heard about it, James and Tilly denied the whole story and Sebastian went off to war hating them. He wrote a letter from the front line blaming Tilly for what had happened. Dodo received a letter, too, and she evidently took it upon herself to exact revenge on his behalf."

This simple summary left even Richard speechless, and I was surprised when Lucinda finally looked up from my dog to ask a question. "How do you know any of this? I barely remember what happened, though I'm sure Tilly told me at some point."

Bella put her hand on my arm to communicate that, for the moment, she would talk. I didn't mind one bit.

"There was a document tied to the war memorial where Sebastian's name is inscribed. Tilly believed that Sebastian was the one who sent the letters and killed James, but he really was killed in the war. Dodo must have been driven insane with hate and jealousy. She clearly blamed your whole family for what happened, though it's hard to say whether she would have gone on to kill you too, Cinders."

Richard looked as though he was trying to solve a brain-teasingly complex calculation and would say nothing for some time.

"What did the document say?" Lucinda shifted her legs beneath her, and Percy had to get comfortable again. "Did Sebastian write it?"

"No, no," I replied. "It was written recently. There are references to the fact that a decade has passed since the events it describes. It only makes sense that Dodo wrote it. After all, who else from our school had such a way with a pen?" I realised that the answer to this question was *Marius Quin*, so I kept talking. "The thing is, there was a lot in the story that Dodo couldn't have known. There are whole sections that seem to have been written from Tilly's perspective, and that told me something important."

When she wasn't talking, Bella watched me in her usual thoughtful manner, but I could tell when she wanted to say something, and so I stopped for her to take over once more.

"You remember Tilly's diaries, don't you, Cinders? You remember how she used to read them to us whenever she had a deep, dark secret to share."

Lucinda's mouth turned up in a smile then, but it did nothing to hide her sadness. "She was so proud of them. I always thought it was rather sweet."

"Well, Dodo must have known about them, too. She stayed at Heaton Manor last night and made it look as though someone had broken in to slash Tilly's throat. It didn't make any sense that your cousin was found in the kitchen, unless of course her companion had convinced her to go downstairs."

Bella paused to let another wave of emotion wash over her, but each time she spoke, she was perfectly composed once more. "With Tilly dead, Dodo used the diary from 1917 to write the account of Sebastian's time in the village. She filled in the gaps in the story that she didn't know, and then sneaked through the forest to hang it on the war memorial when Sergeant Rossiter wasn't looking. It won't be long before the police find the abandoned diary, and I imagine the typewritten pages will match whatever machine is in Tilly's house. Dodo even went so far as to throw the murder weapon over the garden fence so as to suggest the killer had fled the scene."

"It wasn't enough, though," I added. "She must have known that the police would see through her ruse. At the very least, the paper upon which the letters were written was taken from Hurtwood House. It would have been easy for her to take it thanks to her job in the library there."

"But... the letters we received didn't have any marks on them except the text," Lucinda corrected me, and she didn't need to form a question for me to provide an answer.

"I wasn't referring to the ones that came to you. I mean the ones she sent to seemingly random addresses across the country. It was an unnecessarily complicated plot but, essentially, she sent letters to complete strangers asking them to forward sealed envelopes to the three of you in exchange for a small remuneration. It first seemed this was to hide the fact that the letters had been sent from here in Hurtwood, but another possibility occurred to me this morning."

"Oh, yes?" Bella had apparently got caught up in my explanation and forgotten that we were not the ones who were supposed to ask questions.

"I wondered whether that whole scheme had been put in place as, once the first letters arrived, Dodo would be unable to send more without her movements being observed. By sending the letters out and asking other people to return them, they would continue to appear through your letter boxes after the police had been alerted and our investigation had begun."

Bella had a clarification to make. "Of course, we considered the possibility that Dodo was to blame when we learnt about the headed paper, but we should have given it more thought. She always seemed so good. Who would have thought that our dear, kind friend was capable of such a thing?"

Richard suddenly sat upright in his chair as though he was finally aware of the conversation. "Was capable?" He stared at us for a few seconds before explaining himself. "You said that she 'was capable'. In fact, you've been using past tenses and conditionals about Dodo ever since you arrived."

My companion and I exchanged a melancholy glance, and I

tried to answer. "That's because Dodo..." I can't tell you how hard it was for me to speak even these few meaningless words.

Thankfully, the wonderful person beside me on the sofa decided to share the load. "The police just received a call from my father. Dodo was found dead in the library this morning. We think she must have killed herself."

THIRTY

New tears formed in Lucinda's eyes, and it would have been easy to conclude that they were in honour of her cousins who had died, but I believe there was another reason. I believe it was relief that made her cry – relief that the fear with which she'd been living since the first letter arrived could finally now end.

"When I read the story of Sebastian this morning," I began when the time was right, "I knew there was something wrong about it. It gave too much away about the killer's thinking, but when the police located Dodo, it suddenly made sense. The document wasn't written to strike fear into us or confuse the police. It was a suicide note. Dodo knew that there was no escaping what she'd done, she just wanted people to understand why she'd done it."

Lucinda breathed in very slowly and held the air in her lungs for a few moments. "It's hardly a surprise that people hate my family, and I always had the sense that Dodo didn't like me. I just wish that James and Tilly hadn't had to die for that petty little girl to live out her despicable fantasy."

Percy attempted to roll on his back then for his admirer to stroke his tummy, but the trick didn't quite go to plan. He fell off her lap and onto the floor then hurried away irritably as if it was all her fault. I couldn't help but be amused by the funny creature. He was oblivious to the sad topic we were discussing, and as he went to sit in a patch of sunshine in front of the window, I was a little envious of his innocence.

"Whatever James and Tilly did to Sebastian," Lucinda continued, "they didn't deserve to die for it." She shook her head and looked over to the man she'd almost married.

"The poems!" he suddenly barked, which drew a curious look from Percy. "The anonymous poems that were sent to my house; Dodo must have written them. It's the only thing that makes sense."

"Is it?" I said, as I wasn't going to lie to help his cause. "If she was in love with Sebastian, why would she have written to you?"

"Because she hated the Heatons, just as you said. She killed James and Tilly and would have done the same to Lucinda. She sent those poems to drive us apart, knowing how much it would upset my dear fiancée." He went over and knelt before her. "Do you believe me now, darling? Do you see that I was telling the truth?"

She wasn't ready to be happy and could only look down at him through those teary brown eyes. "Of course I do. I should never have doubted you in the first place."

He leant forward to kiss her hands, though, personally, I wasn't convinced by his story and had to wonder whether he was using the tragedy for his own ends. As this happy reunion played out before us, Bella and I waited for the pair of them to come back to us.

"There's only one thing I don't understand," I finally said when the tender embrace had continued for just a little too long.

"What's that?" Richard turned away from his (perhaps) fiancée to look at us.

"When I spoke to Dodo this morning, after we knew that Tilly had been murdered, she said that she heard Tilly going up and downstairs talking to herself as she went. But Dodo was the killer, so why would she have mentioned it?"

The four of us took a moment to consider this odd detail, but Percy was the only one to produce a response. And, no, his yawn did not offer any great revelation on the intricacies of the case.

"If anything," I continued, "Dodo's comment drew my attention to the fact that she'd gone up to Tilly's bedroom to retrieve the diary."

Bella looked a little puzzled but soon offered an explanation. "Yes, but the whole case was unnecessarily complicated. The letters, the document, the poems: it's all the product of a terribly confused mind. It's just tragic."

This was something on which we could all agree. We sat sipping our tea, and I looked out of the window to where Sergeant Rossiter was marching back and forth in front of Lucinda's property. He looked just as angry and unnerved as ever. In fact, he looked quite wild.

"But what if someone else had done it?" I asked when I couldn't hold it in anymore, and, in reply, Richard groaned. "Now listen, for just one moment. What if someone had made it look as though Dodo was to blame? The killer could have crept through the woods to Heaton Manor, carefully broken the window with a cloth around his hand and gone upstairs to threaten Tilly. Perhaps what Dodo heard wasn't the victim talking to herself, but the killer forcing his victim to go downstairs. Once he'd killed her silently in the kitchen, he went up to get the diary and then fled through the woods, dropping the knife on the way."

Lucinda returned to her almost foetal position on her chair, and I supposed I shouldn't have forced her to listen to such speculation.

"I really don't think this is necessary," Richard intervened on her behalf. "You said it yourself; all the evidence points to Dodo."

I really didn't want to be a bore and keep on so but, as Bella didn't stop me, I did just that. "Yes, but there are always gaps in criminal cases. Reading back through old police files, there are usually tiny mysteries that can't be explained – like the diary, for example."

"What about the diary?" my companion asked as if this was a joke we'd rehearsed.

"Well, if Dodo took the diary to be able to complete the document that we found this morning, does that mean she stayed up last night to write it?"

Richard touched his rumpled hair ever so gently, as if he was checking it was still on his head. "That would make sense, wouldn't it?"

Rossiter looked increasingly agitated out on the pavement, and so I went over to the window to watch him as I continued to list the minor discrepancies I'd found. "Dodo killed Tilly between two and four o'clock by the inspector's reckoning."

"Your point being?" Bella sounded both interested and sceptical.

"Well, it would have left her a lot to do. She had to find the diary, and then search out a typewriter in a house that wasn't her own. She had to read through whatever Tilly had written about Sebastian and thread together a narrative that she could then creep through the forest to leave on the war memorial. Obviously before sunrise at, say, half past five to avoid being seen. I'm a fairly swift writer when I put my mind to it, and I'm not sure I'd have been able to do all that in such a short stretch."

Even Lucinda looked curious now, and Percy rolled on his back in case this was the moment I would bend down to tickle his tummy. To his disappointment, it was not.

"You're right, that's not a lot of time." Bella had that eager look in her eyes, and I knew that she was thinking much the same as I was.

"That is a little odd," Lucinda confirmed, and the four of us had another brief round of cogitation to see whether we could explain away this new doubt.

Unfortunately, I landed upon even more questions. "It would also require Dodo to know that Tilly had a typewriter for her plan to work." The sergeant had stopped his nervous pacing, and so I returned to the others to continue the conversation. "Do you know whether Tilly had one in her house, Cinders?"

Her cousin took a moment to consider the point. "There must have been one there when I was growing up. Tilly had little use for it, though, so I haven't seen it in some time."

It was all very puzzling, but I shrugged my shoulders and accepted defeat. "I suppose there's no sense speculating. The police will uncover everything they need to know. The important thing is that the killer has been stopped."

This brought a degree of harmony to the room again, but there was still more to say, and I'm afraid I couldn't resist. "The other thing, of course, is that the document clearly pointed to Dodo as the killer, and yet, when we spoke to her this morning, she denied all responsibility."

"Your point being?" Bella asked once more, and her eye was twitching for some reason.

"That she must have known, as soon as she left her terrible manifesto on the war memorial, that there was no going back. She might just as well have admitted what she'd done, but that's not what happened. In fact, she was remarkably convincing. I spoke to her myself, and I would never have imagined that the emotion she showed was part of an act."

"When it came to it, she must have got scared." Richard rubbed his sweetheart's hand, over and over in tiny circles with the tip of his thumb. "It's all well and good thinking you can face up to the trial and likely execution for your crimes, but then you see the police and your nerves take over and you realise that you'd rather kill yourself in a nice quiet library than live through all that."

"Oh, you're probably right." I took another sip of tea only to discover that there was none left. "Cinders, do you have a typewriter?"

The girl that everyone loved had looked lost and broken ever since her second cousin's death, but something changed when I asked this. There was a sharpness about the eyes that hadn't been there before. She was suddenly more focused and aware.

"I don't... Well, my father may have had one about the house at some point, but I believe I threw it away not so very long ago."

"Yes, I believe you probably did." I paused for just a moment to enjoy the volte-face. "I also believe you will inherit every penny of the Heaton fortune now that your cousins are dead."

Still sitting on the floor in front of Lucinda, Richard looked confused but waited for her to reply.

"Marius, why are you being so cruel?" Her normally melodious voice was higher than normal and sounded quite shrill. "You're looking for holes in the case when there are none to find. Dodo must be to blame. That's why she killed herself."

I heard voices in the garden outside, but I was quite comfortable on the sofa and stayed where I was. "As Tilly's closest confidante, you were one of the few people who knew what happened between your cousin and Sebastian. You were quite possibly the only person she told about the letter that he wrote before he died."

I needed to stop and breathe, but I had too much to say, and the words streamed out of me. "When you'd called off your engagement and were at your lowest ebb, you hatched a plan to get what you felt you deserved. You sent poison-pen letters not just to your cousins but yourself, too, so that no one would suspect you. You created a story that would point to Dodo because you blamed her for sending poems to Richard, though it might just as well have been any of the women he's spent his life charming."

She shot to her feet, even as I continued to enjoy that really very comfortable sofa.

"No, it was Dodo. That's why she killed herself. She couldn't live with the guilt."

My timing was off by approximately five seconds. You can't have everything in life, but it was a bit of a disappointment that, instead of the door swinging open at the very moment I'd planned, I had to fill the silence.

"That's where you're wrong, Cinders." I looked at Bella in case she wanted to say it, but then we heard footsteps, and the door to the sitting room finally opened to reveal my good friend Dorothy Lyle peering in from the hallway.

THIRTY-ONE

The two women stared at each other – the killer and her potential victim. And, while I admit that there'd been a few moments when I was unsure which of them was which, there was no longer any doubt in my mind.

Percy was still sitting in front of the bay window, but the sun had gone behind a cloud, and he looked quite confused as to why everyone was suddenly shouting.

"It's all wrong." Lucinda was desperately shaking her head as she stared down at the floor. "You've got this round the wrong way. Dodo is the killer. She wrote the letters on headed notepaper that she took from Hurtwood House. How would I have managed that?"

We all looked at Dodo, and I felt a little sorry that she was forced to defend herself... oh, and that Bella and I had pretended she was dead to kill time until Lovebrook came back.

"The paper..." she began, before her tiny voice faded, and it was hard to imagine that she would find it again. "I did take the paper from the library. I took it to the school when they didn't have enough for the projects they were doing. But I asked the Duchess, and she said it would be all right."

I got to my feet to answer her. "That will be the school where you volunteer three times a week, isn't that right, Cinders?" I promise I didn't sound too smug saying this. A little smug, perhaps, but not excessively so.

Lucinda was more nervous with every word that we spoke. "But she was in love with Sebastian. She blamed James and Tilly for what happened. I had nothing to do—"

Dodo had found her confidence and stepped into the room with the inspector just behind her. "I never knew what happened to Sebastian. We were friends one week, and he stopped speaking to anyone the next. I thought I'd done something to hurt him. I would have never imagined that Tilly even knew his name. In fact, I had no idea that anything happened between them until Inspector Lovebrook just explained."

The killer – the real killer – looked from one to the next of us before her eyes settled on the only person there she had any hope of convincing.

"Richard, they're lying. You must believe me."

Richard Fairbanks had never been the most assertive man and clearly didn't know what to think, so I kept the accusations flying to help him make up his mind. "The sole purpose of the document we found was to implicate Dodo. In many ways, it stuck to the truth that Tilly revealed to us but added key details to explain why Lucinda's chosen scapegoat would have exacted her revenge upon your family. What it didn't do was provide a good enough reason for her to target you at the same time as your cousins, and that was when I felt certain that the letters were fakes. There was so much history that passed between our circle of friends, and just as Bella predicted at dinner last night, the murders were bound to come down to love or money." I turned back to the culprit who was crying now for a completely different reason. "With you, Lucinda, it's clear which won out."

She marched over to the window to put some space between herself and the policeman lurking in the doorway. She moved so suddenly that Percy got scared and scampered away from her to hide behind the sofa.

"This is insanity. I wouldn't kill my own cousins for money. I had a perfectly comfortable life without resorting to such savagery."

"You had a perfectly comfortable prison." The thought of her two victims rose to the surface, and I showed my anger for the first time. "You told me that you couldn't leave Hurtwood because James and Tilly had all the money. You only had your house and a small allowance. When your engagement came to an end, you plotted all of this just to get your hands on the family inheritance."

I'd finally touched a nerve, and she snapped back at me despite herself. "My father worked just as hard for that money as his brother. Uncle Tom got everything but this hideous house just because he was the oldest. It was completely unjust." She must have realised how this sounded, as she quickly tacked on an addendum. "But that doesn't make me a killer."

It was Bella's turn to show her up, and I was tempted to sit back down on that nice comfortable sofa. I should probably remind you that, while soft yet supportive for sitting, it was not suitable if you needed somewhere to spend the night.

"There were too many contradictions, Cinders." She took a few steps closer to make her point. "If you wanted to make us believe that your chosen culprit was to blame, you shouldn't have made everything so complicated – starting with the letters. Dodo Lyle is the daughter of the postmistress. She wouldn't have needed to make up addresses around the country and hope that they actually existed. Her family own various directories which she could have consulted to find suitable options."

"And Dodo was never in love with Sebastian," I added, to knock a few more nails in the killer's well-deserved coffin. "She was one of my closest friends when we were seventeen and, unless she has a talent for acting that she's never revealed, she only ever had eyes for Richard."

There was one person in the room who didn't frown at this, and that was Richard himself. He couldn't help looking flattered, even now.

Lucinda's breathing had become loud and laboured and she stared down her line of accusers. "Is that all you've got to say?"

"No!" Bella and I replied as one, before she motioned for me to speak. "There are any number of mistakes you made because, despite what everyone had always said about you, you're not perfect after all. You're not the world's best murderer and you're a quite dreadful writer." If you know me at all, you'll know how deep an insult this is. "The version of Sebastian's story that you wrote sounded as if it had been lifted out of a sensational newspaper or a child's notebook. As someone who has read my friend's writing in the past, I don't hesitate to say that she would have done a lot better job than you."

"Anything else?" Lovebrook checked.

I looked at Bella, and it was clear she had a few more observations of her own. "You threw glass around at Tilly's house to make it look as though the killer had broken the window from the inside, but Dodo would have been clever enough to open the door and smash the window from the outside if she was trying to distance herself from the crime. Oh, and you placed the murder weapon in the garden of Tilly's neighbour, when there was absolutely no reason for Dodo to move it from the kitchen."

If you ever have the chance to make a killer feel bad about themselves, I highly recommend taking the opportunity to do just that. I certainly did. "You stabbed one of your cousins through the heart and slit the other's throat. I always thought that there was something not quite right with you, Lucinda."

Those beautiful eyes of hers flashed once more. "You're saying all this because you're obsessed with me." Even as Lovebrook called the sergeant in to arrest her, she turned to shriek at Bella. "You might not realise it, m'lady, but even as he was kissing you, he was thinking of me." It was a fairly desperate ploy and not likely to persuade a jury of her innocence.

Bella was just as unmoved. "You can't stop lying, can you? But it will do you no good. Tilly only ever talked about her diaries with you and me. They were her best kept secret, and I certainly didn't kill anyone." She pushed back her shoulders and spoke with all the strength she'd been brought up to exude. "Everyone loves Lucinda, but it's just like Marius said. There's always been something not quite right about you."

"How dare you speak of me as if I'm—"

"You're under arrest." Sergeant Rossiter looked happier than he had all weekend as he clapped the handcuffs around her wrists. "Stop shouting and struggling, or I will be only too happy to tighten your shackles before we throw you in a police van." I thought he might pull his prisoner away, but he stood there long enough for me to say one last thing to her.

"I think I finally know what it is that's wrong with you, Cinders." I clicked my fingers as the realisation came to me. "You're a Heaton of the very worst kind."

THIRTY-TWO

When the prisoner had been escorted to somewhere less comfortable, the Duchess summoned Bella and me to take tea in the immense day room overlooking the forest in Hurtwood House.

I've never been clear on the purpose of a day room – other than it being a room in which one spends time during the day. I assume it was christened as such because there were so many salons, lounges and parlours in the building that they had run out of names.

In this case, the room was long and bright, with paintings all over one wall and windows all over the other. It was not as ancient in appearance as much of the house and featured functional furniture and low tables. This impression of relative simplicity was undermined by the heavily patterned Shiraz rug that ran the length of the room and the stuffed brown bear in one corner that, according to family legend, had once been a pet of the Duke's grandfather.

"I hear that you've done something rather impressive," Bella's ever-regal mother declared once we were sitting down with yet more tea. What I really needed by this point was a WC, but I wasn't about to tell the Duchess that.

I planned to say something humble, giving the bulk of the credit to my two fellow sleuths, when I heard a voice in the doorway behind us and we turned to see the new arrivals.

"A party and no one thought to invite me? Tut tut." The Duke was rolled into the room by one of the footmen. And when I say *rolled*, I mean he was pushed towards us in a wheelchair, not lying on his side on the floor.

"It is so nice to see you out of your room, Father," Bella told the dear man as Pullman the butler poured an extra cup of tea for him. "It will certainly be nice to play cards with you down here rather than up in your hovel."

"Hovel, indeed." He smiled indulgently at his beloved firstborn. "You've badgered me enough over the last few years. I knew I'd have to give in eventually."

"You know, Your Grace," I began, "this really is a celebration."

He looked about the room before answering. "You're right. The wider world is not quite as dreadful as I remembered."

"Although he's too polite to correct you, my darling," the Duchess explained, "I believe that Marius was talking about the murder investigation."

Bella's mother moved to sit in the armchair beside her husband.

"I know, my angel." His booming voice filled the room. "But if you're not careful with people like Marius Quin, they will develop unimaginably large egos. You should know that better than anyone. After all, you keep me in check."

"I couldn't possibly comment," the Duchess replied. "All I can say is that Marius and Bella have done the most remarkable job of apprehending the killer."

"I heard certain rumours to that effect," the Duke revealed, and it suddenly occurred to me that Sergeant Rossiter himself could have been the source of much of the old man's up-to-the-minute local knowledge.

Bella looked amazed to see her parents interacting so.

The Duchess reached out one hand to touch her daughter's sleeve. "I don't like to think what the village would have been like if that monster had inherited the Heaton estate. James and Tilly were the perfect custodians as they never did anything with it, but that girl is full of ambition. She might well have knocked down every building they owned and built some ghastly blocks of flats."

"I wouldn't have put it past her." Bella's eyebrows knitted together. I could only imagine that she was still coming to terms with the idea that Lucinda Heaton was far from loveable after all.

I was about to drink my tea when the Duchess surprised me once more. "I'm glad you're back, Marius. You certainly showed your worth today. They'll be talking about you in the village for months."

"Thank you, Your Grace. I truly appreciate it." I'd just raised my teacup to my mouth when she spoke again.

"Now, we shouldn't keep you. It's a sunny spring day and young people like you should be off enjoying yourselves."

"Yes, Mother, of course." Bella had a built-in sense of when one was no longer welcome and got to her feet before the Duchess had finished speaking.

I reluctantly put the tea back down and rose to standing. "Indeed, Your Grace. Bella had just suggested a walk in the woods, and it would be unkind to disappoint her."

"Wonderful." The Duke cast a suspicious glance towards his wife as she waited for us to leave.

I couldn't quite tell what had happened. "Goodbye then," I said, in case either of them felt like explaining. They didn't and, once we had left the room, I heard them strike up an intense conversation. I sadly couldn't make out the topic.

"Well, that was... short," I said.

"Don't mind them," Bella whispered as we navigated the maze-like corridors of her home. "What you don't know is that they haven't spoken for several months. Mother thought that refusing to visit him would be enough to get my father to leave his room, but her ploy backfired. He insisted he was enjoying the peace and quiet, but it looks as though you've resolved the stalemate."

"Oh dear," I replied. "Now neither of them will approve of me."

Her eyebrows rose a half inch. "I think it's too late for that." She laughed at me then, and I can't say I minded.

We'd reached the towering wooden doors at the side of the house. They looked as though they had been plundered from some ancient church, which, knowing the history of the Montague family, was fairly plausible.

"I still have some questions for you," Bella said as she hurried a half-step ahead of me towards the Hurtwood. There was a large section of woodland within the bounds of the property, which is where we had spent so much of our youth playing together.

"And in return," I replied, "I hope to give you some answers."

We entered the woods as she began. "I understand the importance of the information Tilly's diary held, but I don't understand why Lucinda decided to steal it last night when she already knew what had happened between her cousin and Sebastian."

"That's a very good question."

She exhaled a happy breath. "I try my best."

"I mean it. That was the thing that took me longest to resolve. I concluded at first that Lucinda had stolen the diary in order to write the document we found. Richard was in her house, though, and might have heard what she was doing if she'd been tapping away on the keys late at night. By writing it in advance, she would have been able to dispose of the typewriter to avoid detection. I finally realised that, although she already had the information she needed to write the fake account, she stole the diary in order to destroy it."

"Oh, of course." She made it sound as though we were both stupid for not realising before... which I suppose we were. "Someone would eventually have found the diary and realised the discrepancies between what Tilly wrote and the document Lucinda had left for us."

It was at this point that we heard a call from behind us. "Marius? Lady Isabella? Wait just a moment, I'd like to have a—"

"Hurry up, Lovebrook," Bella called back to the inspector. "Marius is filling in all the holes in the case."

He was a speedy runner and soon caught up with us. "Have you asked about the diary?" he put to Bella as though they had already discussed this very theme before.

"Yes, she didn't steal it for the information it contained but to make sure it didn't contradict anything she'd included in the document."

"Ahh, of course. It's so obvious when you think about it." He waited politely for a moment, then asked, "And what about the lurker that Postman Ned saw hanging around Lucinda's garden? I felt sure it was Richard Fairbanks and that he'd staged the whole thing to take revenge on the woman who had called off their wedding."

"Not even close," I said before realising I could have been gentler. "I mean, it's a very good idea, but not quite—"

It was Bella's turn to impress us both – and save me from my awkward mumbling. "It was Ned himself, wasn't it?"

"I believe it was."

She clapped her hands together in excitement. "He was always mad about Lucinda. I suppose he must have been worried that she'd seen him watching her through the hedge one day. He reported it so that no one would suspect him."

"That's exactly it," I congratulated her. "And when I saw him on Friday night, he had probably gone there to check she was all right after she disappeared from the pub. He was dressed in black for the wake they'd had for James."

Bella sighed with great compassion. "Poor Ned. I'm sure he meant no harm by it. He's certainly been acting peculiarly since we learnt of the letters. I bet he was terrified that he'd be blamed for everything just because he peered lovingly at that viper of a woman through her living room window."

Lovebrook adopted a more solemn tone. "As long as it was just the living room window and nowhere else. The police don't look too kindly on that sort of thing."

He was such an earnest chap, and I really did enjoy his company. I was about to tell him this when he spoke again.

"I have to say, I fell for Lucinda's ploy. When we read the story she wrote, I picked the wrong culprit. I knew about Dorothy Lyle's job here at the library and the letters on the Hurtwood House stationery. When I interviewed her yesterday, she told me that she'd given piles of paper to the school, but after reading the account of Sebastian Kane's time here, I decided that had to be a lie."

"I still don't see why Lucinda conceived of such a complicated plan in the first place." Bella had stopped by an old oak tree with an incredibly broad trunk. "There must have been an easier way to get enough money to start a life away from the village."

"I'm not convinced that murderers think in quite the same manner as ordinary people," the officer reflected. "It takes a certain *folie de grandeur* to believe you can get away with such terrible crimes."

"I'm sure you're right, Inspector," Bella squeezed his shoulder affectionately, and I had a confession to make.

"There's one more thing that I struggled to comprehend." I cast my gaze around the scenery as I spoke. "Lucinda must have slipped out of her house last night to walk through the forest around the village before making her way into her cousin's garden. But it was very risky for someone who had been so careful in her plans until then."

This time, Bella managed to resolve the mystery. "I suppose it's much like her scheme with the letters. Lucinda knew that she would be watched for her own protection. She could either abandon her plans or go through with them and hope that no one saw her."

"That's just it." Lovebrook whistled a long note as he collected his thoughts. "To benefit from killing James, she had to kill his sister, too. She was always going to have to gamble on the second murder. She was just lucky she didn't get caught in the act."

"She didn't stay lucky for long, though," Bella said with a half-smile on her lips.

I like to think that, with the three of us there together, there wasn't much we couldn't solve. Perhaps we should have put our minds to the problem of world hunger or peace for all mankind, but for the moment, a pair of murders in a small village would have to do.

For Lucinda to have killed the last remaining members of her own family was more than shocking. My old friend James had his faults, but he didn't deserve to die so young. And it really did sadden me to think of the way Tilly had died. She was not a bad person considering who her father, uncle and (worst of all) cousin were. The thought that she had blamed herself for Sebastian's mistreatment showed that she had a conscience that many of her relatives lacked.

"Of course, the one question we may never be able to answer," I began after a few moments' silence, "is what pushed her over the edge? I can't imagine that she had been planning this for years, so what drove her to become a murderer?"

"Perhaps it was her separation from Richard," Bella suggested. "She may have been relying on him to take her away from here and then, when he turned out to be as unreliable as she'd always predicted, she couldn't face her life in Hurtwood anymore."

"Or perhaps it was long-standing jealousy towards her cousins. Imagine growing up as part of that famous dynasty and being the only one without any money. James and Tilly had all they could want and did nothing with it, whereas Lucinda had nothing but a gilded cage."

"Yes," I replied. "That could explain it. But it might just as likely have been something entirely petty. Perhaps she was upset by the idea that her garden really wasn't the prettiest in the village and it drove her over the edge."

I thought there was something darkly amusing in this, but Bella didn't agree. "How very sad. To think that two people could die for something so inconsequential."

We might have fallen into a funk then, but Lovebrook interrupted it. "I must say, it has been an honour to work with you both again, but I had better go back to the house." He turned to look over his shoulder with a frown. "I drove back up here because Chief Inspector Darrington is on his way. I just have to hope he's happy that I resolved a case in record time and not angry with me for poking my nose into business he hadn't sanctioned. Wish me luck." He nodded to both of us in turn before running back through the trees.

"Such a lovely man," Bella said in a gentle murmur. "I really must ask his full name sometime."

Now, this did make me laugh. "I keep thinking the same thing. I feel like we're old friends already, but he's still Detective Inspector Lovebrook to us."

"Perhaps he has a terrible name like Archibald or Aloysius!"

"Spartacus," I said, quite out of the blue. "I hope it's Detective Inspector Spartacus Lovebrook."

I thought this might make her titter, but she stood silently before me and peered up at the branches overhead. "Marius, look."

I followed her gaze and realised that we'd come to the tree house we had built together as children. I say *we* built it, but it was mainly the staff from Hurtwood House who did the heavy lifting. They'd done a good job, too. Well, it was still standing twenty years later at least, and I felt the urge to climb up and see what it was like now.

"After you, madam," I said, pointing to the hanging rope ladder.

She looked a little stern then. "Do you want me to go first to make certain that it doesn't break?"

"That's exactly it. You worked out my ploy." I pretended to be upset as I climbed the ladder ahead of her.

It was quite a height, and it surprised me that we'd had the nerve to climb up there when it was first built. I hadn't forgotten the view through the unglazed window at the top, though. You could see right over the trees to the house itself, which looked so picturesque in the sunshine that I had to wonder if the original owner had built it to be viewed from this very angle.

I was so taken by this sight that I didn't yet think of what had once happened there. Ten years had passed since the day I'd left a note for Bella to meet me in our tree house and then spectacularly failed to ask her to marry me – ten years of ups and downs and lots of middles. The flowers I'd bought were still scattered about the wooden floor, but they were little more than dry brown stains on the wood now. And that wasn't the only thing that had changed.

"I'd forgotten how small it is," Bella told me as her head poked through the opening. "I haven't been up here for years."

Silence fell between us as the clouds raced across the sky

and we looked over her estate. If she was thinking of the last time we'd been there together, she didn't show it. That pretty smile remained on her lips, and I tried to think of something to say that wouldn't make me sound dim.

When I couldn't, she spoke instead. "It's been nice having you back here, Marius."

"I'm glad I came." There were more important things we could have said to one another but, for the moment, this would have to do.

We stood in silence, admiring the way the sunbeams cut through the clouds and the whisper of the trees in the Hurtwood. She was not my fiancée, and I was no longer the man she loved, but for perhaps the first time since she'd come back into my life, I realised that it wasn't the worst thing in the world for us to just be friends.

THIRTY-THREE

After I'd been treated to lunch at the manor – well, in the kitchen with half the staff there asking me questions and casting judgement on the culprit – it was time to head home. Not to London just yet, but back to the village, where a few people were waiting to talk to me.

An old friend of mine was sitting on the bench beside the pub where I'd first seen her two days earlier. She got to her feet when she saw me running down the hill. "Marius, with everything that went on earlier, I didn't have time to thank you."

"You don't need to say anything, Dodo. I'm happy I could help. If anyone deserves someone sticking up for her, it's you."

"I don't know about that," she said, turning to glance at the war memorial on the other side of the road. "But I would like to take you up on your offer."

"My offer?"

Her cheeks had already looked flushed when I got there, but they turned quite rosy now. "To read my writing. I had a look through my notebooks and there are some things I thought were acceptable." She hesitated again and ran her fingers along the hem of her dress. "I mean, they might be good. I don't really know, but I have had some ideas for..." She paused to take a deep breath. "...for a novel, actually."

"That's wonderful news. I'm so happy that you're writing again. I'm certain it will be brilliant."

She had a paper folder under her arm which was bulging with handwritten pages. She hesitantly held it out to me, as though she wasn't convinced it was a good idea to share it with anyone.

"I can't wait to read them, Dodo," I told her and, before I could finish the sentence, she threw her arms around me. My trip to Hurtwood started and ended in much the same way.

She pulled away from me and then dashed off before I could say anything else. As I watched her go, it occurred to me that we never knew for certain who sent Richard the poems. I had a momentary suspicion that she'd loved him from afar all those years and expressed herself the only way she knew how. Either that or Richard had a string of admirers. To be honest, I wouldn't have put it past him.

Two people who never tired of expressing themselves were the old gents in front of the pub.

"Here, Marius," Jeb Paignton called. "I hear you solved the case."

"I did what I could."

"I might even get round to reading your book now. I was given it for Christmas," his friend added, and I realised that Bella really had bought a copy of my debut novel for everyone she knew.

"I can promise that it's a great deal better than anything Carmine Fortescue has ever written." I gave them a wink and a wave goodbye and was about to carry on to my old home when I spotted Sergeant Rossiter standing sentry in front of the killer's house.

"Afternoon, Quin," he said with a frown, and I realised that these were the two most civil words he'd ever said to me.

"Afternoon, Sergeant. You did an exceptional job earlier."

He nodded solemnly. "I was just doing what I could to keep the peace."

This was as much as I would get from him as he'd already turned away. Having known the man my whole life, I thought this showed some progress. Who knows, we might even make it to first-name terms one day.

With a smile on my face and a lightness of step, I carried on to my childhood home.

I'd hardly had a chance to feel anything significant on my previous visits there. I'd either had a dog to control or a body to find and hadn't taken the time to sift through the memories which that simple, cheery façade brought back.

I hadn't thought of my father, out there on Christmas Eve dressed like some sort of gnome, coming to deliver presents but unable to get in through the living room window because the padding on his suit was too big. I hadn't remembered my mother waiting on the doorstep in her Sunday best on the one occasion my family were invited en masse to meet the Duke and Duchess at Hurtwood House. It was my fault we were late, and Mother was heartbroken that she and Father were never invited back.

I thought of these things and more, but the one image that really stuck in my head was of them standing there in the freezing cold on the day I went to the front line. It was the last time I saw my father before he disappeared.

I walked up the path to ring the bell and I could practically feel him there. He was waving goodbye to me, just like all those years ago, and it brought a lump to my throat. But when the door swung to, it wasn't my father who opened it, but his brother Stan.

"Marius, I hear you were amazing!" The house smelt of nutmeg, cinnamon and freshly baked buns. "You solved the unsolvable. And let me tell you, that Heaton girl will get what she deserves." He was so happy he was practically dancing. The only real wonder was that he didn't break into song. "We're all so proud."

"Thank you, Stan. That means a lot coming from you."

I was apparently very huggable that weekend, as my uncle now trapped me in an appreciative embrace. Even Percy (who I had taken the time to escort home before my trip to call on the royal family) looked a little less desolate than normal and ran around me with his tail wagging. It turned out he'd already been fed and walked, so I suppose he was just happy to see me. I gave him a stroke, peeked in to say hello to my aunt in the tiny sitting room, and went upstairs to do something I should have done the second I set foot in Hurtwood.

At the top of the narrow staircase was my father's office. It had shelves on each wall and the files from his time as a solicitor were all there. Every case on which he'd worked for the local community – from the Heaton family's tenants whose houses were under threat of foreclosure to the few cases he'd overseen for the Duke of Hurtwood – was stored in grey cardboard folders. And as I looked at the loose papers scattered across his desk and the pile of legal texts beside the door, I realised just how little I knew about Terence Quin.

It was just then that I heard someone behind me and turned to see my mother standing in the doorway.

"He would be proud of you today," she said as she took a few steps into the room. I thought she would keep speaking, but her words dried up and she looked about the place with a troubled expression.

"You can talk about him to me, you know," I told her. "I don't know why we stopped, but he's my father, and I still think of him every day."

She stretched her arm out to place her hand on my back. "I know, my lovely boy. Not an hour goes by without my wondering where he went." Though her voice remained just as calm as ever, her eyes were filled with glistening tears. "And that's why I've come to a decision."

She didn't turn to face me but kept reading the names on the side of each file in front of us. I wanted to tell her that she could trust me with whatever she needed to say, but I was worried that, if I spoke, she would stop talking altogether.

"I should have told you a long time ago, but it doesn't matter anymore."

I was unsure what she wanted from me, but I found the sudden insistence in her tone alarming. "Mother, I don't understand what you're trying to say."

"Well you wouldn't, would you? I've treated you like a child for years. That was my mistake, and I'm trying to make up for it now." She paused for three ticks of the clock on the wall. "Just before he disappeared, your father did some work for the Heatons. He never wanted anything to do with them, but they made sure that he had no choice."

"Don't worry about that. I already know. The Duchess told me yesterday. It was upsetting at first, but if you say there was no other—"

"You're not listening, boy." She didn't sound like herself then. Her usually warm tone of voice had cooled. "I very much doubt that the Duke and Duchess know anything about what your father found himself doing."

She needed a deep breath, and another quick glance around the room before she was able to continue. "The Heatons made him represent a friend of theirs. I knew it would lead to no good as soon as I heard about the brief Terence was sent. His name was Lucien Pike, and he wasn't just a petty criminal. He was violent. He worked for some powerful people who didn't want him to go to prison, which is why they needed your father."

"But Dad was just a country solicitor. What could he do for a man like that?"

"No, boy. He wasn't *just* anything. When we lived in

London together, before you were born, your father made a name for himself prosecuting criminal cases. His bosses in chambers thought that he was a wizard, but he was so disillusioned by what he saw every day – by the wrong people going to prison and the wrong people walking free – that he decided we should leave the city."

I was finding it hard to concentrate and sat down on the edge of the desk. I couldn't understand why I hadn't heard any of this before, but there was a more pressing question. "Mother, why are you telling me this now?"

Her throat contracted a fraction as she swallowed down a breath. "Because I want you to find him." She walked closer to place her hands on mine. "I want you to find out what happened to your father."

A LETTER FROM THE AUTHOR

Many thanks for reading *The Hurtwood Village Murders*. I hope you were glued to the book as Marius and Bella raced to unmask the killer. If you'd like to join other readers in accessing free novellas and hearing all about my new releases, you can sign up to my readers' club!

benedictbrown.net/benedict-brown-readers-club

If you enjoyed this book and could spare a few moments to leave a review, that would be hugely appreciated. Even a short comment can make all the difference in encouraging a reader to discover my books for the first time.

Becoming a writer was my dream for two decades as I scribbled away without an audience, so to finally be able to do this as my job for the last few years is out of this world. One of my favourite things about my work is hearing from you lovely people who all approach my books in different ways, so feel free to get in touch via my website.

Thanks again for being part of my story – Marius, Bella and I have so many more adventures still to come.
Benedict

benedictbrown.net

 facebook.com/benedictbrownauthor

ABOUT THIS BOOK

The nice thing about a new series is that it offers the chance to do something different. I love my existing characters but my idea with the Marius books was to be able to tell stories that might not have worked in my other two series. As this is approximately my thirtieth murder mystery in four years, it really is more fun to mix things up. Hopefully, that's what I've done in this book.

Trying different forms, like the spring 1917 chapters or Lord Edgington's notes in *A Killer in the Wings*, also helps to make the whole experience more interesting, and I was glad that early readers enjoyed these elements. I also really love it when suspects are already known to our detectives and so we're fitting into an existing world, rather than relying on the detectives to discover everything about everybody.

I put quite a lot of myself and my family into this book. The backstory of the group of schoolmates all in love with one another was inspired by my own highly embarrassing adolescence and, in particular, a trip to Dorset with my English class one spring when I was seventeen. There were six boys and six girls, and everyone was in love with someone, though in many cases not the right people and, for the most part, the girls weren't interested. We stayed in a former borstal in the middle of the most beautiful countryside, drank too much alcohol and all confessed our painful unrequited love to one another. It was just about the most teenage weekend imaginable and perhaps by writing this book I've been able to exorcise it forever. But probably not.

Closer to home, at her eightieth birthday at Hinwick House this year, my mum gave a forty-five-minute speech – which would have lasted an hour if I hadn't politely cut her off – all about her family and growing up in the South Wales mining valley of the Rhondda. It was really inspirational – though I personally thought that my tight-five was funnier. The South Walian Day family in this book is a reference to my grandparents who were bakers, and I also managed to sneak in one of my favourite family anecdote.

My nana, Gwen, who left school at thirteen to work in the family shop, was one of the smartest women I've ever met. She would read incredibly long and complex novels right into her nineties – along with the odd Joanna Trollope. She was also my favourite chef of all time, and her apple pies, roast dinners and, of course, Welsh cakes couldn't be beaten. But one thing she never mastered was driving.

In an effort to teach her, her brothers took her to a place known as Mugs' Alley at the bottom of the hill and left her there with the three-wheeler van from the shop. I imagine they explained which pedal did what but, on her own, her attempt to learn was not a great success. In fact, she managed to turn the van on its side. The most impressive thing, though, was that my five-foot-nothing grandmother simply got out, pushed the vehicle upright and walked back up the incredibly steep hill home. She never attempted to drive again.

Hurtwood Village is based on a real place. My friend Elliot is a keen mountain biker and took us to the village of Peaslake in

Surrey which is surrounded by forest. There are usually twenty
or so cyclists hanging about in front of the pub. I doubt that was
the case in the twenties, but either way, Peaslake has a very
special feel to it, as you have to drive through narrow, winding
lanes in the Hurtwood to get to the village. You really feel
secluded there, and the houses and cottages back onto fields and
woods all around.

I didn't follow the plan of the village exactly, but it was
sometimes funny that I would create something – the bus stop
or war memorial, for example – that would then turn out to be
more or less where I'd imagined them. I used certain geograph-
ical features like the hill over the village – which is really called
Holmbury Hill – but changed the names just enough not to
receive emails from angry locals saying that I'd got it all wrong.
Peaslake is in the best part of Surrey for visiting pretty villages,
and Shere, which has been featured in a hundred cosy English
films, is only two miles away. I can also recommend the lunch
we had at the Hurtwood Hotel, and my daughter Amelie had
lots of fun clinging to the back of Elliot's bike as he went
zooming down dips and hills.

Living away from the country of my birth, I have an added
appreciation for the not always so humble British village. Right
back to the middle ages, in Spain settlements were built with
people living close together, generally in terraced buildings.
British villages are more spread out, which suits a collective of
individuals, whereas Spain is all about the tight-knit community, and I think it's fascinating that our architecture so
perfectly mirrors our common national character traits. There's
the famous saying that "An Englishman's home is his castle",
and that holds true whether the home in question is a three-
room bungalow or a palatial manor house. Of course, the biggest
addition to my version of Peaslake was the massive great manor
house on the hill.

Not so very far away from the real Hurtwood is the

exquisite Wotton House, but I'd used that as the model for my first ever country house mystery, *A Corpse in the Country*. Instead, I used the look and history of the incredible Harlaxton Manor in Lincolnshire for inspiration. It's nothing like the building on the cover (which represents Tilly's house) and I recommend you look online for a photo.

Harlaxton is interesting as it was built in the nineteenth century to look much older than it really is. It mixes several historical styles and exemplified the term the poet John Betjeman coined of *Jacobethan* – being heavily inspired by both Elizabethan prodigy houses and the subsequent Jacobean style. Highclere Castle, of *Downton Abbey* fame, is another example of the Renaissance Revival architecture that was popular in Europe at the time.

I previously included a conversation between Bella and Marius about the original owner of Hurtwood House, but Chapter Six in this book was getting long, so I thought I'd cheat and paste it here instead...

"Dodo's been working at the library and found the diary of my distant ancestor who expanded the old manor that originally stood here. It turns out that he only built it because he wanted to get away from everyone. Montague Montague—"

"I'm sorry," I had to interrupt, "but it's no wonder that he didn't want to see anyone if that was his name."

She continued as if I hadn't said anything. "Monty Montague had no children and never married. His one desire in life was to build the grandest home he could afford and live all alone in it (with a staff of fourteen servants)."

I still hadn't taken my eyes off her house. "And did he achieve his goal?"

"He did indeed. The manor was completed in eighteen fifty-something and he died three years later." Her smile only grew as she detailed her eccentric relative's legacy. "Best of all though, he did everything he could to avoid leaving his fortune to anyone in the family because he hated them so much. He failed, luckily, as the will stipulated that it had to be passed to his nearest male relative."

"Just think," I replied in a sombre tone, "if he'd had his way, you might have been..." I struggled to say the last word. Well, I pretended to at least. "...poor."

"Worse things have happened," she replied with a smile.

Thank you, Bella and Marius.

The real man's name was Gregory Gregory, as opposed to Montague Montague, but the rest of what she said was true. He was a real misanthrope and wanted his family to leave him alone – though he did have a staff of fourteen servants. In reality, he couldn't stop his distant cousin inheriting as the estate was entailed, which meant that it legally had to be left to the next male in line. This story also inspired me to write my Lord Edgington book *The Christmas Bell Mystery*, which was written after this one but came out several months before.

Rebuilding the manor house that he'd inherited was Gregory Gregory's all-consuming passion. He hired two of the most important architects of the day, had a great deal of input on the design himself and travelled around Europe buying up architectural and decorative pieces to finish it, before swiftly dying – as Bella explained –three years after Harlaxton Manor was completed.

As my family and I still live in a rented house and dream of building our own place, I hope we manage it in a more timely fashion.

HISTORICAL RESEARCH

These chapters are long enough without extra waffling here. You know what it's all about, so let's jump right in...

I was shocked to discover that the finger sandwich – that most British of dishes, that staple of afternoon tea – is actually an American invention. The first reference to it in the OED is from 1893 in a publication from New York, and searching on the British Newspaper Archive for the term only gives two results in the 1920s and one of them, discussing an event in Scotland explains, "A novelty in the form of an American finger sandwich was much enjoyed." I suppose our appropriation of this dish makes up somewhat for the movie $U571$.

Speaking of historical inaccuracies, my first historical novel was set in Surrey in 1926, and the police were able to drive out to Lord Edgington's estate without any trouble. However, I recently discovered a line of text somewhere which explained that the Northamptonshire Constabulary – where Inspector Lovebrook was working when he first popped up in my books – didn't have official police vehicles until 1930. From this date, there were only two cars and four motorcycles for the whole county. They were stationed at key places around the area, including one motorbike in Wellingborough where Bella, Love-brook and Marius travel to talk to the gentlemanly artist.

The Hotel Russell chapter which I included in this book was originally written for the previous one in the series. After Bella found Marius lying on the pavement, she picked him up and carted him off for a slap-up meal. The only problem was that it slowed down the opening of the story a lot. I couldn't abandon such a beautiful location, though, and so I plonked it in this one instead – merely adding Gilbert and his bureaucratic ways.

It is not just because the hotel was, and still is, one of the most exquisite in London that I wanted to mention it. Its historical connection to the *Titanic* is fascinating. As clever old Bella explains, the architect of the hotel – the brilliantly named Charles Fitzroy Doll – also designed the dining room on the *Titanic*, which is said to have been a near identical copy of the Hotel Russell restaurant. There is also a bronze dragon called "Lucky George", a duplicate of which was not so lucky to end up at the bottom of the ocean.

Fitzroy Doll designed a sister property which was called the Imperial Hotel, also on Russell Square. The art nouveau building was possibly even more majestic than the first he had built and featured an impressive Winter Garden and some of the most luxurious Turkish baths in Europe at the time. Today, all that remains of this wonderful place is a sign on the street pointing visitors to the now demolished baths. The hotel was knocked down in 1967 and replaced with one of the ugliest buildings in London, which is sadly still there today. This kind of thing makes me so angry. Why did the sixties have the best music but the worst architecture!? The seventies and eighties were also pretty bad. There's clearly a correlation between the two things!

When reading about Harlaxton Manor, which influenced the look of Hurtwood House, I came across the story of a fascinating woman who bought it in the 1930s. Her name was Violet Van der Elst, and she was born to a coal porter and washer-woman but rose to become a successful businesswoman thanks to the cosmetics company she founded, which invented and sold the first ever brush-less shaving cream. She used her wealth to campaign against the death penalty in Britain and saw her goal achieved the year before she died in 1966. She was also a writer, publishing a novel and a collection of ghost stories, and was featured as a character in the 2005 film about the hangman Albert Pierrepoint. Sadly, by the time she died in her eighties, she'd frittered her wealth away in unnecessary lawsuits and died in a lunatic asylum (as they were known back then).

One theme that influenced my first ten or so 1920s novels far less than these books was the Great War. I have been reading more about it since I started the Marius Quin series, and the Imperial War Museum and National Archives are great resources for finding out about the experiences of real soldiers. One thing I discovered was that 1917 – right in the middle of the worst of the fighting – was an incredibly cold year which created appalling conditions for the armies on the continent. The year started with one of the coldest winters of the twentieth century and there were still blizzards occurring with three-metre snowdrifts in Britain and Ireland in April of that year. So the events of the youthful spring that Marius and his friends enjoyed had been preceded by some terrifyingly chilly weather and were then followed by one of the wettest summers on record.

The Battle of the Lys, where Sebastian is said to have died, was notable for being the battle that finally killed Manfred Albrecht von Richthofen, better known as the Red Baron. Richthofen was born to an aristocratic family, hence the nick-name, and would become revered for his incredible ability with his aircraft – which he painted red... hence the nickname. There is evidence that he downed at least seventy-three planes, though the real number is likely much higher. This would put him as the second most prolific fighter ace of the war, behind the Frenchman Colonel René Fonck, who remains the "all-time Allied Ace of Aces". Richthofen had already had one accident when his plane was shot down by an Australian anti-aircraft gunner on 21 April 1918, and his previous injury may have limited his abilities. I think my first knowledge of the Red Baron came from a fictionalised version in the *Biggles* movie when I was twelve, so it was interesting to find out about the real man.

I spent a good amount of time reading up on conscientious objectors and the military tribunals that were set up to decide whether men were fit to go to war. Compared to the six million who served, only 16,000 refused to enlist, not including those who would only serve in non-combatant roles. A good number of them would have objected for religious reasons, and this was particularly true of the firmly pacifistic Quakers. However, over a third of COs spent time in prison for their refusal to enlist and, as soon as they were released, they were liable to be rearrested for desertion. There was great stigma attached to their choice, which accounts for the very low numbers who were confirmed as Conscientious Objectors.

The most famous case is probably the Richmond Sixteen, a group of religious objectors who were first held prisoner in Richmond Castle and then sent to France against their will. They were absolutists who said that even non-combat work went against their principles. On their first day there, when asked whether they would follow orders or risk a firing squad, they all chose the latter. They had to wait a month for sentencing, which was carried out in front of hundreds of soldiers. The judge declared that the punishment would be death, before pausing for a moment and then revealing that their sentences had subsequently been commuted to ten years' hard labour.

The order not to condemn any COs to death apparently came from the prime minister, but the men still suffered greatly in order to stick to their principles. However, by the time of the Second World War, such people were treated more civilly, with only 3 per cent of the 60,000 who refused to fight ending up in prison. I researched all this for a conversation between Sebastian and the others that was deleted after the first draft. Whoops.

It was the job of the military service tribunals in each town to decide whether the COs were genuine or motivated by cowardice. Run by prominent local citizens, such as the Heaton brothers (ha ha), they also had to take into account each man's health, age and circumstances. Potential soldiers could ask to be excused if they were key to maintaining an essential business, but even then there was no guarantee they would avoid conscription, especially as the desperate need for more men increased as the war went on. This led to married men being called up in 1916 and then to the age of conscription being raised to fifty and lowered to eighteen at the end of 1917, which is why Sebastian and Marius would have been sent to fight soon after they came of age.

I often come across or have to search out tiny things that wouldn't fill a paragraph but still interest me. For example, I checked what wheelchairs would have looked like in the twenties and discovered that Queen Victoria already had a rather interestingly designed hand-cranked one decades before. I found an article on a violent crime which equated dementia with madness and assumed the suspect was guilty as a result.

You can consult the complete 1852 *Post Office Directory of London* online, which I did... for some reason I can no longer remember. I discovered that there were, rather surprisingly, cycle battalions in the First and Second World Wars. And, as a last miscellaneous point, the Yorkshire cricket captaincy affair of 1927 inspired great scandal across the UK when a professional rather than an amateur (and thus an aristocrat) was appointed. It was not the most interesting development by today's standards, but it shook Britain at the time.

I took Richard's surname from the actor Douglas Fairbanks Jr. His father was also a famous actor – hence the name – but the son was particularly impressive. His Wikipedia entry is listed as "Actor, Producer, Naval Officer", and as well as playing many adventurous parts in films like *The Prisoner of Zenda* and *Gunga Din*, he went on to become a genuine war hero. He trained with British commandos and won medals from four different nations, including the US Legion of Merit, for putting forward the idea of diversionary units to confuse the enemy over the main point of attack during the Allied invasion of North Africa. I'm really not doing him justice here, but he had an incredibly distinguished military career. He also loved the UK and moved to Mayfair after his service was complete, where he settled into the London social scene and was eventually made an Honorary Knight Commander of the Order of the British Empire.

Speaking of actors, I needed to murder someone without making a noise... I mean, in my book, I needed to murder someone without making a noise, and just as I was about to look up whether this was possible, I got a message from everyone's favourite audiobook narrator, Mr George "The Actor" Blagden. More as a joke than anything, I asked him if he knew whether you can cut someone's windpipe quick enough to kill them without screaming, to which he handily responded...

"You absolutely can! The stunt coordinator on this film I just did had a big discussion with me about it (because someone had to slit my throat in one of the scenes) and I asked if I'd be able to scream. To be fair, the throat slit was with a large knife, very quickly, but basically as soon as air can escape your lungs from a hole lower than your vocal cords, you then can't create any noise! Amazing, right?!"

If only all my research was so easy. Something that took far longer, which I could have totally forgone, of course, was my research into Queen Victoria's dogs. I needed to find out what breed of dogs she was photographed with, and I discovered some interesting facts about her pets.

She kept dogs right from her childhood to her dying day in 1901 when she asked for her Pomeranian, Turi, to be brought in to her. She had any number of different breeds during her life – plus ponies, parrots, a donkey and a pair of Tibetan goats that would go on to make a herd. Perhaps most curiously, though, Captain John Hart Dunne presented her with what may have been the first Pekingese dog to arrive in Britain, which she named Looty. The soldier stole the dog from the Xianfeng Emperor during the looting – hence the name – of the Summer Palace near Beijing during the Second Opium War.

I love reading up on old cars and searching out photos of the most beautiful ones of the time. Marius's red Invicta 3 Litre is a real beauty, whereas Bella's old Sunbeam is, in contrast, pleasantly humble for the daughter of a wealthy duke. However, there are two things with these cars that I'm rarely sure of. 1) do the particular models have keys, and 2) whether they need cranking or had push button ignition.

Car keys were first introduced in 1910 to prevent unauthorised engine cranking, and, by the twenties, locks were added to the doors themselves. However, it wasn't until the late forties that Chrysler invented a key that, in place of the button, would start the engine when inserted into the ignition housing. For some time after, many cars had one key for the doors and another for starting. So now I know.

Next up, that symbol of Britishness, the phone box. Such facilities were first introduced in 1921. The first version was made of concrete, and was considered something of an eyesore, so one town would only allow them if each kiosk came with a thatched roof. There are still fourteen of the original boxes known to exist in the UK, but surely the definitive design, the famous red box, or K2, would arrive three years later in 1924. There was such resistance to the first design that the Royal Fine Art Commission organised first one, unsuccessful, and then another more select competition to choose a better design. The winning entry was by the architect Sir Giles Gilbert Scott, who had designed various Oxbridge buildings, Liverpool Cathedral and, another British icon, Battersea Power Station, which can be seen on the front cover of Pink Floyd's 1977 album, *Animals*, and on my train journey into London from my family home.

Now let's finish with some light entertainment. "Take Me Away From the Streets and the Houses" was written and composed by G. Arthurs and A. J. Lawrance. That's all I can tell you about it, I'm afraid. I can't even find a recording of it online and so, when George has to record it for the audiobook, I will be making up the tune he sings. "Where Did You Get That Hat?" was composed in 1888 by one Joseph J. Sullivan, an American vaudeville performer. This surprised me as, in Britain, it is very much associated with singers from London's East End. However, there is also the possibility – as with almost every Victorian-era song I've come across – that the song was not written by him at all. It is a catchy tune though and tells a funny story, which is good enough for me, Percy and the people of Hurtwood Village.

Thank you for reading (or listening). I hope that a good portion of the above makes sense.

WORDS AND REFERENCES

Get her monkey up – to make someone angry.

Tantalean – the word comes from the Greek myth of Tantalus who was condemned by the gods to stand in a pool of water with a vine of grapes just out of reach and the water always receding as he stooped to drink it. That's also where we get the word tantalising.

All 'Sir Garnet' – everything is in order. The name comes from Field Marshal Garnet Joseph Wolseley who was famous not just for his many military victories across Asia, Africa, the Crimean and (oddly) Canada, as head of the British army, he was also renowned for his efficiency which gave rise to the expression.

Prodigy houses – a stately home built by a wealthy family to show off their might and riches in the Elizabethan era, often in the hope of attracting the Queen to stay as she travelled around Britain with her entourage.

Wollaton Hall – the house on the front of the first Lord Edgington novel – and Longleat are two examples.

Hot-brained – like hot-headed, but it sounds nice and old!

Armadillo's armour – I'd always assumed armadillos had shells, but apparently not. My mother was once given an armadillo's armour by a former student, and we still have the hard, hairy thing at my family home. This is just one of the many odd arte-facts my mother collected over five decades in teaching. She also had a good deal of Second World War memorabilia for the children to interact with which, after she retired, the school foolishly threw away. This also made me very angry.

Kowtowing – To act in an obsequious manner. A word of Chinese origin which literally meant to prostrate yourself by touching the floor with your forehead as an extreme form of bowing.

Upped sticks – to leave where you live and move elsewhere. What I didn't realise before was that the origin is nautical and refers to the raising of the boat's mast in order to move on.

Alewife – landlady / female bartender.

Peeler – slang for a police officer which came from the home secretary Sir Robert Peel who founded the Metropolitan Police. The word Bobby is another reference to him.

Head doctor – psychologist / shrink.

Hedgehoggy – a prickly person. I love this word!

Major Walker – I came across an article in the paper about Major Cecil Walker, an estate agent from Surrey who, in 1922, was blown into the River Nene as he was trying to save his dog. I thought this a bit sad, but now he is immortalised in fiction, sort of.

Heartsick – lovesick.

Sevenpennies – pulp fiction novels that would have cost little at the time.

Folie de grandeur – delusions of grandeur, but that Lovebrook is a bit posh and talks funny.

CHARACTER LIST

New Characters

Lucinda Heaton – talented and capable young woman who was at school with Marius and Bella and is now being targeted by a killer.

Mrs Abbot – Hurtwood Village's school teacher.

James Heaton – Lucinda's brash and bullying cousin.

Tilly Heaton – James's meek, pessimistic sister.

Richard Fairbanks – Lucinda's former fiancé. He's a wiz with plastics, apparently.

Dorothy "Dodo" Lyle – ethereal, hippyish schoolfriend of Marius (before hippies were invented).

Ned Lyle – slow, shy, gentle, postman and Dodo's brother.

Mrs Lyle – their mother and the local postmistress.

Frederick Montague, Duke of Hurtwood —— Bella's rather jolly father.

Sergeant Meldon – a police officer who used to work with Lovebrook in Nottinghamshire.

Mr Aintree – an elderly artist in Wellingborough.

Sylvia Montague, Duchess of Hurtwood – Bella's steely mother.

Sergeant Rossiter – the only policeman in Hurtwood Village.

Jeb Paignton – An old man who sits in front of the pub all day.

Sebastian Kane – a boy who was at school with Marius and his friends in 1917 before being shipped out to France.

Already Old Favourites

Marius Quin – soldier in the Great War with a broken heart, turned mystery novelist with writer's block.

Bertrand Price-Lewis – Marius's publisher and friend.

Lady Isabella Montague – Marius's childhood sweetheart turned friend, the daughter of the Duke of Hurtwood.

Gilbert Baines – Bella's boyfriend, a rather charmless banker.

Uncle Stan – the brother of Marius's missing father, Terence. He was once a baker and may soon be again.

Auntie Elle (Eleanor) – his brainy wife who lost the use of her legs after a childhood illness.

Marius's mum – self-explanatory, but I really must get around to giving her a name.

Detective Inspector Lovebrook – just a jolly nice chap (and Bella and Marius's police officer friend).

Printed in Great Britain
by Amazon